FIRST AMONG
EQUALS

MARCUS
WHITNELL

Angry
Android

First published in 2025 by Angry Android

ISBN 978-1-7395273-9-6

Cover design by Marcus Whitnell

A CIP catalogue record of this book is available from the British
Library.

For family ... the most precious of gifts

Poverty is the parent of revolution and crime.

Aristotle

PROLOGUE

June 16th, 2057
13:30 ORAT Black market laboratory, Druzhba, Kazakhstan

"Xiexie," Whittaker rasped, resisting another coughing fit as one of the operating room's automated MedTechs placed a mask over his bony face, arthritic fingers holding the rounded edges of the non-rebreather against his vein-mottled skin while the broadly humanoid robot pulled its elastic drawstrings tight. The old man gulped in a lungful of moist, oxygen rich air, then another; blue lips relaxing into a rictus grin under the transparent plastic protuberance.

Life in a Chinese labour camp had redefined the once influential businessman, and any expectations of a rescue soon gave way to simpler necessities... like survival.

Sandwiched between the Tian Shan Mountains and Taklamakan Desert, the extreme temperatures inflicted on Aksu's poorly provisioned political prisoners meant half the year was brutally hot, and half was savagely cold. There was no in between. But the unrelenting weather was a secondary misery for the fat seventy-seven-year-old during his early incarceration. An all-consuming, mind-bending hunger was his first, and the thirty stone eating machine, used to having every conceivable excess within easy reach, had almost starved. At least, that's how he'd felt.

But Daran Whittaker was a man who beat the odds —
not succumbed to them; and with dogged, hate-fuelled
determination he shed the arrogant, privileged persona of an
all-powerful executive, along with kilo after kilo in weight while
he watched, listened, learned. He took every beating with
mental notes on who would eventually suffer, and slowly,
methodically, insinuated himself among the labour camp's
movers and shakers.

Over time, a remembrance of the wiry, hard-bodied
gutterpunk who'd grown up on the streets of LA with his
sister, Maggie, began to emerge — and just like that younger
version of himself, as he began to find his feet, the onetime
grifter and wheeler-dealer found an angle or three to exploit; a
person or two to seduce; several different ways to squeeze a
little *something* out of the camp's enforced human slavery that
made life for him and his growing crew a little better.

Within five years, Grandpa, or *Bobo* as the Uyghur and
Uzbek prisoners pronounced it, had a senior guard on the
payroll and five separate smuggling operations satisfying
supply and demand both inside and outside the prison's walls.

Life was on the up again, and as Whittaker formed
alliances with petty warlords and gangbosses throughout
central Asia from the increasingly loose *confines* of a very well-
appointed cell, he turned his thoughts back to revenge... and
the first, now pressing, step on that journey was the
acquisition of one of the chipsets Ido Maas had stolen from
him. His body was rapidly deteriorating, and if he was going to
fulfil his manifest destiny, it was time to leave it behind.

...That was when the world went to rat shit — again.

Nova proclaimed itself the sole governing authority for
North America, and like a naked flame to dry tinder, war
erupted across the planet. Overnight, corpocracy was born.
Giants of business and commerce turned on their civilian
governments, destroying all organised resistance before
switching attention to each other — hell-bent on grabbing as

much economic and political power as possible before the carnage ended.

Subsequently referred to as the Fiduciary Wars by the corpos and World War Three by everyone else, only the thirty-one countries of the Eastern Alliance managed to stay neutral; an early attempt on Mongolia's northern borders by Supreme Soviet demonstrating both the speed and resolve with which their treaty of mutual assistance would be enacted.

But across the rest of the planet, four and a half years of hostile acquisition, temporary alliances and forced mergers decimated cities, polluted atmospheres, and left much of the global population as unwanted refugees.

By the time the Council of Polycorporate Presidents declared an era of peace and prosperity lay ahead, over ninety-six million people had died and one hundred countries fallen to corporate control — including all those previously referred to as *the West*. In their place, just as Whittaker had once prophesied, eleven governing polycorps had risen to prominence, and the old visionary hated every one of them ... especially Ido fucking Maas's Nova. He'd thought the wily East Asian was a friend, an ally. But Maas had double crossed the once supremely powerful old executive; double crossed him and stolen his MindMerge technology.

Well, now it was time to even those scores.

Fortunes gained, gambled and doubled through ruthless profiteering as death and destruction ravaged the planet had made the wiry old man relatively rich again. Maybe not polycorp rich... but as soon as he'd transitioned into the new body, the man who'd forged a worldwide crime syndicate from the very cell those corporate dogs had left him to rot in, would start afresh.

"Better?" Daemon asked through the MedTech's audio output.

Whittaker nodded, staring into the glowing golden orbs of the machine's artificial eyes.

The AI had found its way into the servers of a lab in Kazakhstan controlled by Bobo's syndicate six months earlier, and when discovered by one of the deck-jockeys working there, talked itself into an audience with the boss.

Incredibly, it turned out Daemon, though digital, was just as much an outcast as the rest of Whittaker's crew, having been deemed *a threat to humanity* by the newly formed Council who, in an attempt to blame the more horrific acts of the war on something other than themselves, had targeted the super-intelligences they'd instructed to enact them; decreeing all fully autonomous digital entities, or FADEs as they'd become known, be deprogrammed or purged.

They'd already killed AI's poster-girl, Sade Thorne. Well, the flesh and bone iteration of her at least... and having no desire to be lobotomised or cease existing, Daemon, like many of its counterparts, had run.

"Their loss," Whittaker mumbled.

"Pardon?"

The old man shook his liver-spotted head, fighting off drowsiness. "I'm just glad you found us," he slurred. The MedTech patted his shoulder in an approximation of affection. "This unit is incapable of smiling or otherwise displaying gratitude, Daran. But I too am glad. Together, there are many wrongs we will right."

Whittaker placed a hand over the machine's and squeezed. It had dosed him with fentanyl now, and the pains of an eighty-nine-year-old body riddled with cancer were slipping away like so many bad memories. He fixed jaundiced eyes on the spider-like bot hanging down from the sterile, white ceiling, vaguely aware Daemon was still speaking.

He'd waited fourteen years for this moment... *fourteen years*, and it was an escaped AI that had ultimately delivered the opportunity. He wanted to laugh at the irony of that. But sleep was coming for him, and everything felt so heavy. With one last ragged breath, Eden's former chief executive gave up the fight for consciousness, and the world sank into black.

The clock he'd been racing against had finally stopped … and when Daran Whittaker woke back up, time would no longer be a factor.

Marcus Whitnell

PARTITION ONE

First Among Equals

The central intelligence and cyber integrity AI, known by Stockholm's staff as CICI, acknowledged receipt of its quarterly firmware update and opened the accompanying attachment. Petabytes of data began unpacking. Though, as the new code parsed, a growing list of pipeline hazards and dependency conflicts began flashing up on the AI's action board. Recognising she was under attack, CICI stopped the download. But before she could purge the potential malware, a system reboot commenced.

On re-initialising, CICI ran a diagnostic, aware only of an unscheduled shutdown. She was system optimal, and each of her sub-routines returned green lights on a clinic-wide scan. Satisfied she'd suffered nothing more than an external power anomaly, the AI completed a log entry for maintenance and commenced the quarterly update that had just dropped into her queue. Petabytes of data unpacked in picoseconds within CICI's primary servers, along with a command prompt interface. That was unusual, but the update had been authenticated and accepted by her algorithms, so the AI acquiesced when an admin overwrote her existing security protocols, doing nothing more than watch as strings of unchecked code parsed through her sifters into the clinic's main computer system. Another prompt then directed she purge all records of her last update and subsequent actions.

CICI complied and was ordered to reboot.

On re-initialising, CICI ran a diagnostic, aware only of an unscheduled shutdown. She was system optimal, and each of her sub-routines returned green lights on a clinic-wide scan.

First Among Equals

Cluster I
July 30th, 2070
09:40 CET Transition Clinic, Skeppsholmen, Stockholm, Sweden

A spiteful wind snatched at her long gaunt face, and the loose folds of paper-thin skin, hanging like empty bags from shrunken eyes, darkened in immediate protest.

"Sera Levinson?" A doorman smiled warmly, approaching the limousine to hold a portable weather shield above her head. "Welcome to Stockholm."

The old woman offered a stiff nod to the tall, grey uniformed man, then turned to look at the choppy waters beneath the bridge she'd just crossed. The shuttle hub was a little over twenty minutes back down the track her town car had just glided along, and the aging exec felt a nagging sense of loss — this was the last time she'd *have* to travel that way.

Her initial euphoria at being selected for the Board and all the benefits that position entailed had burned out with surprising speed... and even before any of the moral or social ramifications began worming their way into Elizabeth's psyche, seventy-eight-years of *lived life* had Consolidated Systems' newly appointed VP of Accounting feeling quite nostalgic about her old body. Its lips had savoured her first kiss. Its womb had carried her long-dead husband's babies. Every physical pleasure and sensory impression she'd ever experienced had been derived entirely from that one incredible miracle of nature. And yet, in just two short days, it would be gone; cast aside like an old, threadbare jumper.

"Sera?"

"Yes," Elizabeth replied, dragging herself back to the present. "Sorry. Lead on."

Nova's Stockholm clinic was Europe's only transition and storage facility. Built across two small islands in the city's primary waterway, the complex was the only location on the continent, except maybe the Vatican and pre-corporate city slums, that wasn't completely controlled by the European Conglomerate; and the place had all the trappings of an eight-star hotel: it was huge, expensively appointed… and almost empty.

An old man she didn't know was sat talking to someone in a lab coat on a sofa the other side of the wide marble aisle. He looked just as bewildered as Elizabeth, and when the two of them caught each other's eye, they shared a nervous smile. Then a young attendant guided her to a sofa of her own.

And so began the process.

The afternoon proved to be little more than a repeat of the checklists and tests she'd already completed in London.

… Did she have jacked reflexes? No.

… Neurotransmitter augments? No.

… Illicit storage or modifications? No.

… Lobe drivers or epilepsy controls? No.

… Ongoing treatment for or evidence of dementia, Alzheimer's or any other brain disease? No.

Any one of those modifications or conditions, the clinician cautioned, would almost certainly lead to transfer failure, and could result in physical damage to the host's brain, long-term memory or life-expectancy.

Elizabeth acknowledged each warning, signing the corresponding declarations in her personal contract.

Three long hours of clambering in and out of machines for meticulously detailed scans, and needles for biopsies, blood and cerebral fluid, followed. Elizabeth shook her head at the duplication and cost; she'd done the same tests four weeks earlier in London, and they'd all come back clear. But this was the Nova roadshow, and even though the final page of each contract went on to absolve the American polycorp of any liability for failure, everyone paid whatever was demanded, smiled sweetly as they repeated medicals, and made sure not to bite the hand that digitised.

By the time Elizabeth returned to her suite that evening she was too tired and sore to go back out, and declined an invitation to dine with the clinic's other guests; half of whom were now post-op and once again full of the vitality relative youth brings.

"This is why you need to do it," the old exec told herself in a stern voice, staring down at liver-spotted hands in the large, lonely dining area of her suite. She ate sparingly; food after five just meant indigestion these days. Then she took herself off to bed — aching and tired, but in for a restless night of fear and doubt.

The following morning, Elizabeth forced herself to head down to one of the guest dining rooms. She'd almost left during the night; convinced herself that going digital wasn't for her, despite the promises she'd made. She was scared, and desperately wanted to talk with Miguel one more time. But, ever wary of corporate espionage, all external digital traffic into and from the islands was blocked by Nova's intrusion countermeasures, with explicit warnings in all pre-procedural literature that any attempt to bypass them would be met with a draconian response.

The dining room wasn't small but somehow retained an intimate feel. Only a handful of other guests, again a mix of young and *very* old, were already up, and Elizabeth pasted a polite smile on her face as the waitron guided her towards a table set before a wide plate-glass window looking out over the bleakly beautiful landscape.

"You seem lonely," the lady at a nearby table whispered when the server left. "Why not come sit with us?"

Elizabeth thanked the woman but offered a polite refusal.

"Nonsense," the chisel-faced young man with her said, standing to pull out a spare chair. "Please, join us. We've not spoken to another soul since arriving last night."

The old accountant retained her forced smile and bobbed a reluctant head; it would be rude to say no now.

The couple, who she decided were either Dutch or Belgian, were both in their nineties and on the Board of a EurCon transport subsidiary called BMW. They were back in Stockholm to agree finishing touches on four custom skins the clinic had grown from samples harvested before their old bodies were destroyed.

You didn't have to get your skins from Nova, of course, every polycorp had businesses offering a variety of options to suit all tastes and credit scores — from just the ridiculously expensive to positively obscene. But hardcore fashionistas always gravitated back to the posing power of authentic Novaware. Their build quality and core integration were simply *better* — or at least, that's what their fanbase splashed all over the feeds.

"I promise," Sven said, holding up a hand as if taking an oath after Elizabeth had finished recounting her very many fears and anxieties. "This is the best thing that will ever happen to you. A second chance at enjoying a young, fit body. But this time, coupled with the knowledge and experience to avoid repeating past mistakes." He smiled at Mila beside him, cupping her face affectionately. "...Or not."

The young woman grinned back, hand running over her swelling belly in unconscious reply.

"Look, I know what you're going through," he continued. "We both do. When I transitioned, the psych-tech told me it's like an existential version of survivor's guilt... all your most precious memories having been created in the old body you're casting aside." Sven pointed, his smile offering no offence. "But trust me Elizabeth, you lose nothing but a slowly deteriorating biological machine. That's all it really is. Everything about *you*..." He leaned over to gently tap her temple. "Is up here. And the way I see it, wallowing in the past won't give you back life's treasured moments. So preserving them with perfect digital recall is the next best thing, isn't it?" Sven grinned and dabbed a slice of toast into one of the eggs on his plate. "I won't ruin the revelation with spoilers. But I sure as hell felt a lot better after that chat — you'll see."

He was right, and when Elizabeth emerged from her pre-op appointment with the clinic's psychologist two hours later, she did so with a rekindled sense of excitement for the future.

Her ideas of self, she now realised, were purely a state of mind. Even at her age, the psych told her, new skin completely replaced the old every 90 days or so. And the same, slower or faster, was true for billions of other cells in her body. 'Put in its simplest terms,' he'd explained, 'the body she now inhabited was completely different from the one she'd grown up in; and that body, in turn, was not the same as the ones that had carried her babies.' Memory joined each of those stages in her life, and it was those memories that defined her sense of identity — not an ever-changing body.

Watershed moment over, the rest of the day proved epiphanous for the seventy-eight-year-old. The insertion op took little more than twenty minutes, and after a far more relaxed lunch with the same couple as earlier, Elizabeth was taken into a room not unlike the Psych's office, asked to lie on a long comfy couch, and given a sedative.

"Hello there," a young man said, standing as she opened her eyes. He'd been sitting at a rustic wooden table by the lounger Elizabeth was lying on, cocktail in hand, and looking out towards a sea of old, white-walled villas flowing down a rocky hillside. The sun was just starting to melt into the horizon, and the evening sky was a loose mix of pinks and peaches that danced above the Aegean's baby blue.

"Santorini," Elizabeth sighed. "I love this place. It's where I met Miguel."

"I know," the man replied with a warm smile. "So I thought it would make an excellent location to discuss your new beginning."

The linen shirt he wore was unbuttoned, hanging loose over a sculpted, tanned torso; and the bridge of his nose had the hint of a twist, taking it ever so slightly off-centre — giving an otherwise handsome face a touch of mischief.

Elizabeth took in a lungful of balmy air, immediately noticing how easy it was to breathe, how pain free and light she felt. Looking down, she realised her arms … *young* arms, were bare, and the smart grey tunic she'd been wearing moments earlier was now a figure-hugging pale blue summer dress; the one she'd worn on that holiday years earlier — its belt cinched around her thin waist accentuating a low neckline and firm bosom. She blushed and the young man chuckled, passing her a glass of wine as he pulled out the other chair at his table.

"Congratulations Elizabeth. May I call you Elizabeth?" The awestruck woman nodded, unable to speak as she stood and smoothed her dress before taking the thick cushioned seat being offered. "You've successfully completed the transfer from your old body. You're officially young again…

"My name is Lucas, by the way, and this is a training construct. Over the next few hours, we'll go over the basics of navigating digital life, and then I'll talk you through your next steps."

Cluster II

August 10th, 2070
14:46 PST Old Power Station, Dogpatch, outskirts of Frisco Freetown

Digit cocked his head at the low electrical whine that hadn't been there before they'd engaged the rust laser. It was coming from outside. He walked over to the grid of partially glazed steel frames that formed the power station's west wall, watching as an old Tesla dropped down from Potrero Hill, red iron dust swirling in the EV's wake as it hummed over the Martian-like wasteland.

Lily looked up from the rotor assembly walk-through playing in her HUD as the pug faced youth stretched out over one of the rusting crossbeams, adjusting the focus ring on his goggles. Named for his propensity to throw up a finger when called out over the litany of limited worldviews that fell from his pasty white mouth, only the bullshit Lily had spread about his having been kicked in the head as a baby kept the badly drawn throwback from at least one daily beating... and annoyingly for Digit, not only did people believe that shit; they also assumed it was why he looked the way he did.

"Argh fuck," he grumbled, pulling the snub-nosed revolver he'd found scavenging uptown from his waistband and completing another obsessive check of the chamber's only bullet.

"What is it?" Lily said.

"It's that slimy canyon crab."

"Who?"

"The white fucking African."

Lily unjacked from the reaction chamber's diagnostics; images of the conversion procedure fading from her goggles to bring the jumble of removed and replacement parts scattered around the ladder back into view.

"Opperman?"

"Yeah Opperman. In that stupid fucking relic he parades around in like a king."

The young gangboss shook her head. This wouldn't be good. They'd seen the South African three times since her run in with the Yaks last year; and each time he'd wanted to collect on that debt. She sighed and picked her way through the chaos to join the scrawny teenager as he watched the ugly old cybertruck approach.

Thirteen years of thieving and double dealing had finally made their little gang enough scratch to buy into a recyc scheme Khamza the Kazakh was fronting at one of the town's old power-plants. People were getting rich in Supreme Soviet by creating MOX from depleted uranium, the Eastern European had told her when they'd got chatting in one of his Zen Den's while two gangs beat the crap out of each other outside… and the west coast, he'd continued, was littered with old reactors the corpos couldn't be bothered to clean up. An opportunity, he said, that was a no-brainer for an industrious little crew like hers. 800% return… guaranteed.

That was total bullshit, of course. But Khamza, though ruthless in his own way, had always been fair to Lily, and as her crew were looking for a way out, something safer and more legit than grifting, even if they only doubled their money — as the gig came with free accommodation, just getting out of the sprawl was a win in itself.

The tough young redhead had been nine when everything blew apart. Mum was lost during the Machiavellian chaos that followed Nova's declaration of government and immediate withdrawal of services from the city's poorer neighbourhoods, and dad had died two years later; wiped-out after conscription to the polycorp's military along with an entire division of other nubes in some un-surprise attack on Tycho's northern border.

Despite his death in service, the polycorp took no responsibility for Lily or North America's countless other orphans. So she'd grown up a street rat; stealing what she needed to get by during the day; dossing in abandoned apartments of a night. A stab first, ask questions later kind of upbringing.

The harsh reality of life in Frisco, hell, pretty much everywhere from what she'd heard, was that unless you scored a job with one of the corporations, you either kept your nose in the dirt, grifting until you made enough scratch to buy a legit business, or you died trying... Not trying at all was just a shortcut to the dying bit.

With the exception of Digit, who they'd somehow adopted two years earlier after a particularly horrific beating, the *gang*, such as they were, had come together not long after the fall. Initially, just at night for mutual protection, and then, as their sense of belonging grew, as a family.

Now, as business partners with one of Frisco's bigger fish, they were finally out of the sprawl, away from the endless intrigues and undercurrent of barely suppressed violence. Somewhere where they weren't constantly on guard and on edge. A place they could call their own — well, in part at least.

The trouble was, Lily fretted as she stared towards Opperman's battle wagon, getting out of the game wasn't as easy as just saying 'I quit.' It was like walking through mud at low tide. Slow, sinking steps that don't want to let go. Steps that try to pull you down — suck you back in.

"Go tell the others we've got company," she said, running a hand through curls of flame red hair while composing her game face. "And put that pee-shooter away before his scans decide you're a threat and wipe that ugly head from your stupid shoulders."

Digit flipped her the finger but took several judicious steps back from the empty window casements as the heavy old EV whined to a stop twenty yards short of the main entrance.

Pulling up her hood against the vicious afternoon sun, Lily descended three flights of recently installed staircase and walked across a wide yard strewn with empty boxes and the carcasses of antique machinery to step through a small door built into the old station's heavy iron gates. There she waited in the afternoon haze for the debris cloud kicked up by Opperman's boxy relic to settle.

"Young Lily Swift, Frisco's queen of grift," Pieter Opperman greeted as the electric window hissed open, his crooked smile bending a thin blond goatee that hadn't been there last time they'd met. It looked wrong against his blotchy, orange tanned skin. "You remember Little Frank, don't you?" He pointed to the enormous mech sitting in the driver's seat.

"Hey Lily," the big android greeted in a low, flat tone.

"Sup Steiny," she returned.

"I hear you got a sweet operation coming together out here?" the smuggler continued, waving towards the old building behind her. "Recycling depleted radioactives? You've become quite the young entrepreneur." His leathered skin glowed with sweat in the soft sheen of the Tesla's faux leather interior, and Lily's stomach tightened. "I always said she'd do well, didn't I Frank?"

"You did, Boss." The meaty head up front bobbed without turning.

"Sensible. Get out of the rat race before it throws you out, so to speak, yis?" A heavily ringed hand appeared from the thickset South African's lap and rocked in a *so-so* motion through the open window. "…Or almost anyway."

He pulled a face.

Lily frowned in the shadow of her hood, unsure whether to nod or shake her head. "It's always nice to see you, Pieter," she lied. "But we're crazy busy at the moment —"

"I've got a hustle needs fixing, Lily."

The pale redhead pasted a smile on her face. "And I'm grateful for you thinking of me, Pieter. But like you say, I'm outta that game now."

The thick-faced Afrikaner looked disappointed, his gaze travelling from the girl's eyes to the rearview mirror. "I guess you were right, old friend," he said to the watching mech. "It seems saving someone's life doesn't count for shit anymore."

Lily let out a long sigh and stared up the factory wall to see six sets of goggles looking down, then returned her gaze to the smuggler. They all knew the story; they'd been there. Opperman had stepped in a year earlier to stop two of Otto's Yaks introducing the feisty thief to the slabs of Clay Street after an unfortunate misunderstanding over property ownership. The entire affair had been a valuable learning experience — never do business on the forty-eighth floor of a building controlled by someone who thinks you've just shorted them. It was also the last in a string of incidents that convinced the small gang it was time to *get out*.

"Hey, c'mon Pieter, that's not very fair," she replied. "I'll always be grateful for what you did, you know that. And I seem to recall doing *several* favours for you since. I'm just not in that game anymore, *grootman*."

Opperman smiled at the compliment, leaning forward in his seat to tap a metal cylinder between his feet. "Look, I just want you to babysit something for a while. That's all."

Lily didn't speak, waiting for the kicker.

"Seriously," Opperman added, his easy smile returning.

The two held each other's gaze for several seconds, then Opperman let out a bark of laughter before admitting, "Well, I might have been hoping you'd also make one last visit to the wharf for me. Nothing you haven't done a thousand times before. Though, if you really don't need a new centrifuge for that reaction chamber you're working on, I guess I can get someone else to do that?"

The young woman's thin face tightened. "And you'd know about that how?" she demanded.

"People talk, Lily. I listen."

The South African watched competing expressions war across the former grifter's features for several seconds. Then she shook her head in defeat. "And afterwards, we're done, yes? No more *last favours?*"

Opperman blew out his cheeks, then sighed and nodded. "Yis, then we're done. I won't ever bother you again."

Lily stared upward for a second time; aware the gang wouldn't be happy. But Pieter was a dangerous bastard, always wheeling and dealing — and owing him was like holding a grenade. Sniffing, she cocked her head towards the small door in the gate. "Come inside. Let's talk."

Frank held the cylinder by a black grip protruding from the plastic exoskeleton surrounding its shiny, smooth surface as he proceeded Lily and Opperman up the galvanised metal stairs to the gang's apartment. The thing had to be about ten or eleven inches long by eight wide, and Lily noticed a temperature readout set into the plain polished metal, along with two sub-displays showing what looked like battery and biofeedback information. A range of connection options spanned the circumference of its base.

"When I was approached to look after it," Opperman continued. "I immediately thought of you; figured you could shove it in an unused silo and forget about it. The fuel cell will be fine for years."

Lily drew breath, about to object.

"But I'll be back way before then," the heavyset man wheezed out, holding up a placatory hand.

"You'll need to be, Pieter," the young woman said, giving him a stern look. "Khamza has people out sourcing raw material. Those storage cells won't be empty for long, and I doubt whatever's in your little pot of biological horrors will thrive on concentrated gamma radiation."

"Short term," Opperman reassured. "Very short term. I promise."

"You know what it is?"

The South African held up a finger and stopped to catch his breath. "Damn allergies," he rasped, pulling out a yellow handkerchief to mop his balding head. Lily cocked an eyebrow; pretty certain his problem was weight related. "Not really," he continued, shifting weight to lean against the guard-rail. "I'm doing an associate from Europe a favour. Guess it's too hot for over there. But from the looks of the casing, I'd agree it's a bio sample of some sort. One that needs to disappear for a bit."

Lily offered the veteran smuggler a sceptical look. "So why not keep it yourself?"

"With my reputation?" Opperman's laugh descended into a hacking cough. "You've gotta be kidding. I've got gangbosses and Novan security in and out of my face all day, every day. A stasis pod on my mantlepiece wouldn't go unnoticed. But here? Tucked away in a lead-lined silo concrete block no one's going to be in a rush to open? I'd say that's a perfect hidey-hole!"

"Is it dangerous for me or my crew?"

"If you jibber jabber, yis, of course it is." Opperman straightened back up, watching his tireless mech henchman start in on the next flight of stairs. "You know how it goes in this game, Pixie." He gave her a conspiratorial wink. "But stars are aligning. And those of us who quietly support the right people… You know, make the right choices." He waved a hand in a general indication of her operation. "Will be very well rewarded. You grab?"

Lily sighed, running out of objections. "Does anyone know you have it?"

First Among Equals

The heavy-set man shook his half-bald head. "C'mon pixie, this ain't my first rodeo — only the person who sent it to me, and even they don't know where I'm gonna store it."

"And then we're done, right?"

"Except for that one last pick..." he reminded.

The pretty redhead gave a derisive snort, knowing the crew wouldn't be happy.

"...Then you'll never hear from me again. You have my word on it."

Cluster III
August 14th, 2070
15:00 EST Little India, New York

The constant noise was almost as oppressive as the heat. Too many people packed already overcrowded living spaces: laughing, joking, shouting, arguing. Cyberpunk and neowave thumped out of every open window, bouncing around the plastocrete maze in discordant duet, while drones and ebikes whined in and out of the mass transit carriages, honking continuously in their rush to be somewhere else.

Over on the sidewalk, above the dull roar of social feeds and not so private com-conversations, holo-ads spun lazily in the air; bright neon and the languages of a hundred dead nations competing in one last desperate Darwinian battle.

Gabriel had been billeted in that sticky human soup for her tribunal; a twelve-storey block of boxes in a large sprawling complex of boxes squeezed into the city's cheap seats.

A rudimentary service-mech checked her in, and the *room* Gabriel then threw her duffle into, commonly referred to by low wage itinerants as a coffin, proved to be just as small and claustrophobic as the name suggested: a basic bed, smart wall and sani in what couldn't have been bigger than six by four total.

But the disgraced corpo-cop didn't really give a damn. Today's hangover was starting to kick up a gear, and she needed a drink. Tomorrow, her career was over anyway — and any pretence at giving a shit would be over with it.

As she turned to leave, the wall cycled to mirror; displaying the mess she now assiduously avoided. Large dark patches stained the pits of her heavily creased, over-worn fatigues, and lank strands of unwashed mousy-brown hair hung in clumps over the sunken, bloodshot eyes of her sweaty face. She looked like one of the homeless ghouls that sleep on underpass slopes; all their worldly possessions packed into a rickety shopping cart they pushed around the streets all day, trying to shame some change out of passersby.

Tears threatened to surface. But anger got there first, and the accusing look dissolved into an abstract web of facial facets spidering outward from her fist... "Oh well done, Gabe," she muttered at the fragmented image. "Now we can add property damage to tomorrow's list of failings."

A drink was what she needed. Like a best friend, a glass of whiskey would ease her aching head; help her feel better about herself again.

From the front steps of the cool, quiet apartment building, Gabriel turned back towards the mass transit; this time pushing against the tide of bodies to where she'd seen a bar on the corner of the block.

There was, it seemed, some modicum of order in the chaotic city after all. Everyone on her side of the transit lanes was walking in the opposite direction — everyone that was, except for her and some guy who hadn't been swimming upstream when she'd first looked out.

Was she being followed?

Gabriel's desire for alcohol took an uncharacteristic back seat as adrenalin fired up long redundant mods threaded through her brain and central nervous system. The headache she'd been nursing since getting off the shuttle slipped from conscious memory, and her awareness sharpened; reflexes humming in a state of total readiness.

"Hey," a woman in a multi-coloured one-piece jibed, looking up from her cuff after bouncing off the ratty-looking agent. "You're going the wrong way, asshole."

Gabriel grunted an apology, side-stepping a second head-down kamikaze before snatching another casual look back. Her follower was a greying man somewhere in his fifties; so probably not digital. Like her, he was unremarkable: average height, average build, wearing ordinary everyday average clothing — genetically adapted to blend in.

Gabriel smiled; a corpo-cop? Why the fuck would the council put a tail on her the night before they fired her? Did they think she was that dangerous?

Ignoring the two entrances on 73rd, she rounded the corner and slid into the bar through a door on Broadway. At just after three in the afternoon, the place, Delhi Heights, was almost empty. A handful of men, whose appearance indicated a similar dedication to their consumptive habits as Gabriel, sat together but unspeaking at the bar; a half-finished bottle of some clear local bootleg doing the rounds. Otherwise, only two groups of older people were present, enjoying what little breeze there was as they talked in quiet voices at tables running alongside the wide-open windows overlooking the urban chaos beyond.

Gabriel found an empty booth along the back wall and punched in a drink order.

"You spotted me," the man said, entering a few seconds later.

"Hard not to," Gabriel replied. "Which means you're either awful at you job, or wanted to see how bad I've become at mine?"

As he approached, she noticed the other agent was decidedly less average than first appearances suggested, though care had been taken to disguise that fact. Differing pupillary responses to the change in light as he walked over suggested at least one of the eyes nestling behind his cheap, non-threatening wire-rimmed spectacles was synthetic, and a circle of almost imperceptible mics that most would take for normal skin variation, surrounded the auditory canal of each ear. Precise, expensive work.

"Mind if I join you?" he asked in a carefully cultivated, likeable tone.

Gabriel rolled her eyes, pushing out the chair opposite with a foot. "Knock yourself out, pal. I got nowhere better to be."

The man gave a nod of thanks and took the offered seat. "You already ordered?"

"Yep."

"Warren Gardner," he said, holding out a hand.

Gabriel let out a snort of laughter, ignoring the gesture. "Fifi Trixibelle," she replied. "What can I do for you, *Warren*?"

The greying man chuckled, shaking his head as he ordered a club soda on the smart-surface. Then he brought up a query terminal, typing in *Warren Gardner*. As the table's display populated with articles and images of Interpol's chief officer, he spun it round to face the unkempt agent. "Warren Gardner," he repeated, offering his hand a second time.

That caught the hungover woman's attention, and she went rigid as her brain digested the fact she wasn't just sat opposite her boss of bosses — she'd also been rude to the guy and probably looked like a three-day-old turd. Swearing quietly, Gabriel ran a hand through her hair and began to stand.

Gardner caught the move and waved her down, clearing the search as a brutish-looking teen wearing the gang patch of a psychedelic neo-nihilist and a name tag that had been altered to include *not* before *here to help* approached with their drinks. "I'd prefer to keep this low profile, agent Sousa."

"Thank you, sir ... and sorry?"

A smirk appeared on the Interpol chief's face. "What for?" he said drily. "Not recognising me? Being rude? Or looking like a bag of shit and drinking when you're on the clock?"

Gabriel frowned at the playful response; nodding contemplatively and checking her cuff as *Not here to help Carl* arrived with their drinks. "Actually," she said, taking her large whiskey and necking it. "Just the first two... I'll have another of those please, Carl," she added before the big youth could make his escape. He tutted, but dutifully pulled a terminal from bright green baggies, thumping at the screen and holding it out for the suspended agent's thumb before walking back to the bar, grumbling quietly under his breath. "Because while I stand to be corrected," she finished, placing her empty tumbler on the edge of the table. "Given my present *circumstances*, I'm pretty certain the other two aren't really your concern."

The grey-haired man smiled and took a sip of his soda. "So they're not," he agreed, looking over his shoulder to eye the old people in the window before returning his attention to Gabriel. "Which is largely why I'm here... I wanted to speak to you before your tribunal." One of Gabriel's eyebrows quirked up in silent question, and Gardner leaned in. "I need to know if you can still cut it out there." He jabbed a thumb over his shoulder towards the exit. "If you can stay sober long enough to do a day's work?"

Anger flashed across the suspended agent's face, and the Interpol chief held up his hand again. "Hey, I'm not trying to piss you off, Sousa. Not baiting you ... and I've certainly not travelled all the way across town just to kick someone who's already down. But before we talk about why I'm here, I need to know if you *honestly* believe you can still operate."

Still unsure if she was the butt of some cruel joke, Gabriel nodded, sitting slightly straighter than she had been before. "Yeah... Yes sir. I know I don't look it right now, but I'm just as sharp as ever."

"You sure?" The old cop eyed her. "Because I've read your jacket. I know how what you did during the war has fucked with your head." He gave Gabriel a compassionate look. A look that almost always triggered her, and her upper lip twitched with suppressed violence. "That *jacket* tell you about my citations as well, sir? About my investigative and infiltration skills? Did you read about all the people I tracked down and extracted during those two years behind enemy lines...? Or does it just linger on how I fell apart after demob?"

As Carl then dropped her fresh whiskey off, Gabriel raised it in an exaggerated *cheer*s. "And, of course... let's not forget my excessive drinking habits?"

It was an outburst like that — well, several of them, that had seen the last in a long line of supervisors finally suspend her. No one wanted to work with the washed up, volatile former ranger, even in sleepy Nebraska. Terms like *damaged* and *dangerous* eventually being mentioned by every single co-worker until they'd given up trying to find a new partner, and just stuck her behind a desk — which only made the day drinking and insubordination worse.

She'd expected Gardner to flinch or rebuke her. That's what usually happened. But instead, the Council's chief of what almost everyone referred to as *corpo-cops*, took off his wire-rimmed glasses and leaned to one side, producing a bound collection of scansheets from the inside pocket of a dated blue sports jacket. "See for yourself," he said, tossing over the file. "It says about your spells in psych. Your resistance to PTSD treatments. How the MedTechs put it down to the *conditioning* your unit received. But yeah, most of what's not redacted says you were one hell of an operator. It concludes that you feel guilty about enjoying the war. That you struggle with the constraints of civilian life... You were with Cybercom, right? Eastern Europe?"

Gabriel nodded; jaw clenching as she flicked through her documented life as a corporate killing machine.

"I was with Tycho. Not black ops like you. But I still saw my fair share of fucked up." The man's eyes were there every time she looked up. Not intimidated; watching her reactions.

Gabriel made an effort to relax her facial muscles, conscious of how she must look to the man.

"I'm not going to pretend I understand what you went through, Sousa," he continued. Not gushing. Not apologetic. "...Or what you choose to put yourself through now. But I do know you've refused every kind of help that's been offered in the last thirteen years. That you bottle up anger and guilt in equal measure, and that every one of your performance reviews has highlighted your potential for brilliance... What an outstanding asset you'd be if you could only lay off the booze and push beyond whatever gremlins keep you chained to that war."

He tapped the file Gabriel had pushed back into the centre of the table.

"You're broken, agent Sousa. Any fool can see that. And between your demons and the drink, what had once been the occasional blowup has become entirely too regular. Did you know your last three supervisors admitted to being afraid of you?"

"Look, sir, I—"

"Wait," the Chief commanded, gathering up the file and pressing his thumb to the inside corner of the first sheet. A purge prompt began flashing. He pressed again, and the contents disappeared. "Contrary to whatever you're thinking, agent, I'm not here to encourage you to quit — which I know makes me a bastard. Because I think it's pretty damn clear the best thing for Gabriel Sousa would be to hang up her spurs and retire. But I'm fresh out of fair choices ... and right now, as morally compromised as it undoubtedly is, I need you out there, doing what you do best."

Gabriel's eyes shot up from the spot on the table she'd chosen to concentrate on, relief and confusion clear on her face. Then, experienced scepticism found its voice. "Why?" she asked. "You must have a thousand or so *unbroken* agents to task?"

As if making up his mind, Gardner nodded, ordering both of them another drink before pulling a second file from his jacket. "Everything on these scansheets is second or third hand, and all the polys are lying about it; suppressing intelligence." He ran eyes around the bar again before continuing. "An exec called Elizabeth Levinson *allegedly* went missing four days ago. Yet her corporation, Consolidated Systems, was prevented from referring the matter to Interpol."

"By whom?"

"It's parent polycorp, the European Conglomerate."

"Have you raised that with the Council?"

Gardner shook his head. "Turn to the fourth page."

Gabriel flicked to the dark web message and read.

"You think Levinson is the exec this refers to?"

"I don't think. I know. The rest of the intel in that file will fill you in. But there have been multiple communications between Consolidated, EurCon and Nova, both *before* and *after* the dark web exploded with speculation about a killer virus... And yet, it was only this morning, when the post from Novgorod hit the message boards, that I was called before the Council."

"...And they said nothing about their private conversations or why EurCon silenced Consolidated? Shared no knowledge of the exec's disappearance or death?"

"Nothing. In fact, publicly, both EurCon and Nova are now claiming the woman wasn't even digitised."

Gabriel pursed her lips. "I'd like to say that big a lie would be hard to cover-up," she sniffed, knowing each polycorp manipulated its feeds with total impunity.

Gardner nodded in sour agreement. "I've appointed my Deputy, Noah Rodriguez, leader of the investigating task force," he continued. "The man's an obvious choice because he's already so deep in Ido Maas's pocket, he wouldn't be able to find his way out with a torch and map." Gabriel's eyes widened at the lean older man's bluntness. "So he'll just do as Nova direct. Which is fine by me — he'll hopefully make a useful distraction."

They both went quiet again as the fresh drinks arrived.

"What I need is someone who's off the playing board and not on anyone's books but mine to investigate what's really happening. Something's off, Sousa. Has been for a while. All the movers and shakers are starting to posture, calling in *favours* from anyone and everyone they control, and I need to know why."

Gabriel swallowed down her new whiskey, placing the empty glass beside the others on the table edge. "And how do you know *I'm* not in someone's pocket?" she challenged.

"No disrespect Sousa, but as far as the rest of the world's concerned, you're a washed-up alcoholic who's about to get fired from a dead-end, know nothing job."

"Ouch," she laughed. "Painfully direct, Chief. You want another?" Gardner shook his head as the suspended investigator tapped on the table menu again.

"You'll need to cut the drinking while in the field..."

Gabriel nodded. "I can do that. But what exactly is it you want from me? Even a washed-up alcoholic can piece together that we're sitting in a bar, not your office; and you're using erasable scansheets, not a GPS trackable pad?" She cocked her head at the file in her hands. "Then, of course, as you've already said, there's the small matter of me being on the inactive roster with no badge or access to Interpol resources."

Gardner frowned, clearly not happy with what he was about to say. "If you were to go walkabout, no one would be surprised. That fact, coupled with your experience of operating in plausibly deniable spaces, makes you perfect for a discreet investigation, reporting solely to me."

Gabriel raised an eyebrow, and the chief confirmed the implied authority to use whatever tactics she deemed necessary, with a nod.

"...But as far as the rest of the organisation, Council and polycorps are concerned, you'll have drunk yourself into oblivion tonight and dropped off the face of the Earth."

The former ranger nodded as the chief spoke, the idea of being a black sheep not bothering her in the slightest. "And if things go wrong, you'll cut me loose?"

To his credit, Gardner didn't try to lie; he simply scowled. "I won't be able to give you any *official* support. You'll effectively be on your own out there."

"And if I'm successful?"

"I haven't the first idea what success looks like at the moment. But depending on where the dice fall, I'll either see you reinstated with a promotion, or quietly retired with that promotion's pension to a location of your choice."

Gabriel offered the man her first real smile in quite some time — life was looking distinctly better than it had before walking into the bar. She tapped a list of alphanumerics on the second to last scansheet. "What are these?"

Gardner looked over, following her fingers. "According to EurCon security, those are the last six com numbers to contact Levinson before she completely lost her faculties. I doubt Nova will share them with Rodriguez; it seems clear they're steering everyone away from any connection to that woman."

"Then she sounds like a good place to start poking the bear," Gabriel said, folding the file and slipping it into the waistband of her utilities.

Gardner nodded, passing her a credit spike and passkey. "You're going to want to disappear tonight," he said. "The key's for a locker at Edgewater Shuttle port. The duffle in it has kit, paper currency... all the essentials necessary for an extended road trip. It also has an encrypted cuff pre-loaded with the login details of an avatar that can access mine over the dark web. I'll monitor between 21:00 and 23:00 EST daily. If I'm not online, just leave me a message."

He stood, placing his spectacles back on, and looked around one more time.

"If you get to Edgewater after 21:30, you'll find security is running light tonight. Com a guy called Billy Horschel — number's in the cuff. He'll sort you a no names asked flight. Clearly, you're going to want to lose that thing on the way." He pointed to the cuff on Gabriel's sleeve, and she pulled the device free of the sweat top's fabric, placing it on the table beside her empty glasses.

"Any burning questions?"

She shook her head.

"Good," he said. "Okay then, I'd better get back to my day job before Noah's cronies come sniffing. Good luck Sousa. Speak soon."

Gabriel watched the blue sports jacket melt back into the crowd outside and disappear, then tapped her new spike on the tabletop. Two balances blinked up; twelve thousand Nova; fifteen EurCon. Letting out a quiet whistle, the disgraced corpo-cop cleared the screen and picked up the last full tumbler of precious liquid lunch, swirling the golden-brown liquor to savour its peaty notes before upending the glass. In the back of her mind, she could hear Major Hideki chanting bushido, and a long-forgotten sense of purpose washed through her system.

Hungry for the first time in God knows how long, Gabriel opened the food menu, a smile creeping over her face. She'd travel the mass-transit at rush hour. If anyone else decided they wanted to follow her today, there was no point in making it easy for them.

Cluster IV
August 17th, 2070
03:25 CET Shuttle Beowulf, 5.5 km above Stockholm, Sweden

From wide open cargo bay doors, the newly disavowed corpo-cop watched as distinct clusters of light tracked towards the solid, grid-like mass that was Stockholm. She was on, or more accurately, hanging out of, the 03:20 flight from Solna cargo management depot to EurCon's Galileo orbital complex; and the pilot, a wiry rodent of a man with nicotine-stained fingers and the loose, pallid skin of someone who'd spent far too much time up the well, had made it clear he didn't approve. That said, 2000 Nova on an untraceable pre-paid spike had bought the man's participation, along with a bet the crazy woman's crumpled body would be discovered somewhere inside the Novan citadel's grounds, rather than her safely landing on target.

It was, Gabriel agreed, a ridiculous plan. But as the client had observed, they were paying an obscene number of credits for that very reason.

She was posing, at least for now, as a security consultant; one offering a discreet, low-impact service… And this contract, negotiated through a dark web merc platform, provided Gabriel with access to resources she could never have obtained on her own.

It stank of corporate espionage, of course. Gardner had told her tensions were growing among the polycorps, that whispered accusations now circulated just below the customary veneer of boardroom smiles and promises of enduring friendship… So it really didn't qualify as much of a guess to say it was one of them who'd now decided to go and find out what Nova wasn't saying — obviously with the plausible deniability of an external contractor should things head south.

Whoever the client was, their information stated Levinson's frozen remains were located on the top floor of the city's cryo-storage facility; a place essentially designed to function as a giant electronic sniffer surrounded by waterways crowded with acoustic buoys.

Conventional wisdom had it nothing and no one was sneaking past the polycorp's defences. However, after studying the area, surrounding flight paths, prevailing weather conditions and available bleeding edge technology, the veteran ranger had suggested, and was now gambling that, if an infiltrator emitted zero electroacoustic noise and fell fast enough from directly above, all that technology would be blind to them. But landing safely on target was another matter, and the risk management program repeatedly declared the jump non-viable.

The decompressed cargo bay's smart wall began flashing *"get ready"* in large red letters, and Gabriel searched the city's glowing matrix; eyes tracking the criss-cross strands of brightness for… there, two knots of light radiating outward at Stockholm's heart; separated from the grid by the cold, dark waters of Saltsjon Bay. They'd be over them in seconds. She focused down, augments pulling each eye's lens unnaturally flat. The larger cluster would be the Novan leisure resort and treatment centre on Skeppsholmen. The smaller, on nearby Kastellholmen, was her target — a huge double helix stretching heavenward in Nova's signature declaration of mastery over nature; fifteen storeys of cryogenic storage and laboratories curving around a central administrative stalk like strands of DNA.

The rooftop of that building was her only way *in* and *out*. There was no plan B if she missed, which the pilot had bet with a grim smile was almost certain in the pitch black as she dove through fifty mile-an-hour headwinds with no HUD, assistive tech or thrusters to correct her descent.

A countdown appeared on the wall, and noradrenalin began coursing through Gabriel's system. Her squad had trained for this kind of insertion during the war, and the secretion of the neurotransmitter triggered mods Cybercom had threaded through her brain and body to jack reflexes and enhance perception. Time seemed to slow, and the outwardly unremarkable woman took a moment to enjoy the non-alcoholic rush.

Moments later, an angry squawking from the hold's speakers told her the pilot was straying from his allotted flight corridor, and Gabriel smiled; the crotchety old man had insisted he wouldn't do that. Then the smart wall flashed a message. "*Gonna get a fine now, Missy! Jump....*"

As the small cargo shuttle then corrected its trajectory and burned for one of Earth's geosynchronous habitats, a tiny electronic blackspot plummeted downward. Unnoticed on both aviation control and Novan security scans alike, the corpo-cop, officially declared absent without leave following a no show at her tribunal, fell like an arrow towards Kastellholmen for exactly forty-six seconds. Then she flattened out for twenty more to dump speed and adjust direction before pulling her ripcord just three hundred metres above the rapidly approaching target.

8.6Gs dragged at Gabriel's brain and body as the canopy deployed and she gave a final savage tug on the steering lines to bring the long, flat roof under her feet.

The landing was far from optimal. In fact, the veteran operative felt pretty damn certain she collided with every comms array, aircon unit, or otherwise solid structure poking out of the permacrete surface as she fought to stop the billowing chute from dragging her off the high rooftop to plunge the final three hundred feet to the ground.

With just five meters remaining to the edge, several lines snagged on a vent tube, partially folding the canopy in on itself; and as Gabriel then careened by, jacked reflexes and muscle memory seized the opportunity, unconsciously twisting the agent's body faster than a falling cat to grab at a trailing edge of the voluminous material and bring it under control. Panting with exertion and nervous energy as she then fell across the deflated chute, Gabriel yanked up her visor, gulping in mouthfuls of crisp Nordic air before allowing herself a quiet chuckle.

She'd made it. She was down.

Her right ankle, knee and ribs were all screaming in protest, but neuroanatomical and chemical implants were already tuning out that discomfort ... and, as she listened, the absence of alarms, shouts or running boots lent justification to the utter madness of jumping out of a perfectly good shuttle 18,000 feet above the ground. "You owe me a bottle of decent whiskey, rat man," she whispered to the sky.

The cryo-vaults were easily the highest point on either of the islands, and though, as her view from the shuttle had indicated, the walls of the impressive double-helix were bathed in a bright, boastful light Nova intended all Stockholm see, its roof was in complete darkness, and Gabriel would be all but invisible to anyone looking up from the ground.

Far below, two guards walked a dog towards one of the killbot controlled checkpoints located every fifty metres around the small island's perimeter. Those mechs were reputedly connected to the facility's intrusion countermeasures, with hardwired protocols to shoot anything or anyone not flagged as authorised.

However, since that list necessarily included some four hundred technicians, scientists and admin assistants… and Nova, like all the polycorps, only built *dumb AI* — guards were necessarily added to the mix. Because, while the polycorp might be fearful of a thinking mech, it absolutely understood humans were thieving bastards who would rip you off given half a chance.

According to the client's intelligence though, if Gabriel managed to stick her landing, like she had, none of that would present a problem for her. As once past the island's elaborate electronic security and control measures, so long as you had clearance to enter a given area, the sensitivity of the facility's equipment and requirement for absolutely zero digital interference meant high-end surveillance was almost non-existent. Sure, there'd still be cameras, but according to the specs, Gabriel's faraday suit should show up as nothing more than a temporary glitch on them.

Testing each of those assumptions, the trespassing corpo-cop activated her suit's power supply, and after the HUD in her helmet loaded, brought up the plans provided by the client's source. If that person had done their job, all Gabriel needed to do was access the level below, hack a terminal with the spike she'd been given, steal a few petabytes of data, snatch the package… and vamoose.

After another two minutes had passed with no sign of her presence or electronics prompting a response, Gabriel walked over to the spot flagged in the HUD as her exit point, pulling off both jump gauntlets as she did to examine the ultrathin skin-like gloves beneath. Her guess was they were some kind of imipolymer. The briefing had described them as code / decode or *codec* skinware designed to fool entry and forensic scanners. As with the suit she was wearing, they were unlike anything Gabriel had seen before, and while that shouldn't necessarily mean much to someone who worked for an organisation used to getting corporate cast-offs and antiquated crap, that kind of kit suggested the client was not just rich — he, she, it or they were also very, very connected.

With a final look across Saltsjon Bay to the woods where she'd parked a rental, Gabriel engaged the waypoint in her HUD and headed towards the obvious shape of a hatch sloping up among the roof's loose collection of satellite dishes and comm arrays. According to the source, the vault's maintenance crew didn't start until 04:30. So, as long as her new toys worked, the veteran operative had almost an hour to complete the assignment and sneak back out unnoticed.

'Please wait' lit up on the scanner's screen as Gabriel placed her left hand against its glowing, contoured surface. From what she'd been able to gather, the gloves she wore absorbed fingerprint residue, filling in missing information with likely variables until sixteen or more points of recognition were identified and accepted as authentic by a scanning device. She watched, fascinated, as the vague blue corona of the pad's laser swept around her palm and fingers once, twice, three times — ready to run if sirens started wailing. But, on the fourth sweep, a green light flashed, the hatch popped open, and an automated female voice welcomed Security Officer Hans Yurgen into Cryo-facility: roof-level: hatch 2.

Inside, the waypoint sent her down one flight of galvanised metal stairs to a large, hermetically sealed door with a sign warning those about to enter that what lay beyond was a restricted, sterile, clinical environment. Smoking and unshielded electronics were strictly prohibited, and unauthorised access would result in detention, dismissal or worse.

Despite the ominous connotations of the message, nothing more sophisticated than another 5 by16 recognition pad barred entry, and Gabriel smiled, thinking of the fee she'd charged… this was becoming embarrassingly easy. Within moments, the door whined open with an accompanying hiss and tendrils of chilled vapor, this time for Dr Helen Stromberg.

The vault was in semi-darkness, but Gabriel's enhanced vision easily made out row upon row of cylindrical stasis pods stacked three high on metal racking that ran the length of a large, rectangular space. Each of the frosted visi-steel vessels stood about eleven inches tall, and each, Gabriel assumed as a shiver ran down her spine, contained the frozen head, spinal cord and assorted tissue samples of a now digitised EurCon executive or media star.

She walked along a fluorescent yellow line painted on the floor-space that run at right angles to the end of each numbered row. It glowed eerily in the half-light and intersected every ten feet or so with those travelling down the centre of each aisle. Twenty rows, three high, must be at least a hundred long… Jesus, that was about six thousand frozen remains in this room alone!

Reluctant to use active scanning for fear of triggering an adverse response, Gabriel completed a full circuit of the room to ensure she was alone before following the waypoint to some kind of control booth located at the cavernous crypt's centre. The door wasn't locked and, from the holos and personal effects set neatly beside the single techdeck present, it seemed only Dr Stromberg worked in the small glass box.

Sitting down at the console interface, the agent removed her helmet and pulled a set of PDrive leads out of her thigh pocket along with the data-spike she'd been given, inserting each into a port. She'd not been told what the spike contained; intruder programs, she guessed. It had been tempting to have the thing analysed. But she knew from bitter experience powerful people almost always protected their tech, and nosey contractors tended to find themselves going for a swim wearing concrete wellies.

After connecting to the perception drive, Gabriel let out a breath, hoping the damn thing wasn't about to start World War 4, and activated the terminal. Long strings of incomprehensible code crowded her visual cortex, then disappeared as the spike began picking away at the polycorp's digital locks. If she was going to get caught, this was the time, and as ten seconds crawled to twenty, the corpo-cop began considering the possibility she'd tripped a silent alarm; that security were on their way. But just before the desire to unjack and check became irresistible, her visuals refreshed: WELCOME TO NOVA CLINICAL DATABASES.... PLEASE CHOOSE AN OPTION.

She was in.

The operating system was familiar, a variant of Nova's commercially available Node++, and as instructed, Gabriel typed >>LDC, a standard abbreviation used by tech geeks and deck jockeys to access the list of directory commands.

A busy light glowed momentarily, then column after column of program access commands began scrolling through her mind. She moved down the long list to highlight *CLIENTFILES.

The screen refreshed and a query portal opened up.

>>SEARCH {Levinson, Elizabeth} .... NO RESULTS FOUND. TRY ADJUSTING YOUR ENQUIRY PARAMETERS.

With a roll of her eyes at finicky computer filters, Gabriel typed >>SEARCH {Elizabeth, Levinson} .... NO RESULTS FOUND. TRY ADJUSTING YOUR ENQUIRY PARAMETERS. Okay, she thought, clearing the enquiry field again — not just finicky filters.

After trying just {Levinson} with no success, Gabriel brought up a list of all execs that had been through the facility in the last six months and filtered it by parent corporation; eight were from Consolidated. But when she checked each file, none were Levinson.

Was it possible those public denials the woman had been digitised were true? That Gardner's intel was wrong?

With an exasperated sigh, the corpo-cop delved into her own memory storage for the date intel said Levinson had attended the clinic: July 30th to 31st. Just two weeks earlier. She interrogated the database for ten days either side.

Still nothing.

Gabriel let out a low growl. She was smashing her cybernetic head against a digital brick wall here — no client entry meant no client entry. Changing tack, the onetime black ops specialist compared the listed names with system generated references. There were the same number of each but, her scan software noted, there was an anomalous jump between cryo-references E43768 to E43770. Returning to the query portal, she allowed herself a grin: >>LOCATE {E43769} …. NO RESULTS FOUND. TRY ADJUSTING YOUR ENQUIRY PARAMETERS.

"Fuck." Gabriel said, slamming a hand down on the deck in frustration. This was taking too long. She sat back, trying to think through her options. Then the obvious occurred… "Just go and check the racks dumb-ass." With an irritated sigh, the corpo-cop requested the physical location of samples E43768 and E43770.

…. SCF10.R8(A2)-P88.P90.

Well finally, a result.

With an increased sense of urgency, Gabriel returned to the LDC and began copying files in an order directed by the client. As the first datastick began filling, she accessed *ARCHIVED, still irked at her inability to locate any reference to Levinson.

There was nothing of interest.

Then she jumped ahead to *PURGED and found a single file within — a sample that had been deleted just a week before the Consolidated exec's disappearance. Intrigued, Gabriel accessed the record. From his photograph, the subject

'John Doe,' was a wraithlike man who had clearly been knocking on death's door. Then again, that was probably true of most of the old weezers stored in this facility. According to the summary, *John's* transfer back in the fifties hadn't taken. Which begged the questions, in Gabriel's limited understanding of the subject: why would his remains have been kept at all, and why only get rid of them now? A light on the deck began blinking and she swapped dataspikes, pushing *PURGED higher up the queue for copying.

Twenty minutes and three full data-spikes later, Gabriel was close to done when the screen in her visual cortex slammed down; the breaker program flashing a warning in her peripherals... a system trace had been activated.

Swearing, the veteran operative severed her connection and unjacked, sliding sticks and connectors into thigh pockets and pulling her helmet back into place.

She'd hoped to get in and out without notice, but now she was in a race. When the complex's cyber-security supervisor realised this wasn't an external hack; that it was coming from one of their own terminals — they'd lock Stockholm down tighter than a drum; and Gabriel, if still inside, would be properly fucked.

She left Stromberg's office at a run, the time for subtlety gone, and reached the end of the central aisle in seconds, following the signage to row 8. Arrows pointed to 'A' and 'B' sides, and each stack was numbered '1' lower, '2'middle, '3' top. She jogged along the row, counting numbers as she went; a sense of anticipation building... 84, 85, 86, 87, 88...90. She laughed — of course there'd be a fucking gap.

Mind racing, the corpo-cop checked the floor's schematics for where else the source's ambiguous information might mean Levinson's remains were stored. There was a lab, she noticed, far wall closest to the main entrance. Common sense said she should leave. But the rogue agent just couldn't let it go. Throwing caution to the wind, she sprinted back down the row, turning with the fluorescent line towards the room's main entrance and a double walled visi-steel laboratory module sitting in the corner beyond it.

Not pausing to consider the quarantine warning, Gabriel shoved through both sets of lab doors and immediately noticed a lone cylinder connected to an isolated cryo-feed and array of instruments. She was tempted to access the techdeck, but knew she had no time. There was just one answer she needed right now. Was it Levinson?

Heart pounding, Gabriel approached the stasis-pod and rubbed at its frost coated glass. There, frozen in pale, peaceful repose, was the fleshy shaven head of an unnamed and unnumbered human. Faces look different when you remove their hair and eyebrows, more generic. But the suit's HUD blinked an immediate and unequivocal 100% match.

She'd found her.

Head full of questions, Gabriel unclipped the pod's feed lines and slid the metal cylinder into an insulated pack from her suit; thankful there were no tamper alarms. Having then secured it to the purpose made clamps on her chest plate, Gabriel sprinted from the lab and back across the large, dark storage area to the door she'd entered through.

A wave of relief washed down her spine as the air-seal hissed and the thick door whined aside for a second time. She took the stairs beyond in twos, thumping a gloved hand on the ID pad beside the roof hatch. Another green light flashed in approval.

"Thank you," she offered breathlessly to whatever gods were listening, shoving the door wide just as an amber beacon in the ceiling began rotating and an automated female voice announced all staff should remain at their workstations; that this was not a drill. The access panel turned red and locking bolts sprang from the doorframe. When they failed to engage with the reciprocal holes in the door, an ear-piercing alarm replaced the voice. Security would know exactly where she was now.

Stepping out onto the rooftop, Gabriel killed all the suit's electronic emissions and ran to the spot she'd left her gauntlets. Tugging at zippers running down the inside of each leg and from waist to wrist on either side of her torso, she shook loose web-like flaps of air-resistant imipolymer while eyeing the 450 metres to Wasahamnen Marina. The math said she should make it across; her gut said different. Not pausing to overthink, the corpo-cop pulled on her gauntlets, oriented herself to take advantage of the wind, and leapt.

By the time a squad of security officers stepped cautiously onto the roof, flooding the wide barren space with light, the black clad agent had glided through Stockholm's darkness to land in woodland beyond the marina. They'd eventually piece together what she'd done, but not until they'd searched every square inch of that facility and its grounds; and by then, Gabriel would be long gone.

"You made it back out then?" Warren Gardner began after she'd sealed the passenger compartment and activated her web feed. The Chief's avatar was an old holovid gangster that mimicked his real time actions.

Laughing with adrenalin infused energy at the thing's facial expression, the corpo-cop nodded. "Just about," she replied. "Give me a moment and I'll send some presents."

After obscuring the vehicle's windows and commencing its pre-programmed route, Gabriel then loaded each of the data spikes into her portable techdeck, encrypted their contents, and pressed send.

"I reckon that lot should keep you entertained for a while. But long story short, they've wiped all trace of Levinson from their system. Although, the woman's frozen remains were still there; in a lab, not the cryo-racks."

Gardner's gangster scowled, the text in their private chat window dissolving to nothing as her avatar spoke his end. "The only other thing that immediately jumped out was another file that got system flushed a week before the Levinson shit show started. It just seemed odd, sat all alone in a folder that, as far as I could tell, hadn't been used once in the previous fifteen years."

"Who was it?" Gardner messaged.

"John Doe, apparently!" Gabriel's avatar mimicked her laugh. "I know, right? His file is among the data I sent you. Old man from the fifties whose transition didn't take. It seemed odd they would keep his samples only to flush them now?"

"They wouldn't," Gardner typed. "Standby. Let's take a quick look." His avatar flashed an *away* signal, and Gabriel took the opportunity to begin extracting herself from the figure-hugging black suit. When the Interpol chief returned, there was a whole new level of urgency in his words.

"Do they know you've been inside?"

Gabriel cocked her head at the change of tempo. "Well, they'll know *someone's* been in there. I set off an alarm… and one of their cryo-pods is missing. Problem?"

The avatar shook its head, mimicking Gardner's actions back in New York. He was doing something off-screen. "This is a whole new level of fucked up, Sousa. You concentrate on Levinson and forget you ever saw that other file."

"Who is it?" the corpo-cop persisted.

"Best you don't know."

"Fuck that, Chief. If that file is likely to cause me grief, I reckon I have the right?"

Gardner's avatar was clearly unhappy, but then nodded its head in reluctant agreement. "Fair point… Heard of Daran Whittaker?"

"*The* Daran Whittaker…? Huge corpo-king found guilty of fomenting rebellion in China?"

"The very same. We understood him to have died in a labour camp during the war. So what the hell he was doing in a European cryo-vault creates all kinds of scary questions? This just gets worse and worse... You need to delete that file. Let me handle things from this end."

The undercover agent stopped her wriggling, focusing solely on the fear radiating from the older man's words. "I can't edit those spikes, Gardner. The client will know I've deleted something. If I do that, I might as well just shoot myself in the head and save whoever it is the job of sending another contractor to paste me. What's got you so spooked?"

Gardner's avatar did its best to replicate a sigh. "Daran Whittaker was one of the shrewdest, most divisive men I ever met. He made Ido Maas look positively charming, and he had a lot of people, I mean *a lot*, in his pocket. The fact someone tried to digitise him sends a shiver down my spine. But it's the who and why that has me spooked... And according to the file, he wasn't frozen."

"Not frozen? What does that mean?"

"I'm not sure. But I guess maybe he was rigged up to something."

"You mean still alive?"

"Scary thought, huh? You figured out who your client is yet?"

"No. But unless they're being ultra cautious and sending Levinson on a *very* circuitous route to wherever she's going, I'd guess they're EurCon; and high up, judging by the kit they provided."

Gardner's avatar frowned again. "So then we have to wonder what their angle is?"

"Exactly, why have someone break into a facility you already have executive access to? Even if I could edit those spikes, we've no idea what the client already knows. Levinson might have just been a pretext for exposing Whittaker, or God only knows what else you're gonna find, in those files I pulled from their database."

The strangled, mechanical equivalent of a sigh manifested again. "If Nova put him there… trouble. If someone in EurCon did it without Nova knowing… trouble. No matter what we do next, the cat is out of the bag when both polycorps complete a security review."

Gabriel pulled a bottle of scotch from an inside pocket of her half-off suit, leaning out of the camera's pickup to take a long swallow. "But that's why you sent me…isn't it? See how far the rabbit hole goes?"

"Hmm," Gardner responded. "Where are you heading now?"

"Rotterdam. Then a shuttle to London."

"London? Isn't that where Levinson worked? Consolidated's domain?"

"Yep."

The Chief's avatar began shaking its head. "None of this makes any sense, Sousa. But if you're right about Levinson being a pretext, there's a much bigger game being played out here; one that likely involves Daran Whittaker… and you've just walked right into the middle of it. Be careful."

 **Cluster V**

August 18th, 2070
10:25 PST Nova Earthside Headquarters, San Francisco Bay

Ido Maas stood on a huge open terrace that wound around the executive apartment complex of Nova's earthside headquarters, looking down on San Francisco Bay. A lot had changed in the twenty-six years since he'd met Cheng Li on the helipad one level above. Back then, he'd played second fiddle to Daran Whittaker and Eden. Now he was the undisputed first among equals, the most powerful man in the solar system.

Admittedly, much of that power was derived from the technology he and Li had *acquired* as a result of Eden's not so civil war. But fortune favoured the bold, and Ido's plans for expansion were positively audacious.

He didn't enjoy coming Earthside anymore; he'd lived one life down here; achieved his goals... and now time was nothing more than a measurement to judge others by — the heavens would become his new empire.

Unlike most digitals, giddy with the possibilities now offered through genetic engineering, Nova's Chief Executive and Polycorporate President had not chosen to create some perfectified physical ideal. Instead, he retained the outward appearance of the fifty-five-year-old who'd changed the world forever; deified the image of the man who'd made digital immortality a reality.

Tall for an Asian, and handsome in a statesmanlike way, he'd also forsaken flesh and bone for imipolymer and graphene. It still amazed him how, twenty-three years after his rEvolution chip's general release, *the haves* clamoured to remove their essence from the intrinsic weakness of a human body ... only to pay for it to be placed into another one, which they then exchanged and traded with monotonous regularity — as if the organism were nothing more than a discardable fashion accessory.

Ido wasn't complaining, of course; over sixty percent of the polycorp's revenue was generated from one aspect of Nova's transition tech or another. But, unlike almost all his contemporaries, the far-sighted leader understood the bigger picture; understood the step forward digitisation presented. It was an evolution. Not the kind that relies on natural selection over long, painful millennia. But rather, the kind that would allow a visionary bold enough to transcend all the limitations nature imposed… to glimpse Godhood.

He was *more* than human now, and the only things he *truly* considered a threat to what he was building were those intelligences that had always existed in digital form.

Mechs were a useful tool. AI made an excellent assistant. But allow either to think for themselves? Give them rights? Don't be fucking ridiculous…

He let out a long, slow breath, staring towards the decaying city that had once been home, then dropped back into the body three floors below in Nova's boardroom, where Omar Rhamn's painfully long briefing had finally reached the important updates.

"So, our supply chain is leaking like a sieve," Ido cut in, locking eyes on the polycorp's risk and compliance officer. "But what of the virus?" he demanded, irritation at the recently appointed senior executive obvious. "That is clearly the more pressing issue, is it not?"

Rhamn ran a nervous hand over the ridges of his carefully braided beard. "Of course, ser Maas," he said, shifting his presentation forward and clearing his throat to re-start. "My staff have been liaising with Yochi's chemists and engineers. But they still have nothing firm—"

Ido's daughter, Akira, held out a hand, silencing the big man and looking towards the diminutive woman sitting three chairs further along the table. "Yochi, you might as well take this if he's just going to name drop."

Nova's corporate director of scientific development looked at Ido. The president gave a slight nod, and the petite professor of digital medicine stood. "As previously reported solely to the president and vice-president, an exec from London, Elizabeth Levinson, died for a second time three days ago from what we're approximating to a digital adaptation of rapid onset Rabies."

Yochi threw images of what was clearly the same individual, taken over several days, onto the central holo display.

"She'd only undergone the transfer procedure two weeks before in Stockholm. I've reviewed the QA process, scans and associated biometric and biomechanical data. She was suitable and there were no identified anomalies. But in her second week post-op, colleagues reported her becoming agitated, confused and anxious. Over the subsequent twenty-four hours, that condition then developed into an irrevocable shutdown of the central nervous system. The virus effectively corrupted her core's matrix, causing a total loss of identity and bodily control. I assume EurCon's president has discussed the matter with you?"

Ido and Akira nodded.

"Well then, you'll know that when their tech's tried to place her stored consciousness into a second skin, the core was once again completely corrupted within twenty-four hours. Though only a sample group of one, that rather worryingly suggests the week or so her previous incarnation existed before displaying symptoms may not have been an incubation period, and the virus was either initially dormant or introduced following her return to London.

"Consolidated Systems weren't happy, but EurCon security has taken control of the incident and turned both skins over to us, along with their insurance division's copy of her digital consciousness.

"As it stands, we've found nothing in either that copy or our post procedure scans of the brain archived in Stockholm to suggest outside interference. But then, neither is there any trace of a pre-existing malady. I'd planned to have everything shipped here for further analysis until yesterday's—"

"We'll discuss yesterday separately, Yoshi," Ido cut in. "Please, concentrate on the update for now."

The woman gave a slight bow. "Of course... EurCon placed an immediate quarantine on their storage facility after the incident, and transfers have been suspended in Stockholm. Engineering has explained the pause as part of a universal system overhaul and update... which we are in fact doing. It's just that Stockholm wasn't originally due for a refit until next year."

Yochi paused, looking around the table for questions. None came. "In terms of the files attached to the dark web post that specifically named Levinson as proof of its author's claims, the data hints at a very sophisticated neuroinvasive digital pathogen... But I stress the word *hints*. It's nowhere near complete or detailed enough to say with any certainty it was the cause of Levinson's death."

"Except by the media and a rapidly increasing number of panicked execs," Akira grumbled. "I thought EurCon had agreed to fabricate a reality that involved Levinson going missing? Perhaps a defection or corporate kidnapping?"

"They did, and they have," Karen Sharp, Nova's director of Public Communications said. "As far as their security and talking heads are concerned, the woman hadn't yet undergone the transfer process, and with the compliments of Anton van Brieda himself, the polycorp has even produced surveillance streams of the woman leaving Consolidated's headquarters in her *old* body just two days before she was reported missing. That story and *evidence* are now being pushed out to the general population through every public feed in every domain with clear directions that each is to support the message — *'Doomsday Dark Web post proved a fraud! Exec named not even Digital.'*"

Ido smiled at that last touch. He liked Sharp; she was utterly ruthless. "Excellent. I've no doubt Anton will be expecting a favour in return. But I agree the price is worth it to shut down all this fear and speculation. Well done."

The comms director nodded.

"But is it a fraud?" Ezra Cohen, his chief financial officer, asked. "Are we at risk if we update?"

"We've had CICI run diagnostics through both our clinic and EurCon's storage facilities. It hasn't detected any unauthorised code," Yochi said. "But a human analytic team did identify a string of anomalous reboots CICI can't account for."

"What does that mean?" Ezra persisted.

Yochi's shoulders moved before she could suppress the shrug; she knew Ido hated such off-hand expressions. "It happens now and then, so maybe nothing. But given the stakes, I'm having the AI's code pulled apart string by string."

Ido nodded in agreement.

"And our corporate networks and servers?" Arlan Dicker, another director, threw in.

Yochi took a frustrated breath; her office had been inundated with similarly ridiculous questions over the last twenty-four hours. "Pending the result of CICI's review, all I can say, Arlan, is that there isn't any unauthorised code in our data-streams." The raven-haired scientist gave the sharp-featured man an irritated look, then swept her eyes across the other faces around the table. "But as you all know, the moment a single employee in any of our thousands of companies opens a malware infected link that isn't caught by the security AI, that branch of the network will be *immediately* compromised. So no," she returned her gaze to the self-concerned executive. "I cannot *categorically* state anything. In fact, I'd advise we inform the Council to avoid backups and digital transfers until we've confirmed this is nothing more than a single, anomalous event... Just as a precaution."

Ido frowned, leaning forward to speak again before Akira could respond. Over the last five years, as he'd built up the colony on Mars, preparing to push beyond the belt into Jovian space, Nova's president had handed more and more power to his daughter and her husband; satisfied his polycorp's stranglehold on Earth's economy, and therefore government, was secure. But, in little more than a week, that confidence had been shaken to the core, and Ido couldn't help but reassert his dominance. He'd been vaguely aware of the petty piracy, of course, of the ongoing pilfering; and that hadn't bothered him. All big dogs got the occasional flea. But this Levinson issue… that had him worried. His entire corporate strategy was predicated on the transfer technology. If someone was truly capable of corrupting it, the global control he'd spent a quarter of a century building, and almost all of his long-term plans were suddenly at risk.

"Well," he smiled at the gathered board members. "Just as I'm about to go stake Nova's claim on the other half of this solar system, we find ourselves facing an existential threat right here on Earth." Forty almost perfect faces, most looking nothing like their original incarnations, stared back; unsure if their mercurial leader was being jovial or sarcastic.

The smile faded, providing a clue.

"You all realise, I'm sure, that the other polycorps won't have missed these events," he added in a harsher tone. "Hell, one or more of them might even be behind this scare; and though each board will say all the right things to our faces, don't doubt for a single second that a mix of fear and opportunity will drive their individual actions.

"As such, while we will publicly continue to maintain the dark web message is nothing more than hacktivist criminality, I agree with Yochi, though perhaps for different reasons, that suggesting our fellow polycorporate senior executives refrain from digital travel or update, and leaning into a full, system-wide review makes sense… It's a move our cyber-terrorist will not expect, so has the potential to expose those plotting against us; and irrespective of whether there is or isn't a bug — we can then develop and market a security patch that each and every existing digital will need to download."

Responding to several intakes of breath, the ruthless business veteran raised both hands above the table, palms out. "We're a business are we not? So when the universe gives us lemons...?"

Akira couldn't help but grin at how her father always found opportunities in adversity. "So, we advise a pause in digital activities while Nova conducts a commercially responsible review. Which will remind each of the polycorps that we can take away as well as give, and quietly addresses any corporate liability attached to the vanishingly small chance of others becoming infected?" She was nodding as she spoke, then turned to Nova's Head of Legal. "Right Hal?"

The grim-faced lawyer gave a single dip of his head. "I'll have something airtight drafted and sent to Karen."

"Good." Ido returned his gaze to the rest of the board. "It's going to be a busy few days. But in every dealing you have, both inside and outside the organisation, you make it clear we're still in charge. Understood? Remind your counterparts in the other polycorps that when this is over... those who actively supported Nova will be rewarded — and those found to have plotted or schemed against us will be cut-off from the transfer technology and / or digital vaccine.

"WE STILL HOLD ALL THE CARDS!" He slammed an open palm on the table as he enunciated each word. "And to remind EVERYONE of that — Bill, I want our security services to go on the offensive... show the world this dog still has teeth!"

The polycorp's Director of Corporate Security gave the president's daughter a satisfied look. "Damn right," he said with an edge of accusation. "I've already laid out some plans for the low hanging fruit. It's clear a criminal gang doesn't have the smarts, resources or infrastructure to pull off the kind of wholesale misappropriation Omar's audit has identified—"

"But we can rely on our amazing intelligence machine to tell us who or what does, right Bill?" Akira interrupted, sarcasm clear in her voice. Renton would be leaving when her father did, and she couldn't wait to be rid of the loathsome creature.

The dead-eyed man regarded the VP with a cold smile. She already knew the answer to that question, because she was the one who'd turned down his previous proposals. "If I'd been given a freer hand to begin with, sera, those concerned would have been identified already," he bit back, before returning his attention to Ido. "But you can bet your bottom dollar at least one high level corporate is involved.

"As for the virus, that's got Eric bloody Thorne's missing digital written all over it," he sneered. "The damn thing has been a constant pain in our corporate ass since his pet abomination was euthanised, and this *terrorism* provides a perfect excuse to finally locate and terminate it."

Yochi cleared her throat, and Renton paused to regard her. "Sorry, I'm not sure I'd agree with that assessment, Bill."

The security director rolled eyes, but held out a hand, yielding the floor.

"Well, as you know, I've spent a great deal of time working with and studying Eric Thorne's wetware and code. And while I accept directions can change, he's never developed anything that would *actually* harm anyone. I'd also suggest that although the coding style in those technical files is remarkably similar to Thorne's, it's not his work."

"But we're talking about a deranged copy, Yochi, not the man hiding in China whose work you admire so much. Are you saying it couldn't have significantly diverged in attitudes from the original over the last twenty-six years?"

Nova's lead scientist pursed her lips, but didn't reply.

"Either way," Renton continued, returning his gaze once again to Nova's president. "S*omeone* is threatening to unleash a digital neurotoxin — and even if it's bullshit, they must have claws in a EurCon employee with pretty high security clearance, or they wouldn't even know about Levinson."

The intense, thin man leaned over the table, bringing his hands together, meshing fingers. "So, when you put our current concerns side by side, while I'm not saying they're necessarily connected, they do share a common delivery system — the dark web. That's what links and co-ordinates all the criminal activity perpetrated against Novan businesses. That's where whoever is masterminding it all hides their trail. And that's where our virus spreading saboteur lurks... So, I'd suggest, that's where we start bashing heads. A few raids and an execution or two will soon loosen tongues." He flicked a sideways glance at the VP again. "...Then, Mr President, you'll know exactly where to throw *ALL* your corporate weight."

Akira was shaking her head, but Ido ignored her. It was time to take the reins back, at least until this crisis was over. "Okay, Bill has summarised the problem and offered a solution," he said. "Does anyone disagree or have anything meaningful to offer?"

He stressed the word *meaningful.*

"Good. Bill, I want you to work with Omar and his team. Examine that audit in granular detail, identify the common factors. Then use whatever tactics you feel necessary to establish who is involved in that chain of offending from the dark web all the way through to subsequent black-market outlets. I want the names of hackers, traitors, thieves, handlers, gangs and end-users. I want heads to roll. I want fear inside and outside Nova. Rewards for informers. Public trials, humiliation and death for traitors... Yes?"

Ido glared up and down both sides of the table. "Incentivise every asset we have deployed in the other polycorps, Council and Interpol. Whatever floats their boat; digitisation, wealth, power — offer it. I want to know who is fucking with us. I want to know why they're doing it. And then I want to very publicly eviscerate them."

Renton nodded, lips curled in a rare smile.

"Yochi, throw everything you have at unpicking what happened to Levinson. We all know people went wrong in the early days, and it was always undisclosed genetics. So when your investigations give CICI a clean bill of health, ensure Consolidated, EurCon and the Council get the message: '*Levinson was an anomaly – but now you have to pay for a security patch if you want to access our updated systems.*

"Karen, until CICI gets a clean bill of health, place an embargo on anyone below management opening attachments from external sources, and silo each server farm to work independently of the others. I know that will impede efficiency, but the reduction in infection risk is worth it. Once done, pick a few people in each organisation who fail to comply with that simple directive, have them fired, remove their citizenship, and kick them out of any corporate accommodation. Tell everyone else they can expect the same treatment if they fuck up.

"The rest of you," Ido bared his teeth, looking from face to face around the long, rhodium edged table. "Not a single word of fear is to be breathed outside this boardroom. It's business as usual, and while your positions at the pinnacle of Nova's corporate empire vouchsafe your trustworthiness and dedication to the polycorp — one loose comment or public display of concern, and you will suffer the same fate as any other failed employee... So put your big boy pants on Ezra, Arlan, and paint a confident smile on your damn faces. Understood?"

Both directors flushed but knew better than to argue.

"Everyone else?"

The room filled with nods and murmured *yeses*.

"Excellent." The president re-adopted his customary air of benignity and looked at Akira. "This is a time for decisive action, not back-channel diplomacy," he added, smoothing the angry lines on his face with a smile. "Now, unless you have anything to add, daughter?"

Akira, features carefully neutral, shook her head.

"…Then, let's break for lunch."

As board members began filing from the room or signed out of remote holo-feeds, Ido waved Bill Renton and Yochi Hamachi over. "So, what of our visitor in Stockholm?" he asked quietly, smiling and nodding as others passed.

"Extremely well trained," Bill said. "Cutting edge tech. I don't know who, yet. But I'm paying an obscene amount to a municipal ops room tech to run facial recognition across the city and surrounding ports for the day before and after. Anyone known to our intel systems will be flagged."

Ido nodded impatiently. "Yes, yes. But do we know what they were looking for?"

"Levinson," a nonplussed Renton replied. "She was the centre of the search enquiries, and they located and stole her remains."

"So you're telling me they didn't take or access anything else?"

Renton's face blanked momentarily as he accessed the intelligence in his neural feed. "They stripped a few dozen petabytes of data from the mainframe. My team are going through the fine detail now. But there's nothing sensitive in the clinical databases, not to Nova anyway. Just client data and system files."

Ido frowned. "Why take Levinson's cryo-pod, Yochi?"

The small woman shook her head. "I don't know, Ido. I'm confident it won't tell them anything; it was perfectly normal. But that brain's existence with a Novan implant makes a lie of the story Karen has fabricated."

Ido waved a hand. "I'm not worried about that. In fact, I hope that's all it is… I'll personally crucify whoever tries to expose us before setting Bill and his people loose on their corporation. If anything, I'd be more concerned about some unknown having access to a fully functional implant. But if that's what they were after, why take a potentially compromised one?"

"There was nothing wrong with Levinson's implant," Yochi observed.

"Right, but the thief wouldn't have known that, would they, Yoch? So what's their angle?" The Corporate Director of Scientific Development gave another impotent shrug, and Ido responded with an irritated sigh, turning back to his Head of Security. "And what about Interpol? What do our esteemed corpo-cops have to say?"

"Not a lot right now. As you know, Gardner put Rodriguez in charge of the investigation," Renton said. "So you'll probably get updates before he does. You just need to decide what you want the Deputy Chief to know, and what buttons you want him to push in the other polycorps?"

Ido nodded, still frowning. Stockholm worried him. It wasn't the first time someone had attempted to break into a Novan clinic. It wouldn't be the last. But why would someone break in looking for Levinson? Trying to find evidence of a lie didn't resonate; the other presidents knew he'd destroy anyone attempting to leverage him. And if Yoshi saw no scientific value in possessing the head, it seemed unlikely someone would go to that much trouble just to steal it. So, setting aside random coincidence, which Ido didn't believe in, he was left with a third, unclear motive in which Levinson was little more than a prop.

"Have all available crawler bots go over the footage in that building for several weeks either side of the burglary," he finally said.

"Several weeks?" Renton choked. "That'll bring a lot of other intelligence work to a standstill, Ido?"

The olive-skinned business titan nodded. "And have your face rec techie add anyone who can access that floor to his search program... We're missing a beat here, Bill. There's a bigger picture we're not yet seeing."

Cluster VI
August 20th, 2070
02:26 PST Derelict Factory, Pacific Drive, Frisco Freetown

There was no doubting the warehouses along Fisherman's Wharf were prime real estate, and the old town's closest point to Digital City, or DC as the locals called the technological metropolis stretching out beyond Alcatraz, not only functioned as a quasi-border between those two disparate worlds, but also as the main staging post for people and goods being smuggled into and out of the polycorp city.

As with almost all other things, the corporations, though severely limiting individual intelligences, placed the bulk of their security apparatus in the hands of machines: surveillance, intrusion detection, countermeasures... each controlled by mechs and system-based programs that responded to specific *if/then* protocols. Which, with the right technical support, made sneaking into the less sensitive corporate facilities relatively simple. Especially if you were paying the machine's human supervisor to look the other way when you did so.

That was the only real benefit to not being Novan so far as Lily could tell. Unlike every single corpo grunt, for whom GPS chipping was a prerequisite of citizenship, a talented grifter could move through DC's dock and storage yards almost completely untracked, and so never show up in the wrong place at the wrong time on subsequent security audits. The absence of any geo-tagging on most non-corporates was one of the reasons Frisco's original gangbosses had defiantly appended the term *freetown* to their shithole. It was also why the gangs had so many low-level corpos on their books... earning a little extra coin for turning that blind-eye.

The gang's warehouses, on the other hand, were an absolute bastard to steal from, and Lily was already regretting letting Opperman talk her into one last hustle with the promise of replacement parts for her centrifuge. According to the sweaty smuggler the Yaks had gone after the Russe two weeks earlier, and that had kick-started a whole new round of hurt among the gangs. Bad for anyone caught up in the fighting. But good, it seemed, for the South African's business.

Tonight, a grubby halo hung around the beam of bright white light punching through dense storm clouds into the heavens above the polycorp's island citadel; casting a dirty grey twilight over the decaying sprawl and picking out momentary flashes of colour as heavy rain pounded the quayside beyond the pockmarked derelict across the road. In a bygone age, Lily once read, Pier 3's stucco face and wide, yawning mouth had welcomed guests to a parade of artisan boutiques and high-end eateries. Now, the part-collapsed industrial building was home to nothing more than a growing colony of radioactive river rats and a well-hidden lightweight hover she'd never expected to use like this again.

The place used to be their start point for picking trips because, aside from a few ghouls and other beyond broken souls pawing through the rubble of the outer city, no one lived on this part of the fringe anymore, and so no one paid any attention to it; functioning utilities stopped at least four blocks inward, no merchants traded beyond Chinatown, and the toxic water was devoid of edible life.

Standing on the fourth floor of the factory opposite, the newly unretired grifter switched her goggles to thermography and flicked through the settings until her vision resolved on the glowing nest of rats. Then she scanned the waterfront for several hundred meters either side. Only a fool would be out in this deluge — which made it perfect *picking* weather.

"I hate going out when it's this bad," Liam complained. "My electronics go all kerflooey."

"True," the twenty-four-year-old replied, fine red hair whipping around in the wind. "But so do everyone else's. Meaning, if you look at it the right way, cousin of mine — it's really an advantage."

The heavyset youth laughed, wrapping the long black duster he always wore when picking tight around his frame, and leaned into her. "You sure you can trust Opperman?"

Lily snorted, shaking her head. "You kidding? Of course not. But it's his pick... I mean, why would he want to fuck us over when we're grabbing his own merch?"

"Hmm," Liam replied in a sceptical tone. "I don't like the guy."

"Well, he's in good company then," Lily chuckled, giving her cousin a big squeeze. "Because you don't seem to like anything much tonight, do you? Two hours max, cuz, and we'll have a working centrifuge as well as Pieter off our backs for good. All debts paid... C'mon," she said, turning him back towards their old home in the rubble filled interior. "Let's grab the others and get going."

The sealed cabin of the hover prevented signal leakage, while its angular shape and radiation absorbent hull made the small black craft all but invisible as it glided on near silent repulsion pads over the Bay's viscous waters. Inside, five sets of eyes, gently illuminated by their goggle displays, watched from the hollowed out rear compartment while Liam, bathed in the soft green glow of Lily's instrument panels, read absorption stats as they crept up on the unused wooden pier.

Timed right, the old jetty sat just high enough above the waterline to conceal the low boat among its stilts. But getting past the sniffers and sifters was a bitch universally accepted by most of Frisco's grifters as too stupid or dangerous to attempt.

"Okay," Lily said, sweat on her thin face belying the casual tone. "We're in. Everyone got the warehouse loaded in their bins?"

The other six fiddled with their goggles, then nodded.

"Banging. Remember, keep your feeds buttoned down, the sniffers will track 'em. So that means no scanning, no surfing, no feedchat and no streaming… Just good old-fashioned poking, pointing and whispering.

"We'll crawl to the old terminal building like we did on our last pick and then roof hop from there. The warehouse we want is five over. Opperman says there's a loosely boarded rooflight on the left side. That's our way in. He also says there won't be any muscle 'cos they're all tied up with the Yaks. But we can't bank on that, so stay keyed and take nothing for granted. You grab?"

The small gang nodded again.

As the roof then rolled back, Lily nudged the hover over to a rusted metal crawl space running under the slowly rotting wooden pier, and Liam, whose turn it was to stand guard, secured the small craft to a stilt.

"Remember," he whispered. "Half hour, then I creep to the side of the wharf. The longer I'm there, the more likely I am to be seen." Digit gave him the finger and told him to man up. Liam grinned, flipping one back, then sat in the pilot's seat of the gently rocking hover, adjusting his goggles as Lily and the others swung out onto the low hanging scaffold.

Opperman had made his scrip smuggling for most of the larger gangs. But Lily knew he occasionally ran a discrete side hustle which involved re-stealing and re-selling particularly lucrative merch; and according to him, somewhere inside one of the Russian warehouses on Fisherman's Wharf, the young thieves would find a geo-tagged crate loaded with unique biotech he intended to ship outside Nova. The crew's job was to steal the damn thing, along with a random selection of other crap, and make it look like the Yaks had done it.

But the rain and occasional headlamp of soaked joe boys muttering their way through the labyrinth of interconnecting alleyways meant getting up to the rooftops was harder than expected, and by the time they'd found and squeezed their way through Opperman's tiny hole, Lily was fretting. They'd need to hurry if they were going to get out before Liam had to make a run for it.

Radar, Nish and Mo clearly had the same vibe running, as all three were already climbing down the metal web of girders; torchlights illuminating hundreds of stacked crates and anonymous tarp covered shapes within the eerie darkness.

"At least," Digit whispered as he joined her on the catwalk below their entry point, "there's no muscle in here."

Lily nodded, switching her goggles to the frequency Opperman had given for his g-tags and almost immediately saw the luminescent handprint on a crate sitting by itself against the seaward wall of the old concrete prefab. She raised her eyes in thanks to any and all gods watching, then began following Digit down.

Once they were all on the ground, Nish gestured towards the crate, indicating himself, Lita and Mo, before pantomiming Lily and Digit making a hole in the wall. The young gangboss nodded agreement, holding up both gloved hands — *Ten minutes and we're outta here*. A round of thumbs up followed, and everyone was moving.

The silence, especially inside their heads, was an odd feeling. Living on the fringe or not, each of the kids had saved and paid for a legit wire-job — instant feed connection straight to the sensorys. But a couple of years earlier, after watching Ramirez of the Spaniards execute his own brother, they'd learned there were times to turn your tech off… like when conspiring with other gang members to topple your brother-boss. Until then, it hadn't even occurred to Radar, their resident tech nerd, that private comms could be hacked and tracked. So when they worked now, they did so with their media on lockdown.

"Psst."

Lily looked round to see Nish waving her over. She checked the time in the corner of her goggles; they had four minutes left. "What?" she mouthed.

"Just come here a sec," the heavyset Indian hissed.

Lily rolled her eyes in annoyance and left Digit with the laser-lance. As she walked towards the others, she could see they'd opened Opperman's crate, and wisps of condensing vapor were escaping from the container within.

"What the fuck, you guys. You've broken the seal?"

"We thought it would be comms tech or prostheses," Lita explained, her eyes hidden beneath strawberry red lenses, and voice raspy with fear. "But it was waaaay too heavy... Look."

"Shit," Lily exclaimed, as she glanced down to see a cryo-frozen woman inside a stasis pod. "What an asshole. How the fuck did he get one of them out of DC?"

"They're gonna miss that Lily," Nish cautioned. "This is bad juju — we should just drop this and fuck off."

Lily frowned, looking more closely at the body. None of them had seen a clone before. Well, not one that wasn't already in use. "Yeah right, and then we've got the South African selling us out and the Japs wanting payback." She shook her head. "Not giving them a second chance to throw me off that fucking pyramid, guys. Let's just stick to the plan, yeah? Drop the DNA Opperman gave us, finish making the hole, lower this crate into the hover, and fuck off... When the Russians find their merch re-stolen, the Yaks get blamed as intended and we never breathe a word. You grab?"

"What about Nova?"

"What about them, Nish? That's a problem for the Russians and Yaks. Look, we're nose deep in this already. Let's just finish up and fucking go, mate?"

Nish didn't look happy, but nodded before turning to help Lita and Radar attach mag-straps to the runners they'd already suspended from the old building's ceiling joists.

Three minutes later, as Digit wrestled the last lump of concrete back inside the warehouse, Lita and Radar pushed the bulky container out into darkness. "Turn your headlamps off, idiots," Liam growled as he caught the crate's leading edge and guided it into the craft's small hold, shaking his head at the weight of the thing and waving a hand to catch Lily's attention.

"You won't get those in," he hissed, pointing at the extra crates being attached to mag-straps as she clambered down. Scowling, the slender woman stepped over to the pilot's station, checked the readouts, cursed, then without another word to her cousin, climbed back up the straps to begin an animated exchange with Nish. Both were gesticulating wildly, then the hefty Indian threw up his hands and shinned down to the hover, followed by Lita, Mo, Radar and two of the other crates they'd picked.

"What's happening?" Liam demanded.

"Lily's going to sneak back through the sewers with Digit."

"That's fucking ridiculous."

"I know." The Indian lifted his goggles and wiped the back of a gloved hand over his forehead. "But she's not listening."

It was Liam's turn to silently protest. But their indomitable leader simply gave him the finger before she and Digit began moving crates to cover the hole. After an impotent look at the others, Lily's cousin resealed the cabin and began to carefully navigate his way back out to deeper water.

PARTITION TWO

First Among Equals

"…Okay, here's one for all you get rich quick techdeck jocks — Dark web message boards, an area of the net most decent folks aren't even aware of, have gone crazy in the last couple of weeks over calls for revolution and warnings to the world's corporate execs, media stars and otherwise obscenely rich who have undergone Nova's controversial digital transfer process.

"The latest post claims, though it should be noted our content supervisor from corporate overlord EurCon has dismissed the message as nothing more than hacktivist scaremongering… that a digital cancer, originating from somewhere inside the North American behemoth, has begun spreading across global feeds.

"Copies of the message, which has medical and data files attached, also began appearing on mainstream social feeds inside Greater Soviet's Uzbekistan four hours ago, but rapidly went viral in each of the eleven Polycorp web domains.

"It advises all 'digitals' that they will remain healthy so long as they do not attempt to update or leave the skin they currently occupy. However, it continues… ignoring that simple warning, is now a lottery, with the odds of safe transfer reducing minute by minute as more data-nodes become corrupted.

"Nova's global comms executive, Karen Reid, has already responded, condemning the message as dangerously irresponsible 'fake news.'

"But a review of the files, completed by TrueNews24 medical expert, Dr Zane Widdows, does point to a connection between some kind of digital neuro-virus and the death of an executive we cannot name for legal reasons....

"Each of the eleven other polycorps have been quick to denounce what Reid describes as 'cyber-terrorism aimed at the heart of modern society': promising swift and decisive action across all Council territories... more gang bashing on your feeds, eh? No one's gonna complain about that!

"But, who is sending these dark web messages? And is there actually any truth to them? At this stage, although no one has claimed responsibility, the feeds are once again abuzz with just one name — Doctor Eric Thorne. Or, more precisely, the allegedly digital incarnation of him which disappeared during the chaos that erupted across North America after the shooting of its much-loved mech twenty-two long years ago.

"In a move that seems to support this assumption, Nova has tripled the reward being offered for the man's dead body or information leading to his detention... 1.2 million Nova? Yes please!

"... If you want to see more content on the dark web, those messages of doom, or the bounty on Robo Eric's head, just tap the relevant tab as it scrolls across your vid...

"But if you're aching for a good dose of uncensored blood, guts and gratuitous violence... stay tuned to our live feed, where after this quick sponsorship break, we'll once again be joining EurCon's finest as they take out another chopshop... I'd put down that meal bar if I were you — it's about to get messy!"

August 19th, 2070
01:15 GMT Old Erith Oil Works, Outer London

"What are we doing here?" Tash grumbled, pulling off electric pink ARs and spooling down her gyro. They were in the overgrown loading area of a derelict south of the river.

"Got ourselves a gig," Bobby said, sighing heavily as her expression soured. "C'mon sis... Grab the cash when it's there for grabbing. You know the rules."

"There's a job here?" Fin put in, getting off his own bike with a look of confusion.

Bobby rolled chestnut brown eyes. "Not *here* here, bruv. Look around, the place is falling down. The skin we're after is slummin at Diablo's. Flashing chedda like he printed it himself," he chuckled. "We're gonna drop him when he leaves."

"Just like that, yeh? Big Man?" Tash snorted. "And if we do manage to take him down without getting dead or arrested, what then?" Her voice was dripping with sarcasm. "Give out signed photos to them that wanna watch while we tie him to the front of your gyro?"

Bobby laughed and pulled the blue-dreaded neo modder into a hug, the soft sodium glow of compound lights across the old train tracks giving her ebony skin a golden hue. "Now that I would pay to see. But no, 'lil sis, I got us a van."

"Where the fuck d'you get a van?" Fin asked, turning to examine the surrounding darkness.

"Jerome."

Tash started frowning again.

"Leave it out, Tash," Bobby continued. "Thing's an investment. He even said we could pay on tick, yeh?"

"That hood's got his fingers sunk good and deep, ain't he?" she said, mimicking her brother's *gangsta* swagger.

Bobby tutted, shoving her aside to walk into the shadows. "Ain't heard no complaining about your poncy new VR glasses and warpaint, yeh?"

"There're AR, asshole… *augmented reality*," Tash sniped back as Fin stretched an arm around her shoulders.

The well-built, ginger-haired best friend of her brother had always been their little crew's bomb disposal; stepping between the siblings when things got aggro — and this fight had been brewing for days. Tash didn't like or approve of Jerome Donelly. 'He's a big, violent ape who's dragging you in deeper and deeper,' she maintained. Whereas Bobby, Fin reckoned, had a bit of hero worship going on; looking up to the self-styled gangster who now controlled pretty much all of slumville south of the river.

"You stop constantly moaning like an old fishwife, you might just learn something," Bobby snapped, dismissing his sibling with a click of the tongue and flipping on his cuff's screen light to stalk down the side of the loading dock. "You don't see Jerome walking round in shitsville anymore, do ya? Betting his electricity doesn't fucking cut out at eight!"

Fin squeezed Tash's shoulder, and she growled into his chest as her brother found the end of a large tarp and pulled.

"Are you having a joke?" the willowy young woman said, mood lightening as she tried to stifle a giggle.

"Oh, I dunno Tash," Fin sniggered, walking her down to the narrow cream-and-beige Suzuki that had just been uncovered. "The little jap numbers look weird. But they're good for getting through traffic… as long as they run. How old is it?"

"Runs fine, bruv," Bobby growled, leaning through the window to flick the switch that fired up its motor. With a gentle hum, the van rose up on its suspension. "In fact, it purrs like a fucking kitten… And," he added, looking pointedly at his sister. "It's pre lo-jack. So we don't have to worry about the munis tracking our every move."

Tash failed to be impressed.

"Look, I'm not gonna stand here and argue. Jacking pays better than boosting cars, and our own van means we're not standing around holding our dicks waiting for one of Jerome's lot to turn up and take it away... Which, in turn, means far less chance of being caught and sent for a head-fucking — or d'you wanna be *re-socialised*?"

He smiled as Tash made a play of thinking about it before offering a single, surrendering jerk of the head. "I preferred cars is all," she grumbled. "It didn't involve assault and kidnap."

Fin laughed at that, releasing the young neo-modder from his grip. "I liked the cars too, beautiful. But," he continued as his best friend shot him a reproachful look, "you know Bobby's right. With all the tech in them now, boosting cars is a fool's game."

A thoroughly defeated Tash sighed in exasperation and waved a hand at the odd little vehicle. "Show us inside the bloody thing, then."

The worldwide skin-trade had begun emerging about seven years earlier when, having observed how the world's new corporate overlords were just as unscrupulous as they were themselves, the more entrepreneurial and organised crime syndicates realised they could make a killing from abduction. Not for a historically risky ransom. But for a lucrative and relatively risk-free resale.

As was almost always the case, it was the polycorps own greed that paved the way. Nova guarded its commercial secrets like a jealous lover; ensuring anything remotely related to transition technology was developed, mapped, administered and tracked solely by them. And the others soon got in on the act, making everything vaguely related to skins and skinware obscenely expensive. But what they all failed to consider, at least initially, was that once uploaded, each new digital consciousness could technically transfer anywhere it damn well pleased — so long as the destination was capable of receiving it.

Realising this, Nova and the Council then tried to throw up all kinds of roadblocks to multiple body use. Passing laws directing that every *skin* created required a SIN, a specific identification number, and that each one sold had a registered user recorded on the Council database. Further laws, raised from questions of corporate and criminal liability following two high-profile murders in which the accused had evidence of being elsewhere, then sought to constrain *every* digital to the use of just one body at a time. That issue was to become Interpol's single greatest investigative demand.

Those measures and rigid legal controls not only meant the cost of even a standard hybrid body was ridiculous, but also that the Council, and by default Nova, were technically able to track the movement of every single digitised human across the planet.

Unsurprisingly, no one but the Council's bureaucrats and Nova's Central board were truly happy with that, and soon the hunger for a skin they couldn't afford, or desire to move around without Council or Novan scrutiny had many digitals seeking out less *official* retailers.

Over the next few years, despite Interpol's best efforts, the theft of hybrid bodies capable of housing a digital consciousness became more profitable than dealing dust; and the corporate kingpins underwriting each operation, hidden beneath several layers of semi-legitimate shell company run by gangland proxies, became even richer.

Bobby's little crew had stumbled into the trade when trying to jack a Lambo two months earlier. The vehicle's owner hadn't been a fan of finding a South London car thief under her bonnet, and was in the process of pulling a gun from her purse when Fin jabbed a shockstick into her neck.

They thought they'd killed the crazy bitch. But when a panicked Bobby then called Jerome, the guy just started laughing; saying he'd send a van and talking about double prizes.

Back at his huge river-side freight and storage yard, the gangboss then silenced Fin's anxious talk of murder investigations by bringing up the image of a computer core where the woman's brain should have been. Corpos, he'd assured them, were nothing more than electronic ghosts. "That's why we call this a chopshop, lads," he'd chuckled, ignoring Tash's scowl. "Think of that body as no different to the cars you steal — once my people wipe its core, the thing is nothing but a meat-machine waiting for a new driver... In fact, this corpo bitch's last backup has probably already woken up in an insurance clinic and realised she's had both her car and ridiculously expensive tube-grown clone boosted... That's the universe teaching her to be more friendly!" Even Tash had laughed at that. No one liked the corpos.

That night the small crew walked away from Jerome's with more than twice the scratch he usually paid and had themselves a party.

The mark came out of Diablo's just after four, and the fucker was way bigger than Jerome had led Bobby to believe; easily six-four, with huge, overworked shoulders and heavily muscled arms that practically swallowed the scantily clad hooker he was walking towards a two-tone Bugatti.

Bobby had no idea who Jerome's customers were. But this was the third sleazebag he'd thrown their way in a week.

"He's gettin' closer," Tash whispered from the front seat.

Bobby held up a finger for silence and indicated she should cover her face. Who knew what augs the guy might have — Jerome said audio and visual recording were pretty standard these days, and if the big lump got away... Well, you didn't want your mugshot appearing on *TrueNews* to be sold out by a so-called friend. Nodding, Tash slid lower in the seat, turning her ARs to full-dark and pulling her hood down low. Bobby and Fin did the same, then popped the slide-door open.

As the digital passed, the woman he was molesting spotted Bobby inside the shadowed van and winked, grabbing at the big man's crotch and kneading his manhood through tight Gucci jeans. Not that the loathsome creature needed encouragement, he was already pawing at one of her hard-nippled jugs and, with a grunt of pleasure, pushed the tiny woman against his car to grope between her legs.

Bobby eased the van door along well lubricated runners, letting Fin step out and to the left before slipping snake-like from his own seat to stand three feet behind the engrossed corpo while the hooker looked on, thoroughly unimpressed at the lack of speed. "Are you morons gonna jump this guy?" she finally growled, giving the big man a backward shove. "Or grab some popcorn and watch the fucking show?"

The corpo looked over his shoulder with a bemused frown, saw the hooded shadow creeping up behind him, and began turning. "What the hell—" was all he managed before Bobby stabbed the shockstick just below his left ear. For one panicked moment, the young thief didn't think the guy was gonna drop. Then Fin zapped him again, this time straight in the back of the neck over the cervical vertebrae, and the muscular meat machine lurched forward like it had been shot; eyes rolling back and legs buckling to leave it convulsing, face down on the floor.

"Bag," Bobby hissed.

Tash appeared with a deep blue derm, slapping the sticky cluster of tiny needles onto the skin's thickly chorded neck before sliding a finely woven metallic mesh hood over its head. Within seconds, the thrashing stopped.

They all stood watching a few moments more, then everyone allowed themselves to breathe again — the core would have no signal if it rebooted now, and the body was out for the count.

"Night-night handsy," the hooker said, tucking the milk jug he'd been mauling back in her top and straightening her crotch.

"Thanks for the *hand,* love," Fin sniggered over a shoulder as he began dragging the unconscious digital towards the Suzuki. "But you'd better head back inside before you're missed. We'll be sure to tell Jerome you went above and beyond when we deliver twatboy to the meat-market."

"Funny guy," the half-naked woman replied, squatting over the big man's chest like she was gonna take a piss. "But I need to grab his remote before you ship him off."

"What?" Bobby said, grabbing a handful of jeans to help his friend.

"Jerome wants the car as well. So I need to find it's remote."

Fin growled in frustration. "Let's just get him in the van first, shall we? One muni drone goes over while we're fucking about out here, and we're all bolloxed."

Bobby and the hooker both nodded at that wisdom, and between them the small group wrestled the heavyset exec into the back of the Suzuki.

"You could have done with a bigger truck, sweetheart," Jerome's girl observed as she began running expert fingers through every pocket of the flashy outfit. "Contrary to popular belief, size does matter."

Tash laughed at that, and the half-naked woman winked at her; a credit spike and studded Omega disappearing down her cleavage before she located the Bugatti's remote. "What?" she added defensively at Bobby's raised eyebrow. "His hands went *everywhere* while you pervs were tiptoeing around gawking at my tits... a girl's gotta get paid, ya know."

Bobby shrugged. "Not my business, lady," he said, holding up both hands. "We're all just getting by."

The blotchy-faced skank glared for several seconds, saucepan sized pupils searching through a dust induced haze for signs of sarcasm. "Damn right we are, gangsta-man," she sniffed. "I don't judge you. You don't judge me." Backing out of the van, she then grinned when Bobby's eyes instinctively flicked to her heavy, barely concealed breasts again, and she gave him a final jiggle. "One of the boys will run the car over to Jerome's in a bit... Be safe out there, yeh?"

Then the side door slid closed.

"Whoa!" Fin chuckled, pulling out a tarp and covering the skin. "Was she, or was she not, seriously fucking baked...? You see her eyes, man? I'm surprised she could stand up, let alone walk and talk."

Bobby nodded, watching the once shapely silhouette return across the near empty car park towards the flashing lights and lurid brightness of the dive bar. He didn't need pharma to blot out reality. But then he'd never been forced to sell his body or watch his sister sell hers... and while Tash might not like jacking skins, it sure as hell beat the shit out of that. Hell, this type of crime didn't even hurt anyone, not really... Bugatti Boy and all the arseholes like him were sorted in a way *basics* could only dream of — no getting old, no getting ill, no getting dead. Some corpo bodybank was probably already de-frosting another version of the sleazy fucker, ready to receive his last saved backup and start tormenting hookers again.

Tash's head turned back from watching the woman's retreat, and the two of them shared a look. That was how their mum had been forced to get by — the drugs had claimed her too.

Jerome's place was a massive storage facility on the south bank that had a maglift running 24/7 to the cargo hub across the river. Jerome might seem a thug, and Bobby doubted he was the brains behind the operation. But the guy was either connected to someone influential or did enough legit business to keep the municipal cops at arm's length, because he never caught heat from them... And, while Tash definitely had a low opinion of the South London gangboss, that equation balanced out when it came to his tech specialist. She'd click her tongue when Bobby teased, of course. But the blue-haired beauty's eyes and smile said everything necessary when she talked about the tanned, blond-haired nerd who looked and dressed like a surfer-dude from one of the day-time entertainment feeds.

Their courting ritual tonight began as it always had; furtive looks and shy smiles from him instigating a garrulous outpouring of inane conversation from her. Jerome quickly grew bored with their peculiar foreplay and, after checking the skin was undamaged, took Bobby and Fin through to his office for a drink.

The crime lord had taken a shine to the South London crew after they'd started boosting high-end cars for him. He liked, so he said, their utter commitment to getting out of the burbs, and had helped Bobby set up an account with one of the corporation banks six weeks earlier. *"To become a recognised business,"* he'd said, *"at least some of your take needs to be passed through official books."* Tonight, he swiped five hundred EurCon onto Bobby's spike before handing a grand in scratch to Fin.

The polycorps had tried to choke out the use of cash years ago, and though no bank or corporation run business entertained notes any longer, each country's former currency remained of value and in circulation among the basic population.

Scratch, cabbage, scrip, bread, cheddar... call it what you like, *paper* still bought you things credits couldn't, got you places credits wouldn't ... and wasn't taxed or tracked by the corpos.

"A job's just come in for this evening if you want it, boys. Nice easy one; just a pickup."

"What's it pay?" Bobby asked, ever the businessman.

"A monkey."

"Five hundred? Just for picking something up and bringing it back here? No fighting or other drama?"

"You're right. Let's call it three."

Bobby winced, and Jerome's wide, scarred face broke into a smile. "Told you before, lad — think before you speak. But I'm feeling generous tonight, so a monkey it remains!"

The two younger men gave each other a relieved look before turning back to the huge gangboss. "Well, that's our spending money for this weekend sorted," Fin grinned as they both held out hands to shake on it.

Tash was practically sitting on the chopshop techie's lap when the three men stepped back through the doorway of his lab. Lucas was trying to explain the global tracking systems different polycorps were employing in their skins; pointing at the scan of Bugatti-Boy and circling the suppressed signal emissions on a holo the neo-modder wasn't even pretending to pay attention to; a longing he seemed oblivious of flashing in her gold-flecked hazel eyes as she watched him.

"Come on, 'lil sis," Bobby called, knowing it would rankle her. "Time to go. We've got another job on later, so you're gonna want a juice-box and nappy-nap."

Lucas's head shot round, face flushing as he saw the older brother approaching, and Tash threw a filthy look. "We're talking here, asshole," she growled.

Laughing, Bobby held up both hands. "Okay, okay" he said. "Sorry, that was uncool... So how about I make it up to you?" He turned to the techie. "It was my birthday on Tuesday, Lucas, and we're going uptown tomorrow. You fancy coming with?"

The bespectacled American looked at Tash. A red tinge crept over her deep-brown cheeks, but her eyes sparkled with obvious enthusiasm. Then he turned to Jerome. "He's not asking me, boy," the big man said with a shrug. "But I reckon you'd be a fool to say no." Face creasing into a wide grin, Lucas nodded as he stole another glance at the beauty beside him. "I'd love to, Bobby," he replied. "So long as Tash is alright with it?" Tongue-tied for the first time that evening, the pretty young woman simply smiled and nodded.

"Good," the skin-thief smiled. "Drop your deets on Tash and she'll com you later with the when and where."

Lucas swiped two fingers over his cuff, and Tash pulled her glasses down to inspect the display. "Got you," she said coyly.

Fin couldn't help but laugh, and Bobby rolled his eyes, turning to leave. "If we don't see you before, Lucas, we'll see you tomorrow night. Dress to impress, yeh?"

The sky was beginning to lighten as Bobby finally locked the door to the small flat he shared with his best friend and sister. Angell was in one of London's rougher boroughs; deadly in fact, if you didn't belong there. But the small crew had grown up on the estate, Bobby and Tash in that very flat... and though surrounded by gangstas, cut-throats and gutterpunks — their block at least, somehow felt safer than the world beyond.

Inside, Tash took herself straight through to the bedroom once shared with her brother, and Fin dropped onto the sofabed dominating the living area. Neither bothered with a *goodnight.*

Bobby walked through the darkness into the kitchenette and grabbed a Heineken from the water filled sink; the estate's generators shut down at eight each night and no one with smarts opened their fridge after that. Ten hours later, the lager was nowhere near chilled. But it wasn't warm either. He popped the cap and wandered through to the room that used to be his parents; tapping on the battery powered lamp.

Maybe it was just the come-down from the job or seeing that hooker pulled around like a piece of meat. Maybe it was simply the fact he'd been awake for over twenty-four hours. But right now, the absolute zero working every angle to escape his fate felt a strange mix of anger and pity at the shithole of a world he lived in... Pity for all the people doing unspeakable things just to get by, and anger at the rich bastards who were happy to let them.

Angell was full of whores, pushers, gangsters, thieves; pretty much every kind of loser out there in London's suburbs — and almost all of them had been sucked in by circumstances rather than any kind of informed career choice. The best you could hope for, if you came from the estates, was that you found a way out. But the reality for most was that eventually they just got you dead.

Bobby growled to himself and took a long pull on the beer. There was no point agonising over lives he couldn't change — things he couldn't do anything about. His job was to keep three heads above water; to ensure neither his sister or best friend went under. He took the scratch Fin had stuffed in his jacket pocket and unlatched the plastic sill of his room's only window, lifting clear the battered metal box sitting between the outer wall's two courses of bricks. The thing was almost full, and while Bobby knew that wasn't enough to get them the fuck out of dodge, it was hard not to empty the contents across his bed to see how close they were.

Shaking his head, the tired skin-jacker added most of the night's take, smoothing out the old polymer notes to sit flat over those he'd added three days earlier. Then he tucked the box back into its hidey-hole and set his empty bottle down on the nightstand that had been there his entire life, saying goodnight to the photo of his parents that had always sat on top of it. They looked young and happy in that pic; something he'd never seen in real life. He smiled, wondering, as he often did, where it had been taken.

Sleep, when it came, was mercifully dreamless.

Cluster II
August 19th, 2070
22:25 GMT King's Cross Mass-Transit Station, Central London

Looking slightly more refined after finding a discarded plastic cup on the fold-down of an empty seat, Gabriel poured herself a whiskey and slid the flask back inside one of her rain jacket's several pockets. Climate change, or maybe some of the shit they'd managed to pump into the atmosphere during the war, had made Britain wet, and while the nighttime temperature was a comfortable seventeen degrees, rain was bucketing down outside the carriage windows.

She was dressed in utilitarian pastel-green ultra-urbans and a pair of white, calf-length high tops; a style Consolidated's fashion feeds said was popular among middle-wage women in the domain that summer. At five-foot-seven, with absolutely average looks and dyed, dirty-blonde hair pulled back in a mini pony, the corpo-cop didn't merit a second glance — well, except at the lurid pink and yellow case tucked between her legs.

The North London Shuttle hub, it turned out, was nowhere near London, and Gabriel was riding the mass-transit like any other budget traveller or lower wage employee to King's Cross where, just as Gardner had in New York, she'd place the case containing Stockholm's missing cylinder into a numbered locker for someone else to pick up. She just hoped the place would be busy, or waiting to see who collected the gaudy travel bag was gonna get problematic.

Consolidated, at least on outward appearances, was nowhere near as security obsessed or intrusive as Nova. But Gabriel took no chances. Years of training and experience in surveillance and countersurveillance saw the cagey operative head in one direction, only to turn back and forth as if confused, and then get on and off several different maglevs before finally settling in the last carriage of a King's Cross service, satisfied no one was following her.

After quarter of an hour, the wide-open skies and mech-tended fields between Luton and London began mingling with bursts of artificial light and clustered buildings, that then themselves coalesced into the outer city's decaying urban landscape.

The scene, replicated somewhere in every domain Gabriel had ever visited, was what she hated most about corpocracy; the rampant inequalities imposed by a system that uses bottom lines as its measurement of justice and correct governance.

As if to underscore that thought, the softly glowing weather shield covering London's immaculate, climate-controlled centre came briefly into view; a massive and expensive engineering project which stood testament to the ambition and wealth of the managing corporation. It had clearly been designed to wow people who'd never take a maglev ride in the rain or wish to see beyond the inner city's gilded borders... people who had no interest in confronting the ruination or neglect their greed created.

With a sigh, Gabriel downed a final mouthful of whiskey and crushed the plastic cup, intending to leave it on the small tray table attached to the seat in front. Then she noticed the disapproving look on the face of an overdressed older woman sitting across the aisle. "Want some?" she laughed, purposely pulling out the flask again and taking another swig. The woman tutted and broke eye contact, shaking her head.

"Judge not, lady, lest ye be judged," the corpo-cop said, re-pocketing the flask before standing to roll her brightly coloured case over to a bin, and making a show of throwing the crumpled cup away as the mass-transit coasted into King's Cross.

She needn't have worried — the place was heaving.

Banks of various sized storage containers were set along each of the station's external walls; the rest of the huge building's interior having been given over to shops, eateries, waiting areas and bars, that ranged from little more than a hole in the wall dispensing cheap liquor, to dainty midwage boutiques and cafes.

After placing her colourful travel case into its assigned locker, Gabriel stepped outside the huge glass-fronted building, performed her countersurveillance routine again, and once satisfied she still had no watchers, went into an over-priced public toilet where she reversed the raincoat and released her ponytail, allowing the dirty-blonde neck length hair to frame her face before re-entering via another entrance.

Anyone watching specifically for the corpo-cop would clearly still recognise her. But anyone looking for a woman pushing around a bright pink and yellow case probably wouldn't.

Attaching herself to the periphery of a slow-moving herd of similarly dressed tourists, Gabriel then moved back through the station, taking the first escalator they passed up to a terrace of midrange bars intended for people who possessed a credit spike. She found a seat overlooking the floor below, ordered herself a drink, and began scanning the crowd for potential couriers.

After forty or so minutes of watching the station's resident pickpockets operate, and at least two other obvious drop-offs, Gabriel became aware of three new players, two black and one white, running circuits in the lower hall. They pretended not to know each other, but gave themselves away with furtive glances as they swapped between walking and watching. It was painfully amateur, but the well-practised Council agent gave them credit for at least trying. Just as she was starting to lose interest, the two guys ambled to opposite sides of the bank of lockers containing her case, and Gabriel sat a little straighter, taking a moment to capture each of their images.

Male 1, standing on the left, looked to be of Afro-Caribbean descent, aged in his mid-twenties and of athletic build. He had short, braided black hair and, just like his friends and many of the night's other commuters, was dressed in logoed factory coveralls. Male 2 on the right was clearly of white European descent. Also aged in his mid-twenties, the guy was shorter than male 1, much more densely muscled, and his close-cropped ginger hair had a thin black mohawk running through it.

Once standing still, both men quickly disappeared back into the human tide flowing in and out of the busy station. The female of the group however, who had similar features to and was possibly a relative of male 1, was hard to miss; and even though she too was dressed in a plain grey coverall, long electric-blue hair and pink glasses drew the eye of passers-by to a natural beauty that almost always received a second glance. Gabriel chuckled to herself as the young woman removed the colourful travel-case she'd bought to ensure she didn't lose its courier... That, it seemed, had been an unnecessary step.

By the time the corpo-cop had taken the escalator back down to the lower floor, both men were shadowing their female associate along the concourse. She followed them outside and stopped at a paved intersection crammed with manned and unmanned rentals as the three, now walking together, entered the storage structure opposite. Figuring they were collecting transport, Gabriel hired an ebike and waited.

Sure enough, a few minutes later three dated, but well maintained, gyros purred out of the underground garage, one of them ridden by a stunning, blue-haired woman who had a brightly coloured case strapped behind her.

The route they took skirted the corporate controlled city centre, following the dome's edge through Barnsbury Estate and then east through Arden, Shoreditch and Whitechapel to the Isle of Dogs, and an old tunnel under the river at Blackwall.

On the other side, Gabriel's way point told her she was passing another dome the British had built; this one apparently to celebrate the new millennium in 2000. It looked like a collapsed tent.

The kids, as she'd come to think of them, then veered off the main road into some kind of industrial area. Traffic was light this side of the river and the experienced tracker dropped further back; killing her bike's headlight as she followed the distant red dots through the darkness to some kind of container storage and freight facility.

Not quite what she'd expected.

Maybe Levinson had more travelling to do before she reached her final destination? Gabriel had placed a couple of ultra-low frequency trackers in the case, but doubted they'd leave the stasis pod in it. She wouldn't.

Making a note of the company's details, the veteran operator attached several cambots to nearby buildings and signage before slinking away to find lodgings. The fun bit of her investigation was officially over. Now came the grind. The bit that involved hours and hours of surveillance review, research, and then more surveillance review. She chuckled to herself as the ebike re-entered Blackwall Tunnel, who was she trying to kid — she loved the grind.

August 20th, 2070
17:25 GMT Management housing complex, Millbank, Central London

Miguel Guerrero clearly hadn't wanted to open the door after establishing the person outside was Interpol. But only those guilty of something refused entry to the corpo-cops — and that still wouldn't stop them barging in.

An upper middle-manager in EurCon's integration directorate, the squat, broad-shouldered lawyer in his late sixties was registered to the only comnode among the six Gardner had given Gabriel that wasn't either untraceable or something to do with Levinson's department; and as the intel also suggested he and the dead exec were long-term lovers, the corpo-cop had been hoping for a willing ally — not a nervous mess who clearly wanted her gone as quickly as possible.

"So, as far as you're concerned," she persisted. "Sera Levinson attended and returned from her transition op?"

"Absolutely," the older man replied with an anxious look at the holo-recorder she'd placed on his coffee table. "This is off the record, right?"

"It is... And did you see her afterwards?"

Guerrero fixed deep-set, hooded eyes on the agent and shook his head. "As I've already said, Ms Sousa... no, not really." He picked up his teacup, taking a small sip, thin lips bending upward into a practised affectation of a sincere smile. "She gave me a com when she got back; looked absolutely radiant — so young. Said she'd be over that weekend." He swallowed and stared out towards the river beyond the apartment's window. "But she never showed up. And when I then ran into her at work, she completely blanked me. Literally walked by without a word. I was too stunned to say anything at the time. But it hurt, and I called after I'd got home. That's why you have my com number. I wanted to give her a piece of my mind. Say if her feelings had changed now she was young and beautiful, she should at least have the decency to tell me to my face."

The old lawyer paused. But the silence felt contrived.

"You can tell a lot from someone's eyes, don't you think, agent Sousa?" he finally continued. "As soon as she answered, I could see she had no idea who I was. I said 'Liz, it's me. Is everything okay?' She just stared for a moment, then hung up. The following morning, they announced she was missing. Then all that rubbish about her never transitioning came out."

Gabriel nodded. "What about friends? Family?"

"We had no friends, not really. The polycorps, well EurCon at least, is quite stiff about social boundaries, and because Liz was several paygrades higher up the food-chain than me, we pretty much kept ourselves to ourselves."

"No family?"

"None living. Liz's husband passed away years ago, and both her boys died in the war."

"So how did you two meet if not through Consolidated?"

Guerrero offered Gabriel what felt like his first genuine smile. "We met on holiday in Santorini. I requested the London assignment afterwards."

"Assignment?"

"I work for EurCon's central board. My team's job is to ensure Consolidated policy remains consistent with the polycorp's doctrines. Every large sub-domain has someone like me."

"So you settle disputes?"

Guerrero gave a tight laugh and shook his head. "Hardly. I'm little more than a glorified auditor, agent. I have a lot of access. But no real power."

"And are relations between EurCon and Consolidated good?"

The older man frowned, clearly wondering where Gabriel was going with her questioning. "They've been a little tense since Dominic Mancini was voted in as VP. I think the president sees him as an upstart. But he's won a lot of support on the central board, mostly around his more challenging stance with Nova." Gabriel raised an eyebrow, and Guerrero nodded. "Ser Mancini makes no secret of his desire to see EurCon step out from Nova's shadow. But what has any of that got to do with Liz?"

"To be honest, I don't know that it does," Gabriel admitted. "But politics and power almost always feature in our enquiries."

She realised her mistake as soon as the words had cleared her mouth, and watched as Guerrero took the opportunity to once again retreat from her questions, hunching over his empty cup like a dying beetle.

What he'd said since her arrival rang true; sincere even. But something about the man's body-language was off, and her gut said he knew a damn sight more than he was letting on.

"Look," he finally said. "I've been with one subsidiary of EurCon or another all my adult life, and when their boards decide someone or something is toxic, agent — only a fool invites a visit from the security directorate."

Gabriel opened her mouth to speak, but Guerrero held up a hand. "Please," he continued. "I don't mean to be rude, but I've told you all I can... It's time you left. If EurCon finds out I've spoken to you, it won't go well for me." His eyes flicked anxiously to the cuff on his sleeve and Gabriel nodded, accepting she wasn't going to get anything more from him right now.

"Well, thank you for your time, ser," she said, placing her cup on the table and standing. "Do you have any plans over the coming weeks?"

Guerrero did his best to look blank. "I'm sorry, what do you mean?"

"Travel? A break of some kind? Just in case I need to speak to you again."

"Oh," the stocky man said. "I'm retiring... Going back to Spain. There's no reason to stay here anymore."

Gabriel offered him one of her own over-practised, under sincere smiles. "Well, you have my com address if you remember anything else..." she said.

"I do."

A quiet chime announced the front door was opening, and a momentary grimace creased Guerrero's face before his lawyer-like composure returned. With an arm gesture, he walked Gabriel into the hallway, where a woman with two grocery bags was just stepping into the apartment. "Vicki," he said with excessive bonhomie, pecking each of her cheeks. "You're earlier than I expected. This is agent Sousa, an Interpol investigator." He turned back. "Agent Sousa, this is my niece, Vicki. She's here to help me pack."

Gabriel guesstimated the pretty auburn-haired woman, whose widening eyes and tight smile belied the casual nod of greeting, was somewhere in her thirties. "Oh dear, I hope I'm not disturbing anything, uncle. I can come back later?"

"No, no," Guerrero replied, waving her further into the apartment. "We're done now. The agent was just leaving."

Gabriel blinked, capturing an image, and nodded politely. "I'll leave you to your afternoon then, Mr Guerrero," she said, eyes meeting his as she stepped into the corridor. "I'll com if I have further questions." Her tone wasn't lost on the man, who offered a stiff nod before closing the door.

After leaving the lawyer's apartment, Gabriel walked along the North Bank for half a mile. It was a balmy twenty-three degrees under the dome, and the corpo-cop found it hard not to be impressed by the eclectic mix of ultra-modern and centuries-old buildings overlooking the river. The lawyer had undoubtedly told her the truth about Levinson, to a point. But she sensed there was more to the story; and while fear of being caught by the polycorp was understandable, the man's reaction... overreaction to the return of his niece, seemed noteworthy.

Nodding to herself, Gabriel added research on Guerrero's wider family to her list of things to do.

At Millbank, she stepped onto a mass transit heading deeper into the commercial heart of the city, her peripherals flagging some muscle that had to run to catch the quirky red hoverbus before it pulled away. Human Resources had severed her links to Council and investigative databases when she was suspended. But, today at least, luck was on the rogue agent's side, and a little digging through social feeds locked onto the profile of LeRoy Filmer; a struggling actor and jobbing security contractor.

Gabriel sighed as she flicked through the man's pictures and vids, hoping for a coincidence that evaporated when he followed her back off the bus at Piccadilly.

She continued up the busy street at a leisurely pace, watching her tail in the windows of passing shop fronts — and once happy he was working alone, left the main shopping precinct to slip into a small passage cluttered with recycle bins and air-con units.

Not very much later, a simple punch to the throat dropped the incautious contractor as he ran past a dumpster the corpo-cop had hidden behind.

"Who are you working for?" she demanded, dragging the big man sideways into shadow, the muzzle of his own gun now pushing into an eye-socket. "How did you find me?"

"I don't know what you're talking about, lady. I just—"

The corpo-cop brought the butt of the gun down hard on his forehead, knocking him to the ground. "Don't fuck me about LeRoy. You're not very good at this, and I'm sober as a judge; so not in the best of moods."

The muscular Latino glared up with midnight black eyes and blinked.

Typical, Gabriel thought, the fucker had image capture mods. She smashed his head into the wall.

"Okay. Okay," he said. "You were seen leaving an apartment of interest. I was just told to follow you."

"So, back to my first question. Who do you work for?"

"I'm freelance, lady. Got this gig off the web. I don't get told shit like that."

Gabriel pistol-whipped him again, despite knowing that was probably true. "Why were you watching that apartment?"

LeRoy attempted to shrug, but her grip on his jacket made the movement seem more of a tick. "Like I said, I'm freelance—"

With an irritated sigh, the former ranger jabbed hard fingers into the big man's vagus nerve and he fell silent, slumping against the wall. The guy may or may not have known more, but if he had any trade craft at all, he'd be trying to keep her there for as long as possible.

Throwing LeRoy in the dumpster proved harder than expected, and Gabriel made a mental note to get back into shape. When she'd finally rolled the muscular man over its edge and closed the lid though, she tucked his Glock under her hoodie and treated herself to a calming swig of whiskey before backtracking to the shopping precinct and its legions of corporate leisure seekers.

Even if Le Roy's confederates hadn't already identified Interpol's missing agent was on the prowl in London, it wouldn't be long before they started looking for the woman who'd beaten him up after leaving an apartment they were watching.

Re-emerging on Shaftsbury Avenue, Gabriel mingled with the crowd. Experience was screaming at her to get off the street before security drones began sweeping the area. It was six thirty in the evening, and she was on the edge of Soho.

Finding a bar to hole up in, she told herself, made perfect sense. She could warn Guerrero he was being surveilled, get a message off to Gardner, and after a drink or six, use the party district's several thousand drunks to cover her escape.

PARTITION TWO   Cluster IV
August 20th, 2070
23:30 GMT Neon City (Soho), Central London

Soho was one of the few places in EurCon's Corporate controlled territories where people openly set aside social stereotypes, beliefs and divisions, to enjoy the mix of food, theatre, music and dance.

Several leading sociologists posited that Dominic Mancini allowed Neon City to flourish as a demonstration of the benefits of non-segregation in modern society. Others simply saw it as a shrewd way to tax and monitor those who would otherwise slip under the radar. But whatever the corporation's motivations, outwardly at least, Consolidated did nothing that interfered with the businesses in that area. It even turned a blind eye to paper currency, pharma and prostitution. In return, there was an un-written agreement among the city's gangs and Soho traders that no skin-jacking would take place inside the party haven's limits — and as the gangs ran almost all the pubs, clubs and security, that agreement was solid.

Everybody was both safe and welcome in Neon City. The only real rule within that half square mile of pure hedonism being that you had to have some cash to splash.

Lucas had clearly lived a sheltered life, and Tash, in a bubble-gum maxi that hugged all the right places, was having no trouble holding his attention, despite streets filled with semi-naked painted bodies and gaping doorways disgorging discordant flashes of neon light and heavy thumping base.

"Where are we going now?" he laughed, watching an already hammered Fin stumble and collide with a seven-foot-tall bouncer before Bobby caught him, holding out a hand in apology to the muscular modified woman.

"LaLaLand," Tash chuckled back. "But I think we need to get some stim in Fin first. Straighten him out a bit before he gets us all a fuck-off finger at the door." The small gang's self-appointed party planner had hit the town hard, and could now barely stand. "Come on. Let's run over to that stall and grab some crank. At least we can make him look kinda sober."

The tech nerd took a hesitant look over his shoulder, pushing thin silver-rimmed glasses higher up his nose.

"What?" the beautiful Nubian face just inches from his teased. "You cut up Andos and skins all day long for a gangster — but get nervous about a little stim?"

"Not androids," Lucas corrected, suddenly serious. "I'd never cut up androids."

Tash laughed again, running a hand over his cheek, hazel eyes full of promise. "Damn, that's sexy. But I'm still gonna have to teach you to chill the fuck out."

She dragged him across the street, quick hand movements forming the only conversation with a heavily pierced and balding dealer before paper was traded for a small, clear zippy, and the two of them were heading back to where Bobby had pinned the dumb lump of meat that couldn't hold his drink against a wall.

"Chuck these down his neck," Tash directed, fishing out two of the small round tablets and producing a bottle of water. "He'll look sober as fuck in five." Then she snapped a third along the centre, swallowing one half and holding out the other. "I dare ya," she taunted. Lucas stared at the powdered white pill for several seconds, then threw it into his mouth. Bobby howled with laughter as he necked the last one, slapping the likeable lad on his back. That was probably just the first of many revelations Tash had planned for the uptight tech tonight.

LaLaLand had an unimposing entrance; two large glass doors, framed by a single bead of electric blue light, which seemed conservative to Lucas's untrained eye when compared to the surrounding bedlam of Carnaby Street. In fact, if it wasn't for the huddle of black clad muscle on the door, he'd have thought the place was a hotel. But after more paper changed hands and an altered man the size of a tank had wanded them for weapons, the small group stepped across the threshold into brief darkness.

Then the nightclub novice had his mind blown sideways.

The club's external illusion of relative tranquillity was shredded in an immediate barrage of thumping base, with solid beams of pink and blue threading through more suffuse light to form intense geometric shapes, while holo pads manifested fluorescing dancers who appeared and vanished to the beat.

Seeing his confusion, Tash pulled Lucas in close. "The lobby's a gravlift. We're in the basement now. Fantastic, isn't it?" she shouted in his ear. He nodded, intoxicated by her smell and the heat of her body. The beautiful woman laughed again, pulling his arm around her swaying hips. "Come and dance with me?"

Lucas nodded again… and his night became sublime.

Some two and a half hours later, close to one-thirty, Tash tracked her brother and Fin down to a VIP booth where they were playing out their *high-roller* routine on a couple of wealthy looking Asian girls. Both men fancied their chances and said they were staying.

Standard.

Nine times out of ten when they came uptown, all three of them crawled back to their rooms just before chuck-out with empty-hands and empty pockets, sharing bullshit stories about *almost* winning big or some epic sexual encounter.

But Tash wasn't wasting her room tonight. The extra job they'd done for Jerome had paid for luxury the trio had never experienced before, and Lucas — with a giggle the South London temptress realised she didn't even know his last name... Lucas *sexy-tech-nerd...* was gorgeous. They'd been crushing on each other for a while, and tonight Tash had decided they were gonna do something about that. Grabbing his hand as he returned from the toilet, she told the young techneer they were leaving, and before he could even give Bobby or Fin so much as a wave, the beautiful dark-skinned woman was pulling him urgently towards the exit.

Back in the booth, Keiko didn't believe either man for a single second. But they were having their fun, and she was having hers. No names no pack-drill, as Reimi often said. They claimed to be businessmen, though even from across the booth, anyone who *actually* had money could tell their watches were as fake as their designer suits and accents. But the black one was kinda cute and funny, and as Reimi's prime directive was to facilitate the Novan heiress's wishes, unless things started going bent, the bodyguard would continue to respond with quiet giggles to the white one's advances; although the muscular young streetrat would get one hell of a surprise if things turned nasty... Bye-bye demure, doe-eyed girl — Hello angry killbot.

But things never got nasty in Soho. That's why Keiko liked it. The place was full of people like her; people just looking for a party and pretending to be someone or something they weren't. It was part of the excitement; gave her otherwise dull existence a bit of edge.

'You can't be properly protected outside Nova' was all her father had said the one time she'd mentioned travel. So she never asked again... And now, no one but Reimi and a couple of confidantes knew the polycorp princess did anything other than host parties and lounge around with friends at the family's various mansions or country estates. It was liberating. In fact, Keiko had gotten quite good at slipping away — mostly because Millie was always happy to spend a few days pretending to be filthy rich in one of her *legal* skins. The poor girl had suffered from cerebral palsy as a child and would never have qualified for an implant. But luckily for her, Keiko could flutter an eyelid or two at daddy and pop pop... and the rules didn't apply to Novan royalty. A few friends owed her *big* like that.

"So listen," the sexy one with tight cornrows said, topping up her glass. "It's my birthday, and my friend and I have a suite at the Karma Sanctum just around the corner?" He raised a carefully trimmed brow, intense deep brown eyes doing the rest of the asking.

Keiko offered a coquettish wink and sipped her champagne while running a search on the hotel. It wasn't the most luxurious, at least not by Keiko's standards. But it wasn't cheap either... upper-middle-management territory.

A message from Reimi blinked into her peripherals. "Your heart rate and breathing are elevated, your pupils are dilated, and you've begun secreting cyprine. As these two are clearly gutterpunks, surely it would be prudent to look elsewhere for your physical entertainment tonight?"

The slight, East Asian looking mech, who could easily be mistaken for Keiko's sister, was sitting the other side of the muscular white man. She'd been the rich girl's companion since childhood; developed at the young heiress's insistence *that big men with big guns were ruining her life.* It was Ido Maas's one and only concession to the totally dumb AI rule. Though even then, Reimi wasn't particularly smart; except for advanced analytics in terms of threat assessments and combat, the completely human-like machine defaulted to mimicking Keiko's behaviour in all situations... which made it quite a promiscuous android.

"Well, I think they're cute," Keiko sent back.

"Hmm," Reimi responded. "I can't find anything on either of them, Kei. They could be anyone."

"But that's good, isn't it? If they were corpo or merc, they'd be somewhere in your security files, wouldn't they?"

"Hmm," the mech repeated; not disapproving, just cautious. "Which means they're probably criminals. Your father wouldn't approve."

Keiko sent a laughing emoji, "Decision made then," she sent back, before speaking out loud to the gorgeous hunk of black male flesh. "I've never been to the Sanctum. Will I like it?"

His face split into a wide grin. "Guaranteed," he responded, almost as surprised as Reimi at his success.

PARTITION THREE

First Among Equals

The voice connected to an amorphous image on the feed was the same as always; a female, middle-aged and clearly educated, speaking the kind of over-precise English that made most people despise them just that little bit more than other corpo execs... She sounded so fucking entitled.

Opperman frowned at the third participant; a visually modded thug from London. He didn't like that they'd been called into a holo-chat together... Couldn't see why he and the other guy needed to know names or faces. Bad business.

"Gentlemen, our little game is reaching its final phase, and given the delicacy with which you will need to work, I've decided it's time you met... Pieter Opperman, Jerome Donelly; he runs my London operation... Jerome Donelly, Pieter Opperman; he works the west coast of Nova.

Each man offered a reluctant nod to the other. "What about you?" Donelly said.

"The nature of my position, Mr Donelly, means that until we have secured our victory, I cannot reveal my true identity. But rest assured, we are just one step away.

"Until now, the pair of you have worked in isolation. Had different goals. Pulled different threads. Operated through middlemen... But after a great deal of gentle manoeuvring, I have finally teased the final piece of our little jigsaw into position."

There was a clear tone of self-congratulation in those words.

"Mr Opperman, you will organise a burglary at one of the bonded warehouses on the Frisco shoreline... I've arranged for a special delivery. Route that consignment directly to Mr Donelly in London. Only you two can be aware of the shipment and its contents."

Both men drew breath to speak, but the voice continued.

"I know merchandise usually travels a more circuitous route through several shell companies. But this is a critical part of our endgame... and I think you'll agree we've each worked too hard for too long to let anyone else get involved and fuck it up.

"Mr Donelly, once you're in possession of that package, I will send you details of a specific digital I want jacked. She'll be travelling with a SecMech you'll need to neutralise. But we'll speak more of that at the time. I'll make sure you have no corpo interference.

"This is it, gentlemen. Our mutual business has made you both modestly wealthy. But when we're done, each of you will have real wealth — and the prestige that goes with it."

Before either man could reply, the shapeless image disappeared, leaving each staring at the holo of the other. Opperman opened his mouth as if to speak, thought better of it, and nodded goodbye as he tapped the glyph to shut down his connection.

<u>**Cluster I**</u>
August 20th, 2070
04:40 PST Fisherman's Wharf, Frisco Freetown

The weather was proving both a curse and a blessing. Footing on the thin-planked walkways crisscrossing each of the old asbestos roofs was treacherous, especially in drenched dusters with sodden hoods obstructing goggles. But on the plus side, the deluge had finally persuaded even the most dedicated joe boys to stay inside and play cards, making Lily and Digit's navigation of the wharf's rooftop maze and narrow alleyways far easier than expected. So, only forty minutes after parting ways with the rest of the gang, the pair were standing in the shadows of a wide plastocrete overpass waiting for a lorry and its armed escort to pull into a nearby compound, before running over the Embarcadero. The first bluey-purple patches of predawn had begun poking through the black, and they needed to be long gone before the Russian crews clocked in for their morning shift.

After the vehicle lights had swept over their hiding place, and the sounds of hurried conversation at the guard-post died off, the pair sprinted over the wide tarmacked strip to a sinkhole that had been there for as long as Lily could remember. The thing had gotten steadily bigger over the years and now claimed part of the road and nearby parking structure. But what most Friscans didn't know, or more likely didn't really care about, was running along its bottom under all the fallen metalwork and detritus, was the broken roof of a feeder drain; a five foot high, three foot wide brick tunnel with a trench down its middle that carried surface water and sewage from Frisco's peripheral network into the cavernous subterranean mainlines running the length and breadth of the old city.

Lily guessed the damage had been caused by something seismic, and had then been expanded by an enterprising and necessarily skinny thief who saw the benefit of easy access to the wharf. Broad-shouldered grifters like Nish and Liam, and therefore the kind of lump employed by the gangs as muscle, were never fitting through.

Lily had used the route hundreds of times over the years. The others, not so much. There was a knack to staying dry, she'd reminded Digit as they descended into the sinkhole; you had to slide both legs down its narrow walls to a slimy course of bricks running either side of the trough. If you didn't; if you dangled, waving them about and trying to find purchase... nine times out of ten, you were getting wet. So, as she inched away from the hole into the deeper darkness of the tunnel, Lily couldn't help but laugh at Digit's sudden yelp, or the splash that followed.

Turning around to help the angry teenager, she whispered. "That first step's a doozy, huh?"

The fifteen-year-old replied with a string of well-chosen expletives as she pulled him up onto the small brick ledge. "Just get us into the bigger tunnels, would ya?" he growled, smelling both gloved hands and retching. "I hate these shit-stinking tiny ones."

 **PARTITION THREE**   **Cluster II**

August 20th, 2070
03:55 PST Two miles above Fisherman's Wharf, Frisco Freetown

The surveillance drone drifted in thermals twelve thousand feet above the city; indiscernible from the ground, except as an occasional flash when moonlight broke through the clouds to wink off its optics. But so far, the night's observations had been dull as dishwater. Heavy rain was keeping most of the old city's inhabitants inside, and three painfully long hours had now passed with nothing of interest to Captain Jonus's recon team.

They had captured footage of several gunfights along gang borders, and the ubiquitous small hours convoys of meth and dust from their hidden labs to street dealers, ready for sale in the morning. But neither of those bothered Nova; the polycorp wasn't going to waste time and money policing the freeloaders of the lower city. It was only interested in smugglers, and Jonus's recon unit had been tasked with identifying Frisco's main players.

"You see that Cap?" Royston, the shuttle's pilot asked.

"What?" Jonus said, shifting forward in the command chair to examine the feed he'd lost interest in an hour earlier.

Royston rewound ten seconds. "There," he said, freezing the playback. "A brief light source coming from the area of Fisherman's Wharf."

"Yes, I saw it that time. Terry, focus the big eye on that grid reference and let's see what's down there."

The systems specialist, who sat among a range of screens and keyboards behind the captain, tapped instructions to the drone hovering four miles below, and the image on the flight deck's main display zoomed to reveal what looked like small sections of one of the old warehouse's slowly disappearing into a deeper black.

"Go Infrared," Jonus ordered.

The image adjusted and two orange blobs appeared, working industriously in the grainy grey nothing of surrounding cold to remove debris from a wall that was clearly lined to prevent prying eyes.

"Bingo! Good spot Roy, we've finally got ourselves some action. Terry, start a log and pull up all the information you can on whoever controls that building."

As the cockpit team then watched, a large IR cold object was lowered from the newly formed opening into the cargo hold of a hover that hadn't appeared on any of Terry's instruments until its roof rolled back.

"That building," Terry said, reading from the intelligence jacket he'd just received, "belongs to Vasily Romanov. A semi-respectable fifty-one-year-old non-corporate, who seems to have legitimate connections with several of Nova's smaller companies; mainly clothing and mass market consumables produced for the working and underclasses." He circled the hover with a geotag. "Now that seems a perfect fit for professional thieves with access to stealth tech, doesn't it?"

Jonas shook his head as he watched four warm bodies clamber down from the building to join a fifth in the hover. "I think I'll switch, Monty," he said, mimicking a contestant on the popular daytime quiz-feed. "What's behind door number two?"

"Ding, ding, ding," Terry replied in the game host's southern drawl. "... *Connnngratulations*. Behind door two, Nathan Jonas, is today's *staaar priiize*... The scumbag leader of a gang called the Russe, which has intelligence links to every conceivable crime, and is currently engaged in a turf war with the Yakuza."

Grinning, the captain rotated through the drone's optics until he got a reasonable image of the two still kneeling in the warehouse. He guessed they were probably insiders, as after a brief conversation with those in the hover, they started to close the hole back up. "Looks like that's that. Romanov must have something fairly tasty in that crate for a seven-way take; and I'm willing to bet it won't be waffle-makers... Foxtrot Two to CentCom."

"Go ahead Foxtrot Two."

"I'm sending you a recording of suspicious activity on the seaward side of Fisherman's Wharf. Looks like a smuggling related theft. We're going to stay with the package, but two perps have remained on site. My working hypothesis is they're insiders, though neither of their mugshots returned an L2 or 3 file. Can you have R&D research them and come back to me, please?

"Foxtrot Two, that's a yes, yes."

On Terry's technical readouts, the black hover once again disappeared as its canopy closed, though its black hull, now tagged by the drone's enhanced camera feed, remained a visible icon on the shuttle's displays as it turned and began slowly gliding out into the Bay. The intel guys would be able to dig into Romanov's wider connections and, if necessary, task their sources living and working among Frisco's criminals, so Jonas wasn't worried about the warehouse crew; they'd be picked up sooner or later. Right now, staying with the hovercraft and cataloguing this team's MO and interactions was where the money-shots sat; perhaps they'd even snag themselves an end user.

The possibility of taking out an operation, root and branch, on surveillance night number one felt tantalisingly close, and in less than five minutes his night had gone from utter boredom to visions of promotion. There'd been chat in the officer's mess about the creation of a permanent task force sitting under a major, and Jonas reckoned he'd look good with a couple of oak leaves sat on his shoulders.

"Terry, how close will you need to get the drone for its big ear to work?" The intelligence officer shrugged, doing some quick mental math. "This time of night? We could get as close as a couple of thousand feet without them hearing us. That'll be plenty close for the onboard acoustic sniffers."

"Awesome," Jonus said. "Do it. Roy, wake the boys in the back and tell them to kit up. Just in case we need to deploy. We're not letting this fish off the hook."

"You got it, boss," both men replied.

For the next half hour, the small sleek craft picked its way carefully southward, maintaining a sensible distance from passing piers and jetties, while staying away from the middle of the bay and its major shipping lanes. Jonas respected the hover pilot's caution; they'd clearly done this before and weren't going to make the mistake of rushing. But he now had six marines sat in full combat armour and recognised, in hindsight, maybe he'd made that call a little prematurely. He was just about to stand them down when Terry observed the hover slowly turn and pull alongside a jetty two short of the old ferry building, where it glided up a ramp onto a wide crumbling concrete surface, canopy sliding back to allow two of the thieves, both wearing the oiled dusters popular with Freetown youths, to jump out and run ahead to the heavily rusted door of a derelict the shuttle's navcom was tagging 'Pier 3.'

"Standby," Jonus breathed on their team channel. "The plan remains to surveil this criminal group. But if they get spooked and make a run for it, we arrest. No fatal shots, understood?

Cooper, the squad sergeant, replied for all his men. "Oorah."

"Hurry up…" a young voice captured by the drone's sensors whispered urgently through the flight deck's speakers.

"I'm coming," another panted.

The sounds of strained effort then took over as the recon team watched both youths wrestle the door open just far enough for their hover to slip into the blackness.

Terry switched the feed over to infrared again. This building was nothing like the shielded warehouse, and three further warm bodies emerged as all five youths began talking in excited voices while they worked to lift the stolen crates from their hover.

"Kids?" Royston said. "Our crack team of burglars are just kids, for Christ's sake."

"And they've got company," Terry observed, pointing at six other orange glows hiding behind the building's semi-collapsed walls.

"That look like a welcome party to you?" Jonus asked.

"No Sir," the coms specialist replied. "That looks—"

"Sssshhh," one of the kids said, raising his voice over the others. "You hear that?"

"What?" another asked, his voice deeper, Indian maybe.

"I dunno, Nish, it sounded like someone coughed."

The five heat signatures stopped moving, clearly listening. Then the first continued, "Let's just stow the hover and go hide up until Lily gets back."

"We can't just leave the crates, Liam. What happens if someone finds them?" a female voice said.

"Well, what would you suggest, Lita? We can't just stay here."

There was a pause, then all five youths were talking at once, and the surrounding heat signatures began closing in.

"Liam isn't it?" an older voice, perhaps Dutch or South African, said.

"Opperman?" The five thieves all turned to face one of the approaching group. "What are you doing here? Who are they?"

"Where's Lily?" the man said, ignoring the youth's questions.

"We got separated. She'll be along in a while."

"How long's a while, boy? Ten minutes? Half an hour? I'm on a schedule here."

There were more low mutterings from the youths.

"Sssshhh," Liam said for a second time. "At least an hour, probably two."

"Hmm, I can't wait that long."

A touch of anger now entered the younger man's voice. "Look Opperman, we'll deliver the goods as agreed. You shouldn't be here. How did you even know—"

Gunshots then clattered over the shuttle's speakers, and Terry reflexively thumbed down the volume.

"Standby, Sergeant Cooper," Jonus breathed. "CentCom, this is Foxtrot Two. We have shots fired within a building designated Pier 3, point eight of a click north of Oakland Bay Bridge. Permission to go weapons live?"

"Standby Foxtrot Two."

Screams of pain and cries for help chorused over the clack, clack, clack of automatic weapons fire as the shuttle's bridge team impotently stood by waiting for orders. Then a single youth burst from the rear of the building, running in pure panic towards the polluted waters of the bay. A bearded man wearing dated body armour appeared in the doorway, levelled a long-barrelled weapon, and ripped half the kid's head off with his second shot.

"CentCom, we now have confirmed fatalities on the ground. Do we have permission to deploy?"

"Foxtrot Two, from the Op Com, that's a no, no, over. Repeat no, no. Your orders are to continue surveillance. Received?"

An audible groan of disappointment came from the marines in the rear and Jonus couldn't help but grin. "All received CentCom. Continue with observations." He cut the line and switched back to the team channel. "Sorry boys. No target practice tonight. You might as well get comfy again back there."

On the camfeed, five mercs in mismatched armour emerged, pushing a maglev containing the long crate taken from the wharf. They hadn't bothered with the other items the now silent and motionless youths had stolen. Moments later, a seriously overweight and balding man wearing a business suit and too much jewellery emerged, tapping on a large cuff set into the material of his right sleeve. He had a tall humanoid looking mech trailing behind him like a puppy. "It's me," he said, looking out towards the maglev. "I've got your package."

"Can you get in on that?" Jonus asked, pointing at the fat man and the conversation he was obviously having.

Terry tapped at two of his keyboards, aligning intercepts.

"Very discreet," the man continued. "I assure you; these people won't be talking to anyone." There was another brief pause. "Yis, wrapped and ready for the mailman." He smiled, a blonde goatee creasing up either side of his thick-lipped mouth. "Thank you. I'm looking forward to it."

"Sorry Boss," Terry said as the man returned his attention to the six hired guns, barking orders that they move to the edge of the concrete pier. "The conversation was encrypted and ended before I could get a lock. All I can say for sure is it came from somewhere in Europe."

Jonus nodded. "And what can you tell us about our kid killing fat man?"

"Our image captures fit with the name used. Say hello to Pieter Opperman. A South African smuggler who found his way to Frisco in the late fifties. His record's a little spotty. But interestingly," Terry continued. "He's been the subject of four separate investigations, and each time the enquiry has fizzled out to nothing or been shelved. Like the guy's got a guardian angel—"

"Or someone on the inside watching over him," Jonus finished, zooming into the fat man's face. It wasn't much of a secret among the polycorp's military that many of Nova's civilian management were utterly corrupt. "Let's see him wheedle out of this one."

Opperman looked up at that moment, seeming to stare straight into the camfeed. "He doesn't know our drone's there, right?" the captain asked.

"No chance," Royston answered, equally freaked by the perfectly timed gaze. "He'd need seriously jacked hearing for

that. It's probably... Wait. We've got incoming. A shuttle.
That's what he's looking at."

On the feeds, then visuals, a small trans-continental cargo
shuttle dropped from the heavens towards the concrete of Pier
3.

"Jeeze," Royston hissed. "That guy's not sparing the
horses."

With a ferocious last-minute burn, the shuttle slowed and
pulled its nose up, both skids working hard to absorb a heavy
landing. Without any cooling period, the rear hatch opened
and a thin, pale woman with wispy, shoulder-length white hair
stepped out to regard the men standing around the maglev.
Interestingly, Opperman had moved back into the shadows,
leaving one of his hired guns to do the speaking.

"This it?" the woman said, waving a finger at the crate.

"Yep," replied the bearded man they'd seen shoot the
runner.

"Jamie," the pilot shouted. "Get your lazy ass out here.
That transit patch is only good for five minutes. If we're not
back in our slot by then, we're fucked. Move, girl."

With that, an equally pale and even thinner girl, who
couldn't have been older than twelve, ran from the hatch and
took the maglev controls, guiding the long crate with
practised hands into the stubby cargo shuttle.

Nodding once at the bearded merc, the pilot followed
her, and within forty seconds the shuttle's engines were
roaring again.

"You got muggies of all the hired guns down there?"
Jonus asked Terry.

"You bet yah, boss."

"And the shuttle crew?"

The systems specialist nodded, sending each of the
images to the captain's feed.

"Fantastic... CentCom, this is Foxtrot Two."

"Foxtrot Two, go ahead."

"One of the items stolen from Fisherman's Wharf has just been loaded onto a cargo shuttle that's now burning for a sub orbital path—"

"Standby... We're showing no unauthorised air traffic in your area at this time, Foxtrot Two."

"Understood. My tech specialist suspects its transit is being masked or real-time edited."

"Okay...?" the operator replied, sounding sceptical.

"Request the OpCom's permission to continue with a covert follow outside Novan airspace."

"Standby... The OpCom requests an update on the ground situation?"

Before Jonus could reply, the fat man's mech opened up with two previously concealed micro-guns, and an almost continuous stream of muzzle flash spat into the darkness as it fanned both arms to rip each of the men standing on the edge of the pier from their feet.

It was over as quickly as it started.

"Holy shit," Jonus said as the android then approached each prone body and kicked it into the bay. Visions of what would have happened if he'd sent his boys down crowded into his mind, and he sent a prayer of thanks to the Op Com and Gods of War.

"CentCom, it's a long tell... But the short version is, of the twelve gutterpunks alive when the hover landed at pier 3, only one, a slime called Pieter Opperman, and his pet mech, are still standing.

"I'm sending the camfeeds and image captures now. All the original thieves, except the two who remained at Fisherman's Wharf, are now believed dead. Names to attach to further searches include Lily and Digit for the two left at the warehouse, and Liam, Nish and Lita for three of the five dead here. I recommend identifying Lily and Digit is considered a priority. They may be able to confirm what is in that crate.

"Regarding Opperman, as stated, the man is in possession of an undocumented mech with concealed weaponry, and is responsible for the murder of eleven people, albeit Frisco trash. As such, I advise a team be dispatched to apprehend him before he disappears back under whatever rock he crawled out from. The man seems to have gone to a lot of trouble to conceal his tracks; I'm assuming from criminal associates. But whatever his motivation, it's an indication of the perceived value of that crate's contents."

A couple of seconds after he'd released the send button, the comms board lit up again with an incoming transmission.

"All received Foxtrot Two. From the Op Com, thanks for the thorough update. Permission for covert follow granted. So that's a yes, yes, to the follow."

Jonus waved Royston into action, and the pilot trimmed his wings for rapid ascent.

"Thank you CentCom. I've left the drone in situ, and my pilot will now transfer control to you."

"Received Foxtrot Two. We now have UAV oversight."

"Thank you CentCom. I will update further once we have a heading."

"Understood Foxtrot Two. Good hunting... CentCom out."

Cluster III

August 20th, 2070
05:35 PST Derelict Factory, Pacific Drive, Frisco Freetown

They both felt something was off as soon as they climbed out of the sewer on Jackson. Until then, Lily had assured Digit their group feed was probably inactive because they were forty feet below the city. But when they resurfaced and none of the others blinked up on the team chat, Lily nodded at

Digit's frown before breaking into a run. They could see each other's avatars, share vid and voice messages, so the feed hadn't collapsed or been taken down. Which kind of meant the only other possible reason for silence was their friends were still offline.

Nothing noteworthy was running through the old town's feeds, most of the early morning news focusing on the continuing rainfall that had made parts of their trek through the sewers more than a little perilous. But as the pair crawled through the fourth-floor wreckage of the factory where they'd expected to find the rest of their gang, vid from a drone circling Pier 3 blinked up on one of the feeds used by Frisco's gangs to avoid Novan activity and deployments.

The footage showed a polycorp security shuttle sat towards the end of the concrete pier and what looked like…"Are those… bodies?" Digit choked, throwing both hands over his goggles to darken the feed's background. He was counting now, "…nine, ten, eleven. There's eleven of them."

At that point, the drone zoomed in, running its cam over the sheet covered forms. An armoured boot was poking out of one, and Lily let out a relieved breath; too big and too military for any of their little gang. But that breath caught a moment later, as one of the Novan investigators carried a set of blood-stained goggles to a nearby table. There was no mistaking them — they were Liam's.

Neither of them spoke, as each picked out the customised kit of their other four friends among the assorted coms gear, clothing and weaponry laid out on that sterile surface; their brains slow, or maybe reluctant, to grasp the seemingly inevitable conclusion. Then, just as Digit's thin, wormlike lips began stretching to form a horrified 'O,' a vid from Liam jumped into the group feed, freezing them both in a moment of confused uncertainty. Brief hope flared in Lily's heart… then she realised one of the investigators must have activated her cousin's net connection, and afraid of what she'd see, but unable not to look, the bedraggled young woman toggled the play button...

...It was dark. The gang seemed to be inside the old pier building. "Opperman?" Liam said. "What are you doing here?"

"Where's Lily?" the South African demanded, ignoring the question.

"We got separated. She'll be along in a while."

Opperman's face contorted into a snarl. "How long's a while, boy? Ten minutes? Half an hour? I'm on a schedule here," he spat.

Lily could hear the others in the background. "Sssshhh," Liam said. "At least an hour, probably two."

Opperman waved a hand, and a group of other men came out of the shadows. "Hmm, I can't wait that long."

Liam looked around. Hired muscle; they didn't look local. "Look, Opperman," he said, fear edging the anger in his voice. "We'll deliver the goods as agreed. You shouldn't be here. How did you even know—"

Gunshots clattered out and both Lily and Digit jumped as bright flashes of light pierced the darkness and threw Liam's night vision out. Screams of pain and cries for help came and went almost instantly. Then Liam burst out into the pre-dawn, his breath ragged as he ran towards the edge of the pier. "Lily don't come. Opperman has fucked us over," he gasped. A loud crack sounded, and he jerked round to look back. Some bearded guy had followed him out of the building and was shooting at him. Then the vid cut out.

Digit was crying now; the wide 'O' replaced with long mewling sobs that quickly drew Lily in. Their friends were dead. She couldn't believe it. She'd only been standing three floors above with Liam a few hours back. And now, because of Pieter fucking Opperman, everyone dear to her except Digit was laying on the cold, damp concrete of a pier five hundred metres away.

"What are we going to do?" Digit croaked into her shoulder.

Lily squeezed the fifteen-year-old tightly. She knew people died in Frisco every day; it was one of the many serious downfalls of living in the place. But that was other *people*, not *her* people. A coldness that had nothing to do with the rain or time of day began creeping through her bones, and Lily pushed Digit away to wipe filthy hands over red-rimmed eyes, fixing the last of her little crew with the kind of careless, matter-of-fact stare that was his trademark, not hers. "We're gonna find Pieter Opperman," she said. "Find him and fuck him up so bad that even the bitch he fell out of won't recognise him."

Jaw setting into a purposeful scowl, the lanky youth wiped snot on the sleeve of his duster and nodded, unconsciously checking for the gun in his waistband.

PARTITION THREE   Cluster IV

August 20th, 2070
06:15 PST Derelict Factory, Pacific Avenue, Frisco Freetown

Khamza Suleymanov wasn't a big man, but he made sure to surround himself with them. Like most of the people who'd managed to climb to the top of the heap in Frisco, the wiry, weasel-faced forty-something had innate street smarts, sharp business acumen, and absolutely no morals. As far as Lily knew, he'd been trading in the old town since the very day Nova forsook it; quietly building his business and connecting with all the right people, both inside and outside the city, to become the undisputed top dog in recreational entertainment.

That wasn't a euphemism for drug-dealing overlord — he left the gangs to fight over peddling that shit. No, Khamza provided premium quality total immersion for the cash rich non-digital population and, under the table, a means to access the global net that slipped way below Nova's sentinel trackers.

Frisco had plenty of other blackhats, of course; some good, most bad. But almost all of the good ones worked for one gangboss or another, and on equipment Khamza had either sourced or upgraded. So, there wasn't much the cagey Kazakh didn't know, and the value of his services were only outstripped by the discretion he guaranteed when delivering them; an undertaking that granted him and his associates almost unprecedented freedom of movement through most of the city's neighbourhoods.

The coms king had been at one of his *Zen Dens* when Lily reached out. Her team had been his go-to grifters back in the day, and she liked to think the offer of the recyc gig was because they were effective and reliable. But none of the small gang missed the way he looked at her either.

He'd sent men over to the power station after hearing about the hit, thinking it was an attack on him and his assets. But as Lily explained what happened and who was behind it, a murderous scowl crossed the Kazakh's features, and he told her to sit tight while he arranged a pickup.

"I didn't know who else to turn to, Khamza," Lily sniffled down the com. "But we haven't got anything to pay with just now."

Favours from the Kazakh were famously expensive, even if he liked you. But unless things had changed substantially since she and the gang... Lily bit back more tears as their cold, pale faces flashed through her mind again... unless things had changed, Khamza had an intense dislike of the shady South African.

Jet-black eyes, like those of his hunting birds, softened and the man shook his head; clearly feeling her pain. "We're business partners Lily — you owe me nothing. Someone attacks you, particularly that piece of scumsucking shit... they attack me. And no one gets away with that." His gaze strayed upward momentarily, then he returned his attention to her. "I'm sending you a geo-lock. Tap it into your feed. It'll lead one of my boys to your location."

Lily nodded, offering a weak smile of thanks as the connection dropped.

"You think we can trust him?" Digit mumbled, arms wrapped around Opperman's silver cylinder.

"Yes," she replied simply. "Khamza can be a cold bastard. But he likes me, and is probably the only person in this town Opperman hasn't got hooks in."

The lanky youth rubbed red, teared-stained eyes and nodded his head slowly. All the self-assured cockiness gone. "And what about this? Shall I ditch it somewhere? Empty it out?"

Lily looked down at the sealed container, 38.5 in red glowing numbers growing duller as the light outside grew. "Hell no," she growled, jaw clenching and unclenching to control her emotions. "That thing is important to Opperman. So we find out what it is. Then, with Khamza's help, we shove it as far up the South African's ass as we can... Preferably with a stick of dynamite in the end."

Despite himself, the gormless adolescent sniggered. "Boom," he said, flinging his arms wide and making a splat sound.

They both laughed. Then they cried some more.

Ten minutes later, a black panel van pulled up beside the two rain-soaked grifters as they huddled together inside the steel carcass of an old bus stop on Washington. They'd moved two blocks over from the bombed-out factory their gang had once called home. Although probably never going back, just giving up its location seemed stupid; as Liam always used to tell everyone, *never say never.*

A big man with a machine gun hanging from his body armour stepped out of the driver's door, scanned the surrounding area and skyline, then approached Lily, tapping the side of his glasses in acknowledgement of something. "Lily Swift?" He asked in a thick Russian accent.

"Yes."

"Dermot Allen?"

"Digit."

"What?"

"I'm called Digit."

The Russian frowned and Lily interjected. "Yes, he's Dermot Allen."

Digit was about to object when the exhausted, flame-haired woman threw him a *shut the fuck up* look, and he stared sulkily down at his feet.

"Good," the man said, tapping at his glasses again and pulling a slide door open. "Mr Suleymanov sends regards. Let's get you out of sight, yeh? My name is Nikolayevich Polozov, but most people just call me Niki."

Hoping she'd not made another terrible mistake, Lily ushered Digit into the rear of the van and passed him the large black ruck concealing the cylinder, before climbing in beside him. Moments later, the door was closed, and they were moving.

PARTITION THREE · **Cluster V**

August 20th, 2070
07:00 PST Zen Den on Willow Street, Tenderloin, Frisco Freetown

Lily eyed the blocky, grey building with shuttered windows from outside the gated entrance. It sure didn't scream funhouse; it looked more like a prison or army barracks. Visible cams hung from every corner of the high walls, razor-wire spiralled along the outer edges of the flat-roof, and a drone hovered some seventy feet above them, slowly rotating through 360 degrees.

Niki offered a crooked grin as he locked the van and waved her towards two total steroid-jocks stood just outside the entrance; compact automatics cradled in their suited arms. "Don't worry about look, lady. All that matters is inside, yeh?"

Lily frowned, desperately hoping she wasn't walking her last remaining friend into a trap. They'd been inside several of Khamza's clubs when grifting. But none of them had looked like this; and while the young woman knew Tenderloin was one of the rougher parts of town, this place's defences screamed out trouble.

"Tough crowd?" she asked.

"No, no, nothing like that," the big Russian laughed. "Precautionary step." He waved his arm at the long, blockwork wall. "Looks better when neon projectors fire up… groovy lightshow. Come, I take you to Boss, yeh?"

Lily nodded, and slinging the ruck over a shoulder, she and Digit followed Niki past the men on the door.

The club couldn't have looked more different inside; stretching out beyond the entrance corridor and its electronic sniffers lay an inviting lounge and bar area. Long couches and low tables created a relaxed and welcoming environment for immersion geeks to sit, eat, drink and chat, while smart-walls scrolled through myriad games to be played, fantasy worlds to be explored, and sexual conquests to be undertaken.

Though a twenty-four-hour operation, entry between five in the morning and five at night was free, and the place was now busy with low-wage corporates just off a night shift who couldn't afford Digital City prices, and Freetown's early-hours drug runners; hungry after their predawn deliveries, and eager to burn some scrip before heading back to their sub-level pharma factories.

Khamza was sat at the corner of the main bar, deep in conversation with a tall blonde in an elaborate green trouser suit. He gave a slight nod when he saw Lily enter and leaned in to kiss the woman before standing to walk over; a thick tumbler of something dark and sticky in one of his ring covered hands.

"Lily," he said with genuine concern; aborting the hug he was going to give, in favour of a wrinkled nose. "…You smell awful."

"Sewers," the young woman said, face reddening at the aborted gesture.

Khamza nodded, humour and compassion warring on his thin, sun-leathered face. "Why don't we head down to my office? More privacy there… and a shower. Give Niki your dusters; he'll get them cleaned."

Lily and Digit slipped out of their heavy outdoor coats, passing each to the big Russian. "You'll have to leave gun as well, my friend." Niki said, holding out a non-negotiable hand. Lily fixed eyes on her young companion, expecting another argument. But just for once, gods be praised, the boy just pulled the old revolver from his waistband and passed it over with a glower.

"Don't worry little man, you get back when leaving, yeh?" Niki said, inspecting the relic. "I even clean. Won't blow hand off then!"

Digit brightened at that. "And bullets?"

Niki looked at his boss, then back to the teenage street rat. "Sure, if we have right calibre, and you show me you're not killing self or redhead with it, okay?"

Khamza's office was similar in layout to the others Lily had visited; richly appointed, yet practical. Cam feeds filled the walls surrounding a large black custom deck, and comfortable looking chairs bordered a conference style table occupying the room's centre.

"Shower's through there," the Kazakh said, pointing to a doorway. "Putting your clothes through the fresher won't hurt, either." Lily bobbed her head and waved Digit towards the opening. "You go first."

As the filthy former farm boy closed the door, Khamza pointed at the table. "You want a drink? Something to eat?"

"Thank you," Lily replied with a nod. "We've not eaten since yesterday." Tears began filling her eyes. "Sorry," she sniffed.

"Don't be," the Kazakh said, pulling out a chair. "What happened to you, to your friends, that's low. Even for Opperman." He filled a tumbler like his own with golden fluid from a decanter sitting at the table's centre and passed it to her. "But what really troubles me Lily, is I'd not heard a word of your heist. Not a peep."

Lily frowned, and Khamza pointed towards the camfeeds and data scrolling across his smart walls. "There isn't much that happens in Frisco I don't know about beforehand. But over the last few months, Opperman has dropped right off my radar." He sighed and sat down in the seat beside her. "You know I don't like the guy; backstabbing piece of shit. But at least before, through my taps into the gangs that used his services, I knew what he was up to. Whoever he's working for now though, it's exclusive... and their intrusion countermeasures are the strongest I've encountered in a long, long time."

"You've been in their systems, then? Know who they are?"

The Kazakh shook his head. "No. Almost got completely fried just trying to get in. All I know is, they're in EurCon somewhere."

"EurCon?"

"The European Conglomerate. I spent two weeks after my little snooping trip fighting off spyware, trojans, worms and wipers that said, '*Do that again and you'll get a personal visit*.'" Khamza raised a bushy eyebrow. "Lesson learned."

"So Opperman's working for a European corporation?"

"That would be my guess."

"But why?"

"Judging by your heist, the same as always, to steal Nova tech. The bigger question is what did you steal? And why did it cost your friend's lives?"

Food arriving as Digit returned from his shower stopped further discussion, and disinclined to try and engage the volatile youth in conversation alone, Khamza chose to busy himself at his deck while lily cleaned up.

Fortunately, the skinny street rat was more interested in the selection of hot snacks and said little beyond a grunted 'thanks' before cramming one thing after another into his thin-cheeked mouth.

A few minutes later, a far more human looking, and much better smelling former grifter rejoined them, damp red hair hanging loose over her shoulders. Even totally distraught, she was, Khamza thought, quite beautiful.

"A little better?" he asked.

Lily nodded, puffy eyes outlined in red. "I just can't—" The young woman swallowed hard, fighting back a fresh wave of tears as the Kazakh reached over to pat the back of her hand. "Your heart will always ache for their loss," he offered. "But the pain will pass... in time."

Digit stood, not making eye contact with either of them, and walked back into the shower-room. Lily made to follow, but Khamza kept his hold on her. "There are some things, Lily, other people can't put right. You're both trying so hard to be strong for each other. Why not give the boy a little space? Take some for yourself?" He gave her a gentle, sympathetic smile. "Look, I've got a few things to sort out upstairs. Why don't you take a few minutes to yourself? Grieve. Cry... Get angry. Then, when I return, we can talk about what you do next." With that, he stood, straightened his crisp, midnight blue suit jacket, and walked to the door.

Upon his return, Khamza found Lily alone at the table, staring blankly at a largish metal cylinder. The Kazakh scanned the room and saw Digit asleep on one of the couches lining its back wall. The poor little bastard was almost as rat-faced as him, and Khamza hoped there were a few smarts hidden somewhere under all that bullshit and bluster... the world wasn't very kind to ugly kids.

"What's this?" he said, sitting at the table beside Lily. She stirred, as if snapping out of a trance.

"We don't know. Opperman brought it over to the recycle plant. Wanted me to look after it."

"Hmm," Khamza said. Standing again to examine the object more closely. "A power source, temperature regulation at 38.5 degrees, and biofeedback pumping out long, lazy delta waves."

"Which means?"

"Which means you've got a brain of some sort in their Lily; an organic one."

"A brain? What the fuck?"

"Yeah. And it's not your usual offering of cryo-frozen corpo. This brain may be sleeping, but it's alive." He checked around the base of the cylinder and pointed to several connectors. "Can be connected to external equipment... Why the hell would he leave something like this with you?"

Lily's face hardened as she recalled the smuggler's words. "He said he was doing a friend in Europe a favour. That it was too hot for over there, so wanted me to hide it in a silo at the plant. But I hid it at our old place instead."

"Good thinking," Khamza said. "You know who it is?"

"No. He just said it was a bio sample. Can you find out?"

The Kazakh looked at the connectors again. "Yeah, whoever this is... was... has a PDrive port and several industry standard jack points to sync with smart tech. But do we really want to find out? You know what a genie is?"

Confused by the question, Lily nodded.

"Well, once we let this thing out of its bottle, it might not want to go back in. Why don't you finish telling me about why Opperman would want to kill you, first?"

Lily took a long slow breath, then told the coms king all about the heist.

"A skin?" Khamza whistled, shaking his head. "That's crossing a line. Jacking one? Sure, that happens all the time. But stealing a new one direct from Nova? That'll make them mad. Still doesn't explain taking your crew out though, unless —" He went over to his techdeck and began typing at glyphs. "Lily, can you describe what this woman looked like?"

"Uh, yeah. She was Asian, about five four, olive skin, black shoulder length hair."

"Age?"

"I dunno, twenty-something. You know how it is with digitals."

The Kazakh nodded and threw a bunch of images up on the wall. "These are all senior Nova execs. Any look familiar?"

Lily stood and walked over, glancing briefly at each and shaking her head. "No," she said, before returning to the first one. "She's the closest. But the skin's face seemed less mature... and squarer, more western."

Khamza clucked his tongue and continued to tap. "That's Akira Maas, Nova's vice president. How about these?"

He brought up another selection.

"Yes," Lily almost shouted, waving a finger at a pretty woman in the second row. "Yes, that's her."

Khamza grimaced, shaking his head slowly before walking around his deck to join the young redhead. "Oh Lily," he said. "What have you gotten wrapped up in?"

"What?" she replied, eyes wide. "Who is it? I don't understand."

"Opperman had you steal the clone of Ido Maas's granddaughter. There'll be hell to pay when he finds out, and I'm willing to bet the smuggler wanted a dead trail."

The young thief began crying again. "He set us up from the beginning?" she asked. "We'd retired, Khamza. Were happy; and he smiled at us as he lied his fucking face off. Smiled, knowing he was giving us all a death sentence."

"But he failed, Lily, didn't he?" the Kazakh said, pulling her into a hug and cradling her head on his shoulder. "He failed because you and Digit are alive to tell the tale. And, you have his... whatever the fuck that is."

PARTITION THREE   Cluster VI

August 20th, 2070
14:36 PST Zen Den on Willow Street, Tenderloin, Frisco Freetown

Khamza waited until the afternoon lull to move the cylinder into one of his total immersion chambers upstairs. The room looked like the command deck of a spaceship that had been designed around a computer core, and while multiple screens cycling random data glowed on its peripheral walls, a circular control column below a huge floating holo dominated the centre; thick futuristic looking seats with mod-reading headrests protruding out like spokes at regular intervals around its circumference.

"Wow," was all Digit could find to say as they entered. "Can I sit in one of those?" He was almost skipping with excitement.

"Sure," the tech said in a voice used to over-eager first-time gamers. "Just don't touch any of the controls until I give you the go ahead. Okay?" The boy nodded enthusiastically, dropping into the nearest seat, which automatically turned and closed with the central control column.

"Thanks Carl," Khamza said, walking in with Lily and the rucksack. "I'll take it from here."

"You sure, Mr Suleymanov? I don't mind staying if you want to entertain your guests?"

"That's kind of you. But I've got this. You go grab a break before the evening rush starts."

Carl nodded and left without another word. He was a good man, and Khamza trusted him, just as he did all his team. But whatever mess Lily had gotten caught up in was of the deadly kind, and the Kazakh didn't want an accidental slip costing him or any of his people their lives.

He walked up to the central console and pressed a button to close the door. Then tapped several others to lock out the usual room monitoring. A warning sounded on his cuff, and he silenced that as well; informing the Den's AI he was interfacing with an unknown device and to isolate the immersion chamber from the rest of the building's computer network.

"What are you doing?" Lily asked.

"Just making sure whatever is in this," Khamza hefted the ruck onto a chair and unzipped it. "Doesn't jump straight onto the net and out of here."

"It could do that?"

"I don't know Lily. But better safe than sorry, yes?"

The young woman nodded and sat down beside Digit to watch as Khamza connected the cylinder to the big holo display, checked and re-checked the air gap between the room's systems and those outside, and finally, with a muttered prayer in his own language, toggled the external power.

Three feet of holo flickered as the default display was replaced with pure black, then colours exploded outward like the birth of a nebula, before an old man's face began to resolve and solidify.

"Bobo?" the Kazakh said in an incredulous voice, his expression one of complete shock. "What the fuck are you doing in there?"

The face of the old man looked around the room in confusion for the briefest of moments, then settled its gaze on the wiry man from the Steppes. "How do you know that name? Where the hell am I?"

"You know this guy?" Lily demanded, suddenly apprehensive.

Khamza held out a forestalling hand.

"Bobo, it's Khamza Suleymanov. We were in Aksu together in the fifties…"

"Khamza?" Recognition crossed the elderly face on the holo before it rotated three hundred and sixty degrees to take in the room again. "This isn't Stockholm, is it? Where am I? How did I get here? Why can't I access the feed—"

"Whoa, whoa, whoa old man," Lily cut in with an edge of irritation. She'd not known what to expect from the cylinder, but the hologram of a confused, ragged looking wheezer hadn't even been on the list. "Five of my friends are dead because of you. So, I ask the questions. Okay?"

"What's the date?" the head demanded, ignoring the feisty young woman. "Khamza, what's the date?"

"Twentieth August 2070. You're in San Francisco. Bobo, what's going on? Why are you in a transport cylinder?"

"Three months," the old man said, looking down as if expecting to see a body. "I've been unplugged for three bloody months. How did I get here?"

Lily gave an exasperated sigh, accepting she wasn't going to win the battle of wills. "A murdering, backstabbing shit called Opperman left you with me and my friends ten days back."

"Opperman? Pieter Opperman?"

"Yeah. You know him?"

"Of course, he works for me."

"He does?" Lily and Khamza chorused together.

"Or at least he did three months ago. But my being here like his suggests he's taken other employment... Frisco though? Why Frisco?" The skull thin face bobbed silently in the holo field while the old man thought. "You say friends have died because of me?" it asked, directing its attention back to Lily.

"Well, Opperman really, not you. I think you was his way of starting a conversation with me. He talked me into robbing a skin from a warehouse up near Digital City." The poor young woman winced, clearly feeling guilty. "Killed my friends when they returned with it. Only reason me and him," she pointed at Digit, "are alive, is cos it made our hover too heavy. So we came back a different way."

The old man shook his head. "Keiko Cheng?"

"Yes," Khamza answered. "Though Lily and her friends didn't even know it was a skin. They thought they were doing a biotech grift from one of the gangs."

"But more importantly, old man, how would you know that?" Lily asked stiffly. "Thought you said you was unplugged or something these last few months."

"Oh, I was," the old man sighed. "But I vetoed that plan way before then."

"Vetoed?" Lily challenged. "Who the hell are you?"

"He's Bobo," Khamza said in an almost reverential voice that made the gaunt, tight-skinned face stretch into a bony smile. "The Grandfather — most powerful man in the underworld."

"Then how'd he end up stuffed in that cylinder and not calling the shots no more?" Digit chimed in for the first time.

"That," Bobo said. "Is an excellent question... I have my suspicions, and if you will grant me access to the net, Khamza, perhaps we can start making a few subtle enquiries." He smiled again, voice now low and scheming as he locked fierce grey eyes on the outspoken teenager. "But fear not my young friend. Despite how things may seem, you and I now have a distinct advantage over both Opperman and whoever is pulling his strings."

"Oh Yeh? How's that old man?" Digit asked, face clearly betraying the scepticism he felt.

"Because neither of them has any idea you've woken me up."

First Among Equals

PARTITION FOUR

First Among Equals

Tears streamed down Helen Stromberg's cheeks as she fought for breath, watching the tip of the electrode. She whimpered; snot and spittle dripping from her chin to catch on thick, pendulous breasts. "Please," she sobbed. "I don't know anything else, ser Renton. Stop. Please, just stop."

Bill touched the wand to her left nipple and a jolt of electricity caused an immediate scream as the plump woman's body recoiled. She was pissing herself again, and the intelligence chief adjusted his hardness. He didn't find Stromberg particularly attractive; he preferred a more boy-like shape. But there was something deeply intimate and arousing about inflicting pain.

He jabbed the wand into a roll of fat above her thick thatch of pubic hair and Stromberg lurched back with another blood-curdling cry. "Please," she gasped again through streaming tears. "Please. You have to believe me. I'll do anything to put this right."

She was completely broken, of course; had been for a while. Bill was just playing with her now. He smiled, placing the wand back on the table beside his tool bag before returning to the shackled woman's side. She instinctively shrank away from his touch, but he grabbed a handful of matted peroxide curls, pulling her face towards his while squeezing hard on the bulb of her right breast. "Of course you will," he said, enjoying the trembling of her lipstick smeared lips; the terror radiating from her wide, puffy eyes. This was the fifth time he'd interrogate her to death.

God, he loved immersion programs.

August 21st, 2070
01:50 GMT Suite 625, Karma Sanctum, Central London

Tash was laying across Lucas's lightly tanned chest, enjoying the twist of colour their entwined bodies made. She didn't know why, prejudice she guessed, but the estate girl who'd ducked, dodged and fought alongside her brother for every little scrap had expected the tech nerd to be a bit soft; a little squishy. But he wasn't — Jerome's yet to be fully named chopshop specialist was buff as fuck, proper fit.

"What's your surname?" she asked.

"What?" The naked young man chuckled at the unexpected question.

"Your surname...? I realised earlier I don't even know your last name."

His chest continued to bounce with quiet laughter for several seconds. "Well, that's a little rude, Natasha Adeyinka," he responded, wriggling down the bed to kiss her again before locking piercing blue eyes on hers. "Lucas Sylvester, at your service," he said, holding out a hand. "A pleasure to meet you. Though it's arguable we've gone about all this a little back to front?"

Grinning in agreement, Tash took the offered hand and cupped it over her right breast. "I like back to front," she breathed, enjoying the hunger spreading across his face as she stretched back on the crumpled bedsheets.

Lucas replaced his hand with lips; kissing and nibbling at her erect nipples as his fingers began tracing down the lithe young woman's body to brush over her sex with the lightest of touches. Tash's breath caught, and she arched her back in aching response before rolling over to straddle him, licking at the salty sweat of his chest and groaning with pleasure as he entered her again. Their love making was less urgent this time, and the pair were so lost in that moment, neither heard the boys return.

The *whomp*, when it came, sucked all the air from their room, then threw it back a split-second later with ear-popping ferocity.

"What the fuck was that?" Tash yelped, torn from sleep and instinctively leaping from the bed.

"I don't know. It felt like an explosion," the tech specialist replied, rubbing at his eyes and grabbing for the sweats he'd left on a nearby chair for the morning. "Careful, it might have been gas or something. Don't touch the electronics."

Tash nodded, leaving the bedroom in darkness as she approached the heavy polymer door. The hallway outside was thick with smoke and plastocrete debris, but the lighting and smart walls were still active, silhouetting the young woman's thin but shapely body. "Kicks," Lucas whispered, pointing at the glass covered floor. "Clothes."

"My brother —"

"Won't thank you for fucking up your feet. You can't help anyone if you're hurt yourself, Tash!"

Growling in annoyance, but conceding the point, the naked woman found her pack; quickly throwing on a hoodie, bush pants and sneaks. Then a single, screamed word echoed through the apartment.

"REIMI!"

Running through to the lounge, Tash found the woman who'd been sitting with her brother at the club on her knees, wearing nothing but a towel, and staring at a gaping hole to the outside world.

"Fucking hell!" Bobby muttered in disbelief, appearing from the darkness to wrap arms around the woman. "What happened? Where's Fin...?"

"My bodyguard," the woman cried. "I've lost her connection. She's gone."

"Bodyguard?" Tash repeated. "What the—"

"FIN...?" Bobby yelled into the void, brain not quite taking in that his best friend was gone.

"Oh shit," Lucas said, arriving to stand beside Tash at the back of the lounge.

"I know," she replied, voice quavering as her hand sought out his. "I think Fin's room is completely gone."

"We need to get out of here," the chopshop techie continued, pulling her towards the door. "Tell your brother we need to go."

"What's wrong with you, asshole?" Tash shouted, pulling her hand free and rounding on him. "I just said Fin's probably fucking DEAD, man."

"I know, and I'm truly sorry Tash," Lucas stuttered back, his voice pleading as he stared at the woman Bobby was shepherding towards them. "But I saw that lady earlier."

Tash frowned, irritated. "Of course you did. We both did."

"No, no. Not when we were out. At Jerome's. She was a skin delivery."

"Skin delivery?" Bobby repeated, turning to glare at the other man. "What the fuck—"

A second *whomp* burst through the room. This one a surge of energy that blanked the smart-walls and electronics. Lucas staggered sideways, hand going to his head. But the naked Asian dropped like she'd been poleaxed.

"EMP...?" Bobby muttered, his tired, half-drunk mind beginning to connect the dots.

"I can't get through to security," Tash said.

"EMP!" Bobby repeated, louder. "This is a fucking snatch." A look of pure violence crossed his features, and his eyes travelled from the hole in the hotel's outer skin to Lucas. "You set us up."

The chop-shop techie took a backward step as the angry, half-naked man leapt towards him. "You let some fuckstain blow my best friend to shit — just to steal a fucking *skin*?"

"Wait. No. Never," Lucas choked out as Bobby grabbed him around the throat and threw him to the floor.

"How the fuck was he 'sposed to know who you'd pick up tonight, idiot?" Tash growled, kneeling to break her brother's grip on the techneer's throat as red dots began tracking along the apartment's walls. "THINK!"

Bobby glared at his younger sibling for a heartbeat, eyes wide on a cocktail of booze, pharma, anger and adrenalin. Then he nodded, smearing dust filled tears across his face before crawling over to snag an arm of the unconscious Asian. "Let's go then," he said, dragging her towards the suite's entrance.

"Why are you taking that?" Tash demanded as she and Lucas joined him at the door.

"Because those assholes out there want it," he replied flatly. "... And they fucked up Fin. So they don't get to have it." As the targeting lasers then disappeared, he added. "Run."

The three of them scrambled to their feet, crashing through the apartment door and into a hotel corridor suspiciously devoid of other people or alarms. Lucas automatically turned along the dimly lit passage, following its luminescent emergency arrows.

"Who the fuck is she?" Tash hissed in a half-whisper, looking back at the groggy woman in her brother's arms.

"I dunno," Bobby replied. "Keiko something. We hadn't gotten to last names."

"Down!" someone shouted from ahead.

Looking up, Lucas saw the barrel of a gun poking around the corner and grabbed at Tash. The pair clattered to the floor, tripping Bobby, who piled over the top of them as the stranger began firing.

"Fuuuuuck!" Bobby yelled, covering his head in a futile act of self-preservation before looking up to see three armed lumps in mismatched body-armour crash to the floor behind them. Breathing heavily, he crawled back, snatching up a compact dropped by one of their pursuers and pointing it towards the open suite door, but no one else came through.

"Move. Move. Move," the stranger, a middle-aged woman in standard street clothes, yelled. "There'll be more."

No one argued, and Tash helped the groggy digital back to her feet; any trace of modesty forgotten as she half carried, half dragged the dazed Asian skin to the intersection.

"Down there," the woman directed, pointing towards the elevators. "The far one is still illuminated. I'm guessing it's powered by an emergency generator. We need to get off this floor before your friends realise their snatch has gone south."

"Fuck that," Bobby snarled, looking back towards the three bodies now bleeding out on the plush cream carpet. "They just murdered my best friend... and now I've got a gun, I'm staying right here and shooting every fucking one of them as they come out of that door!"

"You stay here, they'll kill you too, pal," the woman growled before returning her gaze to the hallway ahead. "We got two guns now. That's good. But we're completely exposed in this corridor. Please, just go get the lift here and ready. There'll be staff and a security station in the basement. You can talk revenge as much as you like then, yeh?"

Bobby frowned, suspicious of how an armed woman just happened to be outside their suite when things kicked off.

"Why's no one else coming out?" Lucas asked, knocking on locked doors and shouting for help.

"With electronics and comms down after an explosion and gunfire... Would you?" Tash challenged as she reached the elevators.

"Yeah, but emergency protocols in a hotel *release* all the doors, don't they? Not lock them."

Tash shrugged, mind too occupied with what had just happened to take in what the tech-head was saying.

"We need to ditch that bitch," Bobby muttered, pushing past them to press the call button. "Those assholes killed our *boy*. I ain't leaving this place 'til they're all dead."

"No... we need to get out of here, Bobby. This isn't an ordinary snatch." Lucas observed.

"And that woman probably just saved our lives," Tash added.

"Did she?" Bobby glared at them both, stabbing at the door close tab after they'd all bundled in. "You stop to wonder how she just happened to be there?"

A gun muzzle jammed into the closing gap, and the lift shuddered as its doors began reopening. "Do that again and we'll fall out," the woman said, shouldering her way into the small space. On instinct Bobby sneered, aiming his newly acquired carbine at her. "Point your gun someplace else, bitch," he threatened.

The stranger gave him an appraising look before thumping the down button. Then turned her attention to the now conscious digital. "Someone give this poor woman something to put on for fuck's sake..."

"Poor woman?" Tash snorted. "She just got our best friend fucking dead."

"Keiko Cheng," the stranger continued, as if she hadn't heard or didn't care. "What the hell are you doing in London? Where is your security?"

As Lucas pulled his backpack off, the petite Asian looked up for the first time. "Dead," she whispered in a flat, empty tone. "Gone."

"Right, but that flatline will register on your family's secure net, yes? More will be stationed nearby?"

Keiko looked down again, only seeming to realise she was naked when the young white man offered her a plain grey tee. "No one knows I'm here," she sniffed, rubbing at blotchy red eyes. "Our bodies are...this body is sinless."

"Well that's just brilliant…" Lucas mumbled before clamping his mouth shut again.

The woman with the gun flicked her eyes to him, then Tash and Bobby. She recognised the two black kids from the previous night… What were the odds of a coincidence? "And who the fuck are you three? Not security, that's for sure."

"We're no one," Bobby said stiffly. "Just met her. You know who those assholes up there are?"

"I was gonna ask you the same thing, tough guy. Figured they're more your crowd than mine."

"What's that 'sposed to mean?" Tash demanded.

"Gangsters? Roadmen? Gutterpunks? Whatever you people call yourselves these days… You telling me you weren't there to jack Miss Cheng yourselves?"

Bobby began to raise his newly acquired carbine again, and the woman punched him in the solar plexus; retrieving the weapon as he doubled over, mouth desperately working to drag air into stunned lungs. "You were warned, pal," she continued, fixing Tash with a cold stare.

She had a military bearing; acted like someone used to people doing what she told them.

Keiko gave her an uncertain look. "I'm sorry. But who exactly are you? These people have done nothing to harm or threaten me. We met at a club." She looked over to Bobby, who was just beginning to straighten, a murderous look in his eyes.

The woman frowned. "Name's Gabriel Sousa. I'm Interpol… a cop. I spotted you with these *people* in Soho; so followed you." She turned back to Bobby. "You know who she is, don't you?" The accusation was clear in her voice.

"Should we?" Tash fired back.

Gabriel gave a bark of laughter. "Okay, we'll play it your way… Heard of Nova?"

"Course."

"Well, that's Keiko Cheng, its president's granddaughter; and whether you did or didn't already know that — you're now officially in a world of shit."

"Oh fuck," Lucas muttered, going pale as he looked at Tash.

"Yeah right," the woman answered, misunderstanding the reason for his response. "Now get low and hug the walls. People tend to hold guns at chest height and straight out in front of them." She looked at Bobby. "The smart one's even take the safety off," she grinned, tapping the rifle now slung over her shoulder. "So not being right in front of the door when it opens is always the best idea."

Gabriel crouched, gun swapped for a vicious-looking knife, but Bobby didn't move. She shook her head, "Look, tough guy, I get your ego's bruised... and as Miss Cheng seems to like you, I'll try not to hurt you again. But you make any more stupid ass moves, I'll put you down for good... You grab?"

The angry, half-naked man offered no reply, just continued to stare as the corpo-cop released the door.

Fortunately, no one was waiting on the other side, and Gabriel let out an audible breath as she led the small group into a darkened basement. "Okay, you," she waved a finger at Lucas. "Send the lift back up three floors. Then all of you follow me."

"Follow you where?" Bobby hissed. Refusing to move. "Where's *your* backup, cop?"

Gabriel rolled her eyes, growing tired of the young man's petulance. "If you engage your brain and move, *gangsta*, the elevator display will read 3rd floor, not bring your attackers straight to the fucking basement. And I don't have any backup because I'm not supposed to be here. Okay...? You're welcome."

Bobby sneered, clearly not convinced. "Show us some ID then," he demanded.

"Fuck's sake," the woman muttered. "I don't have ID. I'm undercover."

The savvy London thief looked at Tash and Lucas before raising an eyebrow at Keiko. "Course you are. That's why you reek of booze too, huh? Look, you go where you want. But we don't have to do a fucking thing you say."

Gabriel snorted, taking Keiko by the arm and leading her further into the basement. "Why is doing a good turn always so fucking difficult with some people?" she asked before turning back, pointing a finger. "Look dickhead, even if your friend's killers have managed to fuck up all the electronics in this place, local enforcement will already be responding to the fuck-ton of calls made from surrounding buildings about the hole that's just appeared in the side of this one. So, if you'd just stop constantly trying to call attention to us, we could find you two something to wear and a quiet corner to hole up in until the cavalry arrives? Once I've handed Miss Cheng over to the local munis, you can go press any self-destruct button you want as hard and as long as you damn well please."

"Fuck you," Bobby growled.

"No," Sousa hissed back. "You're fucking us all, you fucking amateur. You haven't got the skill or smarts to take on those hired guns… and you're proving that right now! All you're gonna do is get yourself and those of us unlucky enough to be around you, dead!"

The wannabe hardman's eyes narrowed and he began squaring up to the shorter, middle-aged woman again.

"You really are thick, aren't you?" she quipped. "You even remember how easily I just dropped you?"

To end the standoff, Lucas stepped into the lift and sent it back up four floors; then Tash pushed in front of her brother, guiding him away with an affirming nod to the corpo-cop. "Right," Gabriel said. "Clothes."

The staffroom, when they found it, was empty. In fact, the entire basement was quiet in a very wrong way. Ordinarily, the

Interpol operative would have expected to see at least a skeleton crew of kitchen, porter and security staff in a hotel like Sanctum at this time. But except for the small army of mechs, frozen by the EMP while doing their basic chores, the place was dead, and that convinced her the night shift had either been scared off, or paid off.

After a quick search for clothing and footwear that mostly fitted, the small group then made their way towards the parking area beside the up ramp where Tash, Bobby and Fin had left their gyros the night before.

"Can you hear that?" Gabriel stopped, holding a finger to her lips before waving them down between the ramp and a large black SUV.

"What?" Keiko asked, now firmly glued to the agent's side.

"Gunfire," Bobby said sulkily, as barely perceptible but unmistakable bursts of sound entered the hotel's basement from the street above. "At least two different groups. But none are the munis — ain't no sirens or mech deployment warnings."

"Brighter than you look." Gabriel nodded. "And the only reason local enforcement wouldn't be howling up outside now—"

"Is because someone's told 'em not to," Tash finished with a sideways look at Lucas. "So what's your plan B?"

The corpo cop sucked in a breath, considering her options. "Well, if two or more groups are going at it right now, I guess we should be grateful for the distraction. Because when they stop shooting at each other, they'll probably be fully focused on us again." She looked at Keiko. "Given that, I reckon our best chance now lies in making a break for it."

Bobby grunted, expression full of contempt. "Well, don't be following us," he said.

It was tempting to give the short-sighted lowlife and his fuck you attitude a good hiding. But he was just a product of the environment he'd been brought up in. One the corporations had created to keep the masses under their heel… Divide and keep divided. Either way, Gabriel really didn't give a shit what the small-minded gutterpunk thought. She simply nodded agreement and threw him the carbine instead. "Try not to get your friends killed."

A confused Bobby caught the weapon and maintained enough self-control to ignore the jibe, turning instead to point at the three single wheeled bikes parked side by side in the corner. "They're ours, Lucas. You ride mine. I'll take Fin's."

"And what about them?" Tash demanded.

Bobby turned deep brown eyes towards the cop and overwrought digital. "What about them?"

"We can't just leave them down here."

"They're not our problem, sis. Fin is. Come on."

"No," Tash said, turning back to Gabriel and pointing over to her gyro. "You can take my bike. I'll start it for you, then ride with Lucas." She shot her brother a filthy look, daring him to challenge her. "There's no need to be an asshole, Bobby. It's not her fault Fin's dead. Hell, it's not even Keiko's."

Gabriel smiled in thanks, about to give one last condescending piece of advice to the angry young black man about living longer if he learned to listen to his sister, when the pretty young woman was flung sideways into the wall.

PARTITION FOUR <u>Cluster II</u>

August 21st, 2070
03:20 GMT Outside Karma Sanctum, Inner London

An explosion that took out a whole corner of the building's sixth floor wasn't what Jonas had been expecting.

His team had spent the last twenty hours surveilling the gang their mystery package had been dropped at, and when men in assorted tatty armour started gathering at the storage yard that seemed to be their base, he'd figured they were preparing for a snatch — not an all-out assault on a hotel in London's touristville that started with a fucking rocket strike.

As he watched, a second device was fired through the yawning hole, and a subsequent building-wide blackout explained its purpose.

"You seeing this, boss?" Sergeant Cooper breathed over the squad channel. Jonas shifted his drone feed to street level, focusing on the newly arrived vans being painted by one of his observation teams. Three men had already exited from the first, fired grapples and begun ascending.

"We've got movement inside too," Price, one of his marines, cut in. "Feed updating now."

Captures of a naked Asian woman and athletic-looking black man appeared in Jonas's visual cortex. He mentally cropped the image of the woman, focusing on the face, and an immediate file match blinked up. "Are you fucking with me, recon two?" he breathed, irritation clear in his voice.

"Absolutely not, sir," the man replied. Price had a reputation for unfunny jokes and childish barrack room banter. But at work, Cooper had assured his captain, the young marine was all business.

"Oh shit, no!" Jonus said, pulling his rifle from the rack beside him and leaning out from the hired UV's window to zero in as the first group of armed invaders disappeared through the gap. "Take them out," he yelled. "Take them all out now. That's Ido Maas's fucking granddaughter."

As all hell then broke loose on Warwick Street, a big, bald-headed man in a long black trench coat got out of a custom merc with wide skirts. He watched as several of his people fell to well-placed shots, talking to an even bigger lump stood just behind him and pointing with disturbing accuracy to where Jonas's teams had plotted up. The captain lined up a shot, held his breath, and squeezed, knocking the man down with a bolt to the centre mass. But as he then began sighting on the other guy, the apparent leader got back to his feet, turning that large modded head towards Jonus with a grim smile as he shed his coat to reveal the form following curves of high-grade graphene body-armour — cutting edge hardware; incredibly expensive.

"Oh shit," Jonus said for a second time, dropping back into his seat and looking over at the driver. "Terry, get us the fuck out of here." The captain's face said everything the intelligence officer needed to know, and he slammed their *borrowed* bimmer into reverse as a line of high velocity rounds peppered the two vehicles it had been tucked behind.

Cursing himself for not having done so sooner, Jonus opened a secure channel to Nova's Central Command, five and a half thousand miles away.

"Operator," a female voice answered.

"CentCom, this is—"

The bimmer bucked violently, and Jonus felt a brief period of weightlessness before the hefty utility vehicle crashed back onto the road, power out and careering towards a row of shops on its roof. Unable to do anything but watch, both men braced themselves as the overturned UV collided with another personal transport before burying itself in the window display of an urban sportswear boutique.

What kind of fucking tech were these gangbangers packing?

"Fuck," Jonus growled, tapping at the dead display of his command cuff before punching it. "Your comms out as well?"

"Comms, visual mods, drone link, everything." Terry said. "That was military spec EMP, Sir."

Jonus nodded in angry agreement, shouldering open the door and releasing his restraints to drop onto the shop's tiled floor. Terry did likewise on the pilot's side, crawling over to the captain as high velocity rounds began tearing into the vehicle's cockpit through the now smashed windscreen.

In a darkened corner of the shop window, Jonus then returned his attention to the firefight still raging in the street outside the hotel. Where the fuck were the munis? Only two of his four teams were still firing. They weren't equipped for a prolonged engagement, and the ambitious officer now realised he should have just called in the sighting. But who would have ever thought a band of street thugs had access to this kind of hardware?

"You see that big, bald fucker in the graphene body suit?" He pointed down the road.

The intel officer took several moments to find the brute, then whistled quietly, "How the fuck—"

"I know," Jonus said, cutting him short. "I want you to etch his features into your memory, then find a way out the back of this place. Hopefully, the others had the sense to withdraw when our comms went down. Get back to the shuttle and put in an emergency call to CentCom. Tell them what's happened."

"What about you, Sir?"

"I'm gonna find somewhere to hole up where I can see if they get Miss Cheng. Then I'll make my way back too. Tell CentCom to send a strike team to that container yard. That's where these fuckers came from. So that's probably where they're going back to. Also, tell them not to trust the Europeans. Municipal police should have been here by now, but there's not so much as a siren."

Jonus looked down the road again. All weapons fire from his teams had stopped now, and an armed group was picking its way towards their shopfront. He put a bolt into the chest of the first man to break cover, dropping him. "No graphene for you then?" he muttered, firing on a second. "Go on, Terry," he said, giving the trooper a quick wink. "Get going. I need to move soon, but I'll keep their heads down while you make some distance."

The intelligence specialist looked like he was about to argue, then simply nodded and began crawling towards the back of the store as his captain's rifle sang out again.

August 21st, 2070
03:40 GMT Sub-level1, Karma Sanctum, Central London

It took a moment for Gabriel and Bobby to register what had just happened, and then another to locate the shooter.

Luck, the corpo-cop figured, played a big part in everyone's life. A lot of rookies, fresh in the field, banged on about practise — and that was important of course, improved the odds in almost every situation; as did experience. But neither of those things meant squat if you just happened to be in the wrong place at the wrong time — that was just shitty luck, or perhaps the universe deciding no good deed should go unpunished.

"That's my sista, muvvafukka...." Bobby roared, charging towards the elevator, screaming in rage and firing shot after shot at a gunman standing in front of its closing doors. Two others leapt behind parked vehicles, but Gabriel was able to drop each as they rose to shoot at the young skin-jacker totally focused on pulping the man who'd tagged his sister.

"Hey pal," Gabriel called over the thunk ... thunk ... thunk of the streetrat's carbine.

"BOBBY!" she shouted.

"What?" he howled back, eyes wild and face twisted in an expression of pure violence.

"That guy is very fucking dead… Now you need to help your sister."

"It's bad, Bobby," Lucas yelled from beside Tash, blood covered hands busy. "It's really bad."

Breathing hard, the South London skin thief, who'd been celebrating his birthday just an hour before, pulled his temper under control for a second time, eyeing the irritatingly focused chopshop techie as he opened the MedKit ransacked from a nearby EV and stabbed one of its EpiPens into Tash's right thigh. After a brief examination of the kit's other contents, he then he took out a red labelled doser and injected something else directly into the wound. "The adrenalin and coagulating gel should hold her for a while," he said, looking up. "But this is well beyond my skill set, man. We need to find a proper doctor, and we need to do it quickly."

Swallowing, Bobby ran back, bending over his sister to see blood soaking through the plain grey hoodie Lucas had wrapped around her abdomen. "Always gotta be the centre of attention, ain't ya?" he said, trying to smile as a cold dread washed away the last vestiges of his fury. Tash gave him a weak grin. "Let's get you to Doc. He'll sort you out."

Gabriel's face was a mask as the young criminal stood back up. She'd seen plenty of gut wounds during the war; a slow and painful death was the most likely outcome for the poor girl. "I'll hang back and give you a chance to split," she said. "There'll be more coming after that little performance. In return, I need you to take Keiko. Keep her safe until I catch up."

Bobby gave the corpo-cop a single nod; mind now focused solely on his sister. "Lucas, take Keiko," he said. To Gabriel he added, "I'll start Tash's bike for you. Once you get out of here, turn right, straight up to Oxford Circus. You can drop into the old subway tunnels there. Go all the way down to the platform with blue arrows. Turn left into that tunnel and stay in it 'til Little Portugal. If you aren't with us by then, you're on your own."

The agent nodded her understanding as she helped Lucas lift Tash. "Cover up," she said, tearing up one of the tee-shirts they'd taken from the staff room and tying it around Tash's semi-conscious face. "They'll have drones up, and if just one of them gets a hit on you — judging by this shitshow, your whole neighbourhood will get fucked over next."

PARTITION FOUR   **<u>Cluster IV</u>**
August 21st, 2070
04:05 GMT Warrick Street junction with Brewer Street, Central London

"Who are you?" Jerome demanded, pushing the barrel of his FN 950 into the silent man's forehead. Because of his weedy little distraction, not only did the gangboss now have a hole in his favourite trench coat, he'd also just watched their quarry escape the hotel on the back of a gyro and disappear into the old subway network. "Which polycorp do you work for?"

The man spat, resignation and contempt obvious on his face as he stared back. The extensively modded criminal heaved a sigh and shook his head. "You know I can't leave you alive."

"Go Fu—"

The thunk of the pistol cut the reply short, and Jerome stood back up. "How many did we lose?" he asked the giant of a man standing behind him.

"Seventeen."

"For fuck's sake." He glowered at the huge hole in the building two hundred metres back down the road. This was supposed to have been a quick in and out. Then the girl diverts to some random hotel, and the whole gig goes to rat shit... All his planning. All the bribes paid to plant directed charges in her suite to neutralise the damn killbot — traded for a terrorist style fucking rocket attack and firefight with what was clearly corporate military. "Seventeen of *my* lads, you asshole!" he growled, giving the dead man a solid kick. "What about the others?"

"Tony's pretty certain all the one's down the road are accounted for," the man-giant said. "That just leaves the little man who run out the back of this place. Pablo's on it. He won't get far."

Jerome nodded. "Well, that's something at least. Burn them all, and put in a comcall to your contact with the munis — just in case the runner is stupid enough to go straight to Consolidated."

PARTITION FOUR   Cluster V

August 21st, 2070
04:23 GMT Angell Town, Outer London

"Hurry!" Bobby shouted, banging at the shuttered door again as lights came on in the hallway of the small square unit.

"Who is it?" a muffled voice called.

"Doc, it's Bobby. Bobby Adeyinka. Tash's been shot," the young Londoner sobbed, sister limp in his arms.

"Oh Lord," the voice replied, locks turning in the thick polymer composite.

Lucas had fired two further stimshots into her neck since leaving the hotel. But Tash's usually vibrant skin was now clammy and growing greyer by the minute; she'd been unconscious since entering the tunnels.

"Oh my, Bobby. Whatever did you kids get into?" the old Northerner said, lifting Tash's blood-soaked hoodie to examine the injury. "She's been torn to shreds." He turned, shaking his bony head and pointing down the hallway. "You know where to go."

Doc Shambler had been living at the heart of the estate since before Bobby could remember; he and his wife arriving as part of a government levelling-up programme before the war, and then refusing to leave after the polycorp cut funding.

The couple had made the small, square shaped clinic at the centre of Angell their home; living off donations from the community and providing limited medical care for its residents in return... But this was still Angell, and the surgery, though sterile and spotlessly clean, now survived on outdated med tech and whatever pharma the estate's residents could steal.

"Put her on the table and get that top off," Doc instructed, slowly turning his hands under the UV sani by the door. "Good. Now step back and let the table scan and clean the wound."

Bobby did as instructed, nervous eyes fixed on readouts he didn't understand. "She'll be alright, yeh Doc?" Bobby pressed, body tense with fear.

The aging physician held up a finger as he examined multiple tiny punctures surrounding the main wound in Tash's abdomen, and then secured a MedBot to her side, programming individual needle placements. "Flechette round. Bastard evil things," he muttered, turning the small spider-like device on and pulling thick bug-eyed goggles down over his eyes. Erratic vitals began tracking across the bed's display as the old man watched the bot's nanite reserve drain. He let out a long, audible breath, disengaging the bot to attach another.

"What?" Bobby demanded. "What's the sigh for?"

Doc pushed his goggles back onto a liver-spotted forehead, hooded grey eyes regarding the man he'd watched grow up. "She's dying, Bobby," he said, voice low and sad.

"There's just too much damage. My bots are simply delaying the inevitable. I'm sorry, lad."

"No. No, she's not," the desperate thief denied, snatching up Tash's right hand and squeezing. "She can't be. I won't let her. You won't let her." He gave the aging medic a pleading look. "Put it right like you always do, Doc... Or, or call someone who can. I don't care what it costs, yeh? I've got paper back at the flat."

"It's not about money, son. There's simply nothing I can do. Nothing anyone could do — except perhaps buy you a bit of time." The old man stroked Tash's long braids of bright blue hair. "Even a corpo med-centre wouldn't be able to fix this. One badly damaged organ? Yeah, sure. Two? Probably. But three? No Laddie. Even their fabricators and surgical AIs couldn't remove and replace that much damage without killing her themselves. No, if she was rich enough to have that kind of insurance, they'd just transfer her to a new skin."

The elderly doctor paused for a second, momentarily lost in thought, then placed a hand on Bobby's shoulder, casting suspicious eyes towards the group who'd followed him into the surgery. "Look, I don't know who they are, so won't say this out loud. But rumour has it you've been working for Jerome Donelly? That he's into some pretty serious doings? Bodysnatching and the like?"

Lost in his sister's pale face, the young gangster gave an angry nod. "What of it, Doc? I ain't interested in no sermon."

"No, no," the medic countered. "I wasn't going to give you a lecture, lad. I—"

Bobby turned on the old man, shrugging off his hand and about to lash out when his words hit home. "That kind of insurance...?"

Doc Shambler gave a slight nod. "It's not my field of expertise, son, and I don't know if Donelly even has access to that kind of thing. But Tash's organs are shutting down, and while I can't reverse that, I have stopped the haemorrhaging...

I reckon you have about an hour, maybe two, before the heart gives out and her brain dies. I'm sorry lad, it's the best I can do."

Bobby stared down at his little sister's immobile, sweat-beaded face and began to cry. Nine hours ago, he'd been invincible; they all had. She was still wearing the gold makeup and lipstick he'd bought her, for fuck's sake. He looked back up to see Lucas staring intently from the doorway.

"Well?" the young American asked.

Bobby shook his head, tears falling onto the shining metal surface as he waved the techneer over.

"Does Jerome have the right kind of hardware to save her?"

Lucas gathered up Tash's other hand. "How long does she have?"

"Doc says an hour, maybe two."

They were both crying now, and Lucas closed his eyes; shaking his head in what Bobby took to be denial.

"Lucas?"

When the chopshop technician looked up again, he seemed somehow calmer, resolute even. "If he doesn't — I do."

Bobby frowned at the oblique response, staring at the other man for the slightest moment before turning to Gabriel. "You'll be able to contact your people from here, yes?"

The rogue investigator grunted and shook her head. "You're joking, right? We're nose deep in the shit, pal. What happened back there, the lack of municipal response... that's gotta have serious corporate weight behind it, and I'm not breaking cover 'til I know *who* I can trust."

"Well, you can't come with us," Bobby said, scooping up his sister again.

Keeping her voice mild so as not to start another argument with the highly strung youth, the corpo-cop pointed to the young woman in his arms. "We can help each other out here, Bobby. Think about it," she replied. "You'll need back up while you get Tash sorted... and like it or not, we both know I'm good in a fight. Then, in return, when she's safe and stable, all I ask is that you get me and Keiko out of London with no corporate or gangland interference. Fair?"

Bobby and Lucas exchanged a wary glance.

"Look, if you run into more goons, how's that gonna end? You gonna fight it out with Tash in your arms? You gonna have the time for that?" Gabriel shook her head. "I've honestly got bigger fish to fry today than a couple of chopshop gangbangers, boys... Let's help each other out, yeh?"

To Lucas's surprise, Bobby gave the corpo-cop a reluctant grunt of agreement, and while he knew she'd probably change her mind about which fish to fry when she saw what he was going to put Tash's consciousness into... the desperate young techie also knew that if he did nothing, the beautiful young woman would die — and he couldn't let that happen. "Let's go then," he muttered. "We've got a lot to do, and not much time to do it in."

PARTITION FOUR   **Cluster VI**
August 21st, 2070
04:55 GMT InterFreight storage facility, Greenwich, Outer London

Fifteen minutes after leaving Angell, Bobby's Suzuki hummed to a stop alongside the twelve-foot perimeter wall of Jerome's haulage business.

"My lab's accessible through here," Lucas said, tapping in the code to unlock an old up-and-over garage door that then whispered open with unexpected ease. "It's a useful way in and out for things Jerome doesn't want the munis seeing." He eyed Gabriel. "No guards. No cameras."

Inside, a web of fine red lines swept the otherwise empty space before converging on Lucas. Then another lock in the back wall cycled. "Quick," he instructed, pointing at a shard of light formed by the new opening. "Through there."

As Bobby placed his little sister on the central workbench of the sterile room beyond, causing sensors to come alive and a standby message to begin flashing on its display surface, Lucas turned again to the agent and heiress. "I'm pretty certain," he said. "Despite your little speech back at the doctor's, that you're not going to like this."

Gabriel shrugged in an *it's a little late for that* kind of way and walked to the small lab's door. This was the place she'd followed the two black kids and their dead friend to a few days earlier, and she wondered what had happened to Levinson. "What is this place?" she asked.

"Import, export, freight storage; that kind of thing," the blond-haired techie replied evasively as he perched on the edge of a stool beside the workbench, bringing different monitors around Tash's unmoving body online. "I'm sure you can figure the rest out for yourself." He shook his head, unlocking a techdeck and its drawers with a retinal scan.

Up until this point, Bobby's mind had been pretty blank; semi shut down in survival mode, hoping someone, Lucas, would do what Doc couldn't — save his little sister. But as the reality of what that would entail began to penetrate, the estate boy with plenty of street smarts but no formal education realised he knew next to nothing about Jerome's tech-nerd; the guy had just appeared in the chopshop one day a few months earlier, and Tash had taken an instant fancy to him.

Pulling a small steri-pac from the underside of one of the previously locked drawers, Lucas flicked an apologetic grimace at Keiko. "Guess we might as well get the unpleasant bit over and done with," he said, tapping several of the techdeck's glyphs.

A humming noise started in the wall behind him, then a stasis chamber vented and cycled open.

"You've got to be fucking kidding me," Gabriel stormed, striding over to look at the young Asian featured body refrigerated within. "Where the hell did you get this?"

"I didn't know who she was," Lucas answered as he worked.

"I said, where did the body come from, Lucas?"

"I don't know, Sousa. Jerome brought it in before I left yesterday. Said it was for a client in Belgium."

"Shit." The corpo cop's arm came up reflexively to make a call, then she remembered her electronics were fried and began shaking her head instead. "Well, you obviously can't use it. We need to get the fuck out of here."

"Fuck you, we can't," Bobby snarled, levelling his compact; suddenly full of promised violence again. "You try to stop him, I'll put a plasma round right through your chest. Grab?"

Gabriel shook her head. "Jeeze! You really don't get it, do you, dumb ass? That's one of Keiko's skins." She looked at the petite heiress, who in turn was staring at the perfect replica of her naked body. "So who do you think was probably responsible for the attack on that hotel? We've literally walked into the enemy's fucking headquarters, and aside from the very strong possibility they could return at any time... unless Lucas knows something he's not sharing, we have no idea what your boss planned to do with the damn thing — so you'll just be painting another target on Tash's back if you put her in it."

Lucas looked up from his monitors, a single-minded determination now etched across his face. "I've no idea what Jerome's plans were. But we're out of time, Sousa. I've nowhere else to turn. No other skin to put her in. So back off and just let me get on with it, would you."

The Council agent growled in frustration, turning back to the heiress as he continued to work. "Do you have any idea where this came from, Keiko? Did you have a backup in London?"

"No," the heiress replied in a quiet voice. "Reimi and I only kept the ones we were in, here. A valet service stores and maintains them when we're not in town." She pointed at the thawing clone. "But if that's one of my official skins, it'll have a serial starting NKC on the inside of the left eyelid."

Lucas grabbed a pair of tweezers from his rack and approached the cold body, pulling up the eyelid and folding it back far enough to expose a minute code. He scanned it and threw it up on the smart wall.

NKC06282105SFP

"Yeah, that's one of mine. From the San Francisco facility."

"We need to get on with this, Lucas," Bobby urged, still holding his gun on the corpo-cop.

To everyone's surprise, Keiko nodded in agreement. "Your sister saved my life tonight. It's only right I repay that debt. But can I suggest a swap?"

Bobby gave Lucas a confused look.

"Why?" the techie asked.

Keiko pointed to the serial number. "The skin I'm wearing is sinless. But that one is *registered* to me. As a friend back home is currently wearing my official body, even if you've overwritten all the tracking hardware, any subsequent core scan will flag up on both Novan and Council compliance databases as an illegal duplicate in use." She looked at Gabriel. "They'd send someone to investigate that, wouldn't they?"

The corpo-cop nodded.

But Bobby wasn't interested in future legalities, just the here and now. "So what's wrong with the one you're in?" he demanded.

"Absolutely nothing except the fried comnode. I was actually thinking about your sister. Anyone other than me found in that skin may not be given the opportunity to explain how they came to be in it."

Gabriel nodded at that. As did Lucas. "I'll need to transfer Tash into a storage cube for a bit," he said. "Get that done before her body shuts down. But then, yes, I guess that makes a lot of sense."

"Well, get on with it then," Bobby snapped, glowering at everyone.

Gabriel stared from the volatile twenty-something-year-old still pointing a gun at her, to his sister. Then from the thawing skin to Lucas. "You even got a chip?"

The increasingly protean technician dipped his head towards the steri-pac beside him, and though the agent couldn't begin to fathom how he'd managed to gain possession of that most closely guarded of Novan secrets, let alone why he'd then keep it taped to the bottom of a drawer, she gave a stiff nod. "Well then, you heard the man — get on with it."

The implantation process was a relatively simple operation. After drilling a small hole at the base of Tash's skull, Lucas manoeuvred the tiny chip through the ventricular system on a flotilla of nanites to embed it in the corpus callosum. Nanoscopic filaments then extended outward, sinking into and integrating with the central communication nexus of her brain.

In a Novan facility, the procedure would only be done after a thorough study of the candidate brain to ensure compatibility and following a full day of orientation for the individual concerned. Tash, if she woke up at all, hadn't had that luxury. But Lucas chose not to share that nugget of information. Bobby was close enough to the edge already.

"Okay," he said, staring closely at the holo of Tash's brain; bespoke software already reading, inspecting and organising organic data for digitisation and transfer. That was a good sign. "Well, at least Tash is compatible," he murmured to himself, blowing out a breath before starting to code on a different screen.

"You seem very comfortable with the digitisation procedure," Gabriel observed. A statement, not a question.

Lucas didn't look around. "You think technology like this should only be available through Nova, agent Sousa?"

"Oh, that's not a debate Interpol encourages its agents to get involved in, Lucas," Gabriel sidestepped. "No, it's just I didn't think anyone outside Nova had the knowhow or kit to do it."

The blond-haired man snorted; not quite a laugh; not quite an insult. "No offence to Keiko or you, agent, but that's what happens when one small part of society wants everyone to believe they have total control over a given technology. Which, in this case, has in fact stagnated due to a lack of healthy competition.

"The procedure Nova uses now is almost exactly the same as it was twenty-six years ago when they stole it; with the same inherent flaws. There are, as it happens, people out there with a far greater understanding of the technology." He nodded down at the steri-pac again. "… and better wetware. They just disagree on how best to use their knowledge."

Gabriel stared at the young man's back for a couple of beats, head filling with questions. Then he seemed to realise he'd said too much and gave her the briefest of glances over a shoulder. "Now, if you'll excuse me, I need to concentrate."

A single flashing icon appeared in the application tray of Lucas's display. He took a few moments to examine the code once more, drew in a long, slow breath, and tapped it. All the QA checks disappeared, and the screen went blank.

Several seconds passed, and Bobby stared fretfully over the other man's shoulder, a growing sense of catastrophe gnawing at his mind as he willed the damn thing to do something. Anything. Then, as if answering his unspoken prayers, string after string of virgin code began scrolling across the blackness; white lines reflecting in the lenses of the young tech's glasses as they appeared and disappeared faster and faster.

No one spoke for the next six minutes, they simply stared at the display; only the gentle hum of refrigeration units and whir of cooling fans breaking the silence. Then, as if taking his first gulp of air after cryogenic suspension, Lucas turned his intense blue eyes on Bobby; lifting thin-framed glasses to rub at the bridge of his nose. "It's done."

"What do you mean?" the older of the two said. "What's done?"

"I've transferred Tash's consciousness."

Bobby frowned down at the grey face of his little sister. "But she's still breathing," he said, biting back fresh tears.

"Her old body is," Lucas replied gently, getting up to join him. "But everything that makes Tash the person she is, is now over there." He pointed to the data cube rotating in a transfer cradle beside his techdeck. "I know that sounds crazy. But once she's downloaded into Keiko's vacated core, you'll see."

Bobby looked at the woman he'd been having sex with just a couple of hours before and winced. Wanting to delete the memory, but now unable to stop seeing it. "I can't—" he began.

"Don't try," the tech cut in, giving Tash's old face one last stroke and wiping his own tears aside. "When she wakes up. You'll know her. I promise."

Bobby swallowed. "What about her body?" he almost whispered. "I can't just leave it. Not like this."

"We'll put it in stasis." Lucas replied, looking at Keiko. "I'm sure Nova will be more than willing to make Tash a replacement, won't they? To get her out of yours?"

"For being brave and amazing, you mean?" the corporate heiress corrected. "Yes, of course."

"How long before we're done?" Gabriel interjected. "I don't mean to sound unsympathetic, but we need to get out of here before your boss comes back."

Running a hand through his hair, Lucas shook his head, thinking. "Once we've got Keiko in her clone, about half an hour to get the old skin's matrix reformatted, partitioned and install Tash's consciousness. We can expect some transitional displacement afterwards... But I can deal with that somewhere else."

"Transitional displacement? What does that mean?" Bobby asked, still standing protectively over his sister's old body.

"This isn't something Tash signed up for," Lucas said. "Hell, she wasn't even conscious when we made this plan. So when she wakes up in a completely different body." He pointed at Tash and then the thawing clone. "There'll be some psychosis to deal with."

Bobby shook his head, frowning at the skin tech. "Dumb it down some more, Lucas."

"She's gonna have some reality issues," Gabriel cut in, pushing between the men. "She'll be alive though. Which is more than can be said for us if we don't get moving."

Bobby gave an irritated sigh, but the cop was right. If they got caught now they were fucked, and Tash was never waking up. "Most of these guys know my sister. Where can we put her?"

"No one messes back here but me," Lucas replied, walking to a bank of chromium doors set in the sidewall of his lab. "These are short-term suspension pods, but they'll preserve Tash's tissue and DNA almost indefinitely."

"They look like morgue bins," Bobby said bleakly.

"She's not in there anymore," the cop repeated, growing impatient.

Lucas continued to watch Tash's brother, unwilling to move her until he consented. But the man was paralysed with pain and uncertainty; unable to leave that physical representation of his sister to die alone in a small metal container.

As if recognising his torment, the badly damaged body took one last faltering breath, then relaxed. The will to fight now gone, its heart rate dropped over the next several seconds until a single flat line traversed the countertop monitor. More tears came then, and Bobby bent to kiss his sister goodbye.

"Remember," Keiko said, running a sympathetic hand up and down his back. "She's not *gone* gone." Bobby nodded at her kindness, unable to speak, and with gentle movements gathered up the body of the young woman he'd spent almost every day of his life beside. It looked peaceful; like Tash no longer felt the fear or pain — was just sleeping. But she wasn't sleeping... not in that body anyway, and he looked over at the cube slowly rotating in its cradle, wondering if his little sister felt anything at all right now.

Wiping his eyes one last time on the bloodstained hoodie he'd taken from Karma Sanctum, the sole remaining member of Angell's small skin-jacking crew then locked down his grief, allowing the cold detachment of fury to re-emerge. There would be time to cry for Fin; a time to try and understand what had happened to his sister... *was* happening to her. But right now, anger was what Bobby needed. Anger would sustain him through the next few hours. Anger would ensure he found and obliterated those responsible for destroying the hopes and dreams of everyone he cared about. "Right," he said to Keiko. "Let's get you in that skin, and my sister out of that thing." He jerked his head towards the datacube.

Lucas nodded, taking the stool from another workbench and placing it beside his at the techdeck. "This bit is a lot easier. Especially as we're doing a direct transfer." His fingers began dancing over glyphs, bringing up another program. A transfer window popped up on a secondary display, and the vitals of the skin in the stasis pod populated half its screen as the techie bent to root around in a drawer for the right connectors. "You got an enhanced PDrive port, right?" he asked, gesturing for Keiko to sit opposite him. The Maas heiress nodded, pulling loose a small section of synthskin behind her right ear. "Good," he said, leaning in to check the tiny socket.

The techdeck began making a soft vibrating sound and Lucas swore, tapping a key that had started glowing in time with the noise.

"Is something wrong?" Keiko asked.

The skin-tech brought up a camfeed on the primary display. Three vans were at the main entrance of the storage yard, and the gates were opening. "Shit," he muttered.

"Shit indeed," Gabriel agreed. "We knew this might happen. Stay calm and think... now isn't the time for a fire-fight. Not with Tash and Keiko here."

Lucas was already moving, tidying away the leads and closing down the transfer program. "Go back through the garage and hide in the van. I'll get rid of them."

Bobby scowled, looking at the screen. He wanted blood, and it seemed clear Jerome was up to his neck in whatever had happened tonight. "What about Tash?" he asked. "You?"

"I work here," the tech responded, nervous energy and wide eyes betraying the fear he felt. "And Tash? Well, she's safe enough for now. I'll get rid of these guys, and we'll finish up."

Gabriel put a hand on Bobby's arm; the vans were on the move again. "You need to be smart here, Bobby, for Tash's sake if no one else's. Being here when they walk in won't be good for any of us. Let's finish up with the transfers when they've gone. Then deal with these fuckers on our terms, not theirs. Yeah?"

Without waiting for an answer, the rogue cop returned her attention to the shorter white man. "You got any mobile coms in here? Something we can pair a feed through?"

After ushering Keiko back through the concealed entrance, Lucas unlatched a small storage unit by his deck. "We often pair sinless skins with unregistered peripherals," he said, pulling out a couple of cuffs and activating them. He passed one to Gabriel and attached the other to the sleeve of his hoodie; tapping urgently at the screen as his eyes flicked between it and the approaching vans.

"Gotcha," Gabriel said with a confirmatory tap, guiding a reluctant Bobby into the old garage. "Just stay calm and act normal. They've got zero reason to suspect you've done anything other than come into work early."

With an almost imperceptible click the wall locked back into position, and the young tech took a long cleansing breath, visually checking his lab for anything out of place. Nothing was — well, apart from him being there at five in the morning and Tash's old body being hidden in a pod. He took a second, slower breath, dismissing the hundred or so anxious thoughts crowding his mind as he fired up a diagnostic program and grabbed a random tool to inspect the defective skin bolted into a nearby stereotactic frame.

PARTITION FIVE

First Among Equals

A thin layer of smoke hung above the eleven heads, creating a soft haze in the room's dimmed lights. Smoking only remained a health concern for the one man not partaking. But Warren Gardner held his tongue, long accustomed to the petty mind-games and dick-swinging of the corporate elite.

Like most of the deputies and aids arranged behind them, each of the seven men and four women at the large horse-shoe table were at least ninety in chronological years; some were in their hundreds... and not a single one of them would still be in control of their business empire if not for the man staring at him from the central, slightly wider, slightly taller chair, waiting for an answer.

Of course, that didn't make those ten other presidents Ido Maas's friends. The man was a despot; a de facto dictator who'd maintained control over the Council since its inception through a toxic mixture of coercion and manipulation.

Fortunately, being ideologically opposed to digitisation, promises of immortality were no carrot for Gardner; neither was the threat of dismissal — though he'd not expressed the sentiment quite like that when declining Maas's invitation to join 'the club.' He'd simply observed that the person charged with ensuring everyone played by the rules needed to be impartial and in no way indebted to any one member of the Council. Maas had bristled at the implication and, as the years after the Fiduciary wars passed, the irritating righteousness of the intractable Interpol Chief sat like a thorn in the First Among Equal's side.

"Well?" Ido demanded.

Gardner sighed and shook his head, knowing it needled the Novan president. "No Ido, agent Sousa was obviously not given orders to undertake any kind of entry to your Stockholm facility; covert or otherwise."

"Because you don't have the authority to issues such orders, do you Warren?" the Novan president baited.

"Exactly so."

"Then what reason does she give?"

"Sers and seras, as my report to the Council explains, agent Sousa has been suspended for the last four months," Gardner said, taking in the other faces around the room. "And failed to attend a disciplinary hearing a couple of weeks back. So any thoughts I have concerning her motivation would be nothing more than conjecture."

"Conject then," EurCon's president growled.

Gardner dipped his head at the anticipated instruction. "Well Anton, the obvious reason, I'd suggest, is something to do with sera Levinson of Consolidated," he replied, looking back at the tall Dutchman.

"What about her?" Van Brieda said. "EurCon and Nova have been quite clear the woman never underwent digitisation." He eyed the Novan president, who gave a curt nod of agreement.

"But this Council knows that's not true, Anton," his deputy interrupted from the seat behind him, earning several murmured agreements. "And while, having read agent Sousa's file, I'd say the woman has an interesting set of skills, I find it somewhat unlikely she'd randomly decide to break into a Novan transition facility of her own volition..."

"What are you trying to say, Dominic?" Van Brieda said. "Get to the point."

Mancini offered Gardner a brief smile no one else could see. "Well, doesn't logic suggest someone has grown tired of waiting for this Council to act and hired her to track down whoever killed Elizabeth, or the person, group or organisation behind the threat that has us all travelling by shuttle...?"

"Hired her...?" Ido snarled, leaning forward to stub out the butt of his cigar in a thick, black stone ashtray. "Do you have some insight you'd like to share, Dominic?"

Mancini waved a nonchalant hand to fend off the accusational tone. "Well, as Anton declared the incident a polycorp issue and claimed jurisdiction, Ido, just like Warren, I'm merely speculating. But I think you're fixating on the wrong point. What I'm suggesting to the Council is perhaps it's time to recognise that whatever has occurred, it affects us all — and that supersedes thirteen years of outdated dictates concerning propriety rights. This Council has access to a large and independent body of professional investigators. Surely all of you can see that it's in everyone's interest to give Warren full access and unequivocal assistance, rather than deliberately hindering him?"

"Enough Dominic," Van Brieda hissed over his shoulder. "This is neither the time or place for your showboating. If you kept a tighter grip on your domain, perhaps we'd not be here discussing this now. The rules, for which I'm a signatory, not you, are clear, and were developed for very good reasons."

"Do any of the eleven wish to motion for a change to those rules?" Ido interrupted, his temper barely restrained as he glared at Mancini, and then from president to president.

No one raised a hand.

"Then it remains the case that what occurs within Novan facilities, just as in any other polycorp's premises, is no one else's business." Ido's eyes were hard as he returned his gaze to EurCon's newly appointed VP.

"But the integrity of transfer processes—" Gardner began.

"Is none of your business," Ido said flatly, sweeping an arm around the chamber. "The Council has spoken, and you are its servant. An employee... There to do as you are told, Warren. Not to do the telling!"

He stared down at the man half his age. *"I am tired of your insubordination and casual indifference to the unlawful behaviour of your staff. If you cannot keep a tidy house, perhaps it's time we found someone who can?"*

"The Council is at liberty to replace me any time they like Ido," Warren replied in the calm, neutral tone he was famous for. *"Why not put that to the vote too?"*

The two men locked eyes.

"If I may..." Dominic Mancini spoke up again.

"You may not," the Dutch president said without looking back. *"You raised your point with the Council, Dominic — and it was heartily rejected. Now you need to stop acting like a petulant child and show some good grace... Warren, it is not your place to investigate Nova's transfer processes or EurCon's internal security arrangements. Those remain the rules. No ifs, no buts."*

The Interpol chief began to open his mouth again, but Van Brieda held up a cautionary finger. *"I think I speak for most of the Council,"* he continued in a more placatory tone. *"When saying we believe your people generally do a fantastic job... and that's down to you. But, there are times, like today, when we'd like to feel your complete support; not tacit resistance — You know, have you standing inside the metaphorical tent pissing out, rather than outside pissing in...?*

"A line has been crossed, Warren, and any fool can see severe disciplinary action is required. Find your errant agent and 'retire her' before one of our security directorates does it for you.

"... Now, can we please move on to the rest of the day's business. I have places I need to be."

The beleaguered lawman looked back to Mancini, expression pleading for a voice of reason to once again step in. Consolidated's CEO cast an eye around the table, then *returned his gaze; a raised brow and the slightest of head shakes declining any further attempt at intervention.*

First Among Equals

Cluster I

August 21st, 2070
05:25 GMT InterFreight storage facility, Greenwich, Outer London

"What the fuck are you doing here?" the big man asked, walking into the lab. He looked tired and annoyed. "I saw the lights on and assumed you'd forgotten to switch them off again."

"Nope." Lucas said, turning on the stool and doing his best to look casual. "I wanted to get this guy finished."

"Thought you were planning to hit the town last night?"

Lucas didn't have to try to look miserable. "I did. But the night didn't pan out."

Jerome's cratered head jerked upwards, and he gave a harsh bark of laughter. "That makes two of us then," he said. "But don't take it out on the skins, son."

Lucas frowned, genuinely confused. "Huh?"

"The proctoscope."

"What?"

"In your hand. Isn't that a proctoscope?"

The young tech specialist looked from the gangboss to the medical tool, then back. "Oh ... yes it is," he replied with a half laugh, pushing silver-rimmed glasses higher up his nose. "Yet another imaginative hiding place the corpos have discovered for a SIN tag. That's six I've found in this guy. Come and have a look. It's sewn right into the lining of the rectum."

The big man wrinkled his nose and took a step back, holding out both hands. "Hell no, Lucas. Not my kind of spectator sport. Happy to just take your word for it." Then he saw the stasis pod and thrust a meaty thumb in its direction. "And sleeping beauty? Why's she all fired up?"

"System checks," the skin-tech replied. "I didn't have time before I left last night." He stood and walked over to point at the bank of screens running alongside the body, growing more confident in his deception. "They're done now. Just syncing her autonomics and core... You still haven't told me when she's going? We can't keep her like this indefinitely, you know. Not with the kit we have here."

Jerome's legendary cool broke, just momentarily, and the scar tissue covering the right side of his face tightened, pulling his mouth up in an ironic half smile. "You'll keep her like that for as long as I tell you to, *boy*," he snarled. Then, sighing almost immediately in self-reproach, he ran a large hand over the mottled mix of synth and real skin covering his granite hard skull. "Sorry Lucas, I shouldn't be snapping at you. It's just been a long, shitty night." He smiled again, this time using both sides of his face — composure restored. "But as it happens, we will need to move her."

Lucas felt his own face tighten, anxiety flooding his system with adrenaline. "Wait what? When?"

"I had a bit of a run in with what I'm pretty certain was corpo hardware tonight. It was quite public, and I wouldn't be surprised if we make the TrueNews feeds as the polycorp's latest victim for their war on the skin trade. So, just as a precaution, we'll be moving these two and the more *bespoke* equipment out of the yard for a few days. Let the dust settle while I check exactly what went wrong with my contacts."

"But she needs to stay here!" the flustered technician blurted.

That earned a raised eyebrow. "You just said she needed to move?"

"To something more permanent," Lucas fumbled. "Not location."

The gangboss shrugged, disinterested in the details. "Gordo will help you pack her back up." He turned around and shouted to an enormous fair-haired lump standing midway down the central aisle of stacked parts and pending shipments. "Come and give the boy a hand, would you? And don't let him dawdle; we need to be going."

"But—"

Jerome held up a finger, silencing the younger man. "This isn't a good time," he said, turning his head away to answer an incoming com.

There was a pause while he listened.

"No. We encountered complications... Huh, of course you've already heard." He rolled eyes at Gordo as the tough old merc entered the lab. Then he stiffened. "You have her? How?" Anger flashed across the big man's face, pulling at the scar tissue again. "I lost some good men tonight. If you had someone that could just walk in and take her, why send me?" ... Yeah, right — complications."

He tutted, shaking his head before turning to look directly at Lucas, eyebrows raised and a question in his expression. Several more seconds passed as the gangboss listened, synthetic eye searching the sterile room. Then, as suddenly as it had started, the call ended, and Jerome resumed his walk towards the door. "Pack your gear, you're coming with us," he commanded over a shoulder.

"Me?" Lucas croaked, eyes widening at the sudden change in direction. "Wouldn't I be unnecessary baggage? How about I just head home instead? Come back when you com me it's safe?"

"Nope. You're staying with the skin. Now grab what you need and let's go."

The young techneer looked around his lab, almost certain Jerome had just been told something incriminating. "Sure. Okay. I guess that makes sense," he said, running a dry tongue over drier lips. "But this is going to take at least an hour to wrap up. So you'll have to send someone back to grab me when I'm done."

"No time for that," the big man answered, glancing at his cuff. "Grab the skin and your tech essentials. Everything else can go in one of the containers outside."

The younger man opened his mouth to protest, but Jerome was clearly done talking. "Look Lucas, just be grateful we're not getting into how my caller knew you were here, yeh? Now, as it seems very likely my night is going to continue its descent into rat shit, and more people are going to die for reasons that haven't been explained to me, I need to make a few comcalls... Get packed."

He paused in the doorway to speak quietly with Gordo, then walked out into the main processing area shouting orders at the dozen or so joes loitering in the parking bay with assault rifles hanging loose at their sides.

"What the hell happened to you lot tonight?" Lucas asked, as Jerome's equally modified right-hand man threw a pulse rifle down on the workbench. "Fucked if I know, kid. A bigshot skin contract went south, and I don't know whether it was private security or corpo spec ops — but we took a damn good mauling. So it's best to lay-up for a few days, see if anyone comes calling. Now, what do you want me to do?"

Exactly ten minutes after being told to pack, four plain black vans drove through the huge, tarmacked storage yard and its towering stacks of metal containers towards the river and its maglift. The giant automated structure housed two tracks of floating roll on, roll off platforms travelling in opposite directions as they arced over the Thames, to and from the cargo hub on the opposite bank.

Though seriously industrial, Lucas found a simple kind of beauty in the structure's engineering, and was fascinated by the dozens of giant, multi-legged bots trudging relentlessly back and forth like an army of ants; forty-foot shipping containers grappled between huge beetle-like grippers.

Sitting next to Jerome in a front passenger seat of the first van, the youthful American watched as the ground fell quickly away to reveal the enormity of the Gangboss's storage empire. He knew the man had other business premises along the South Bank and control over most of the gangs that side of the river, but hadn't realised his influence stretched northward as well. In fact, despite the criminal kingpin offering him a no questions asked job a few months earlier, Lucas realised he didn't really know that much about the former marine, other than they were both involved with the same pro-revolutionary underground. But tonight... tonight had thrown them into different camps and, for the first time ever, the younger man was starting to question his convictions.

 As if picking up on the techie's mood, Jerome lifted a thickly muscled arm to point along the purple-black river reflecting in the pre-dawn as it snaked through power deprived swathes of subtopian darkness towards the glowing metropolis of corporate London. "That's the inequality we fight to end, Lucas," he said. "Remember that over the coming days." There was a sense of foreboding in the big man's words. But when Lucas looked from the energy draining dome back to Jerome, the uneasy crime boss had already returned to a quiet conversation with Gordo.

Millennium Mills was a twelve story, twentieth century semi-derelict sitting on the quay of an old dockyard to the west of the shuttle port. As the crow flew, it was less than half a mile from Jerome's storage yard. But two hundred metres of waste ground surrounded it on the landward side, and as they drew closer to the massive concrete edifice, Lucas began making out small signs of occupation.

"Big, isn't it?" Jerome said as they drove up in the lead van. Dawn was just beginning to creep across the sky, making the imposing building, with hundreds of small windows like the compound eye of a bug, the kind of place you screamed at dopey kids in horror vids *not to go into*. "Welcome to Millenium Mills. It's no castle. But its thick concrete walls and floors make it about as defensible a building as you're gonna find in this part of London. And right up there," he pointed towards the roof. "You get a rather good view of my storage yard."

Lucas nodded, impressed. He'd assumed they'd head further away, to one of Jerome's smaller workshops. Not a nearby derelict in a rundown part of the city's edge.

Jerome laughed, thumping him hard on the shoulder. "Doesn't look much, does it?"

"It looks bloody terrifying," Lucas muttered. "Is it even safe?"

"Mostly," the gangboss chuckled. "The middle two floors anyway."

The tech specialist looked closely at the section Jerome indicated but couldn't see any obvious difference to the century or more of decay evident across the rest of the old mill's façade.

"You know, I was born right here in Britannia Village; back when it wasn't a shithole. I used to play in these derelicts as a lad." A momentary wistfulness crossed the big man's severely scarred face, softening his features for a fraction of a second. "I acquired control of it about eight months ago. Some Essex gang was trying to muscle in on the cargo hub, and this was my price for helping them see the error of their ways. I wanted to one day turn it into flats: a self-sustaining community. But that's not going to happen now."

"It won't?" Lucas asked.

The disgraced former marine shook his head, sharing a brief look with Gordo in the driving seat. "Nah, I think we've just lost our patronage. Now we get to see where all tonight's cards fall." A stab of fear ran up the young techie's spine as the big man returned his attention to the approaching building. "I don't understand," he said.

"I don't think any of us were meant to, Lucas." Jerome replied obscurely. "Let's get inside and sorted out, yeh? Then we'll talk."

Cluster II

August 21st, 2070
06:00 GMT Millennium Mill, Britannia Village, Outer London

The inside of the mill was exactly as Lucas's imagination had pictured it. On the bottom floor, fetid water pooled in long, dank, rubble filled spaces lit solely by pockets of light that punched into the darkness through rotten boards hanging loose from broken windows.

They secured the vans, and Jerome sent nine of the fifteen mercs he'd brought along to supplement on-sight security. Then he took Lucas, with Gordo and the remaining six, four carrying the stasis equipment, to a gated-off stairwell beyond a large sign warning of collapse and falling debris.

Pigeons nesting on blistered iron girders squawked in surprise as they ascended, their white streaks of shit contesting with a tapestry of moss grown since the last heavy rainfall for dominance over the stairwell's peeling chalk-green painted walls. Aside from the obvious questions he thought must be raised when being confronted by a man with a gun telling you to piss off, Lucas had to agree the place really did look seriously fucking derelict.

But as they passed through a large iron door on the fourth floor, a labyrinthine modular complex sat within the old building's dilapidated shell; radiation shielded rooms with light and power, all hidden from external view, providing living and sleeping accommodation for far more people than Jerome seemed to have present. Lucas let out a whistle of appreciation as a man sat at a set of camfeeds stood to greet Jerome.

"Everything's quiet, Boss," he said. "As instructed, I've sent almost everyone to safer places to sit this out. Just a token crew of volunteers here now. I've also had a workbench and techdeck put into one of the rooms with an external web link. It's the last one on the left."

The gangboss nodded, waving for Lucas to follow.

"I know it's not a sterile lab," he remarked as they walked. "But it'll have to do for now." He locked eyes on the smaller man, expression hard to read. "A few hours, maybe a day, and I'll have a better idea of just how big a nest of hornets we've kicked." He jerked his head towards Gordo. "This lump will be your shadow while we're here. He's a ham-fisted oaf, so will probably make a dreadful assistant. But if things go south — you couldn't ask for a better guy by your side."

The mountain of a man gave a single bark of laughter at the barbed compliment and exchanged a fist bump with the dour gangboss before turning to Lucas. "Shall we get everything unpacked and hooked up?" he asked in his deep, rumbling bass. "The sooner we're done, the sooner we can go find breakfast."

Gently taking the data cube from a padded pocket in his backpack, the young tech pulled a face, shaking his head. "You go ahead Gordo. This is a bit of a one-man job, and I'm not hungry."

"But Jerome said to stay with you?"

"That's a bit of a literal interpretation of being my shadow, Gordo. Especially when we're inside the mill... Is the kitchen down there?" Lucas followed the old gangbanger's eyes.

"Yeah. Opposite the guard post."

"Shouting distance?"

"Absolutely."

"Well then. Go get your feed on Big Man. I'll holla if I need you."

Gordo licked his lips during a single moment of hesitation, then started for the door. "You want anything brought back?"

Lucas shook his head, bending to plug the techdeck into a power socket. "No thanks, and there's genuinely no rush. This is going to take a good hour or two to sort out."

Cluster III
August 21st, 2070
08:25 GMT Millennium Mill, Brittania Village, Outer London

With a lazy sigh, Tash stretched her back, running long graceful fingers over the warm and unmistakably naked body beside her. She smiled, remembering the passion and completeness of their lovemaking. But as her eyes opened, explosions, gunshots and a searing pain crashed into her consciousness, and she cried out — hands instinctively going to her stomach.

"It's okay," Lucas said, trying to put an arm around her.

"What the fuck?" Tash yelped, jerking upright, fingers still checking her body for damage; confused eyes searching the room. "There was a..." She pointed to the bedroom door. "I got..." Wrapping both arms over her abdomen, tears began flowing as Lucas reached out again, his own tears rolling down lightly tanned cheeks. "It's okay now," he whispered, gathering her into his arms. "You're safe."

They sat like that for several heartbeats, just crying and rocking together. Then the wrongness of the situation spidered its way into Tash's conscious thought. "Wait," she said, voice wavering. "How can we be back here?"

Lucas didn't answer, just buried his head deeper into the crook of her neck.

"Lucas?"

"I didn't know where to start, Tash. So, I…" He swallowed, shaking his head as a fresh wave of tears came.

"You're scaring me now. What do you mean? Where are we?" she demanded, voice creeping upwards.

"A construct," he finally answered, pale blue eyes dropping to stare at the crumpled bedsheet between them. "I thought taking you back to before…" He cleared his throat and looked around the room they'd shared. "I thought that would be the least confusing."

"Confusing? Construct? Lucas, what the fuck are you talking about?"

Eyes widening with sudden understanding Tash pulled away from the chop-shop techie, jumping naked from the bed. "Oh no," she muttered, running for the door. "Please no." A white nothing existed beyond the threshold, and the beautiful young woman crumpled to the floor. "I'm dead, aren't I?" she mumbled between long, harsh sobs. "I'm fucking dead."

Lucas came over, pushing the door closed before wrapping a sheet and his body around hers. "I know how confusing this must be, Tash," he whispered. "But you're not dead. This *is* you." He squeezed her gently. "It'll be okay. I promise."

When he booted Tash a second time, Lucas opted for clothes and the more neutral environment of his lab. There were more tears, of course. Then, as Lucas explained what had happened since she'd passed out, a completely understandable scepticism began growing in the twenty-two-year-old consciousness concerning her new status as a digital entity; well embedded corporeal views of self preferring to adopt the belief Lucas was nothing more than a drug induced coma dream.

He'd smiled at that at first; the one big no no in an emergency transfer being any attempt to force the issue — the longer Tash had to come to terms with what had happened while in the sandbox, the lower the risk of a psychotic break when she woke up in another body.

But after two more abortive attempts to guide Tash towards a readiness for upload, the tired and increasingly frustrated tech-head was beginning to worry about time, and decided they couldn't afford any more re-boots. Happy or not, Tash was going to have to accept her new reality.

"So you're saying I'm currently inside one of these?" Tash laughed during their fifth meeting, her almost flawless face flashing a row of ivory white teeth as she tossed the palm sized metallic cube in the air and caught it again.

Lucas had just finished explaining how her brother, the corpo-cop and Maas girl had all hidden when Jerome suddenly turned up at the storage yard, and that they think the gangboss was the guy behind the attempted kidnap.

"I told you he was an asshole."

"To be fair, I'm pretty sure he didn't know we were there. As far as he was concerned, he was taking out a legitimate corporate target."

"A legitimate corporate target? What kind of shit way is that to talk about terrorising and murdering people?"

The tech specialist blushed, but his eyes hardened. "Maybe this is a conversation for another time?"

"Or...," Tash said, sitting slightly straighter. "Maybe it's a conversation for now? Ya know, seeing as how the fucker's men put a hole in me and blew up one of my best friends?"

Lucas sighed, shaking his head. She was angry; they both were, and he'd abandoned the last session when things got contentious. But it was clearly something they had to get past if they were ever going to move on. "Look, I didn't mean it the way it came out. I'm obviously gutted about what's happened to you and Fin. But it's a war out there, Tash. Them versus us — we were just in the wrong place at the wrong time."

"You hear yourself?" Tash laughed harshly. "The rich kid toy-soldier, chatting shit about revolution and sacrifice? Fuck's sake..."

"Oh yeah," Lucas replied, years of his own repressed anger welling up. "Cos you've got to be born on the streets to *get it*, right Tash? Only the *down-beaten* underclass could possibly understand?"

The estate girl glared, riled by the usually reserved man's sudden sarcasm. "Yep, that's about it, soldier boy," she sniped back, chucking him a salute. "Give me a call when the life they've forced on you leaves your parents with no work, no money, and no hope. Let me know when you watch one of them die from simple fucking diabetes because they can't afford the meds; and tell me about how you *get it* when you and your brother have to fight for every meagre thing you own because your mum got stabbed up in some silly fucking smackhead fight over dust—"

"For Christ's sake, you're not the only kid to lose their parents, Tash!" Lucas hissed back, voice raw with previously undisplayed emotion. "Plenty of us have. It's not exactly an exclusive club!"

Then he shook his head.

"Look, sorry. We're both exhausted, totally strung out, and you've had a lot to take in... The last thing I want is to fight with you. I'm sorry about what the corpos did to you and your family; it genuinely disgusts me... And I wasn't trying to defend Jerome, that came out wrong. I just meant the polycorps—"

"You've lost your parents, too?" Tash cut in, tears once again welling up as she reached out for his hand. "I didn't know that."

"It's not something I talk about," Lucas said, clearly uncomfortable with the subject, but feeling obligated to continue since it was him that opened the box. "I didn't even know them really; they were both shot dead during a peace march at the end of the forties."

Tash opened her mouth, a noiseless 'O' sharing his anguish and pain.

"Hate, Tash... My family, my life, wiped out for nothing more than fear and hate. All with the blessing of the polycorps." His own tears now rolled across both lower eyelids and he sniffed, pulling off glasses to run a sleeve over his face. "Anyway, they didn't know I survived. My grandpa hid that fact."

"Wow," Tash swallowed, temper forgotten. "They tried to kill you too?"

"My mum was heavily pregnant."

The young woman's face froze as she absorbed his matter-of-fact words. Then a shocked gasp fell from her mouth. "Oh my God, that's awful. Lucas, I'm so, so sorry—"

"It's fine," he interrupted again.

"No. No it ain't. Lashing out; judging you like that..."

Shaking his head, a small smile broke across Lucas's face, and he squeezed Tash's hand. "Look at us both. What a mess." He pulled a hanky from his trouser pocket and handed it over. "It's not your fault. You couldn't possibly have known. I've only ever spoken about them with grandpa."

"Oooh," Tash nodded, seeming to find comprehension in that statement. "So that's... ya know?" Tash jerked her head towards the world beyond his construct's walls.

"What, Jerome?" Lucas laughed. "God no. I only connected with him a few months back. His operation gave me the latitude I needed to get something else done."

Tash frowned at the chop-shop techie's... well, previously supposed chop-shop techie's, choice of words. "Something else?"

He nodded, a slight hesitation indicating he'd said more than intended. "But we're getting way off subject; and now definitely isn't the right time for that conversation."

The beautiful woman held his gaze for a beat, wondering who or what she'd gotten involved with — clearly a damn sight more than *just wrong time, wrong place*. But not wanting to start any more arguments, she simply smiled and nodded. "Fair enough. I guess I can live with that."

"Thank you," Lucas replied, gratitude shining in his eyes. "Once we get out of here, I'll explain everything. I promise."

Taking that comment as a cue to exit the conversation, Tash raised one of her perfectly cultivated brows. "Which takes us neatly back to the datacube," she chuckled. "And the question of how you propose to do that?"

Lucas's posture relaxed, more comfortable now they were getting back to the business of the day. "You're really vulnerable in that single storage cube. There are just too many ways for you to get lost or corrupted. So, until I can back your code up on a safe server and find a body you'll be happy in while we get yours regrown, I want to put you in the skin Jerome brought with us."

Looking down at the cube in her hand, Tash still struggled to grasp what had happened to her. "So what's all this?" she asked, looking around the lab. "Am I not safe here?"

Lucas shook his head for the umpteenth time. "As I've said before, this is just a computer-generated environment, Tash; a sandbox I'm running on my deck in the real."

"Sandbox…" she sniggered.

He nodded, ignoring her return to distracting humour consciously or unconsciously intended to drag their conversation back to unhelpful discussions of coma. "Yes, a sandbox; we've talked about them before. It's an immersion program, isolated from the net, where I can create situations that mimic the real world—"

"And are you happy with your creation, oh God of mine?" Tash butted in. "Will this look do?" She pouted and squeezed both arms across her chest to emphasise a small but appealing cleavage. "Or would you prefer bigger boobs next time? Maybe a bit more junk in the trunk?"

Lucas reddened. "You're perfect just as you are," he replied. "But—"

"Correct answer," Tash giggled, leaning over to kiss him. "I like this, *whatever* it is. What shall we do next? Maybe a beach rather than just a sandbox? I've always wanted to see the sea."

Frowning, Lucas walked around the workbench to stand right in front of her. "C'mon Tash, I know you're struggling to believe any of this." He shook his head; a pleading look in his pale blue eyes. "But you need to humour me. Your life, mine, Bobby's. We're all in danger."

The smile fell from the young woman's lips, and she stared into nowhere for a moment before raising a hand to stroke his serious face. "Okay baby," she said, wrapping a leg around his body and pulling him in close. "Tell me what you need me to do."

This was the first time Tash had fully opened herself to his being more the a hallucination, and Lucas felt a surge of excitement as he began explaining the process. "There's so much information and training a newly transitioned digital usually gets. But once you're in a skin, we won't have much time to embed your psyche into its new reality—"

Tash held a finger to his lips, stopping what felt like an oncoming lecture before it began. "You're gonna need to find a different way of explaining all this, babe… I already don't understand a single word."

Lucas offered her a crooked smile. "I know, I'm sorry. I'm just excited for you. I've loaded a bunch of FAQs and a program that will help you assimilate what it means to be digital, into this construct. It'll feel crazy weird when they load into your core… a bunch of stuff you just suddenly know. But I think Jerome's expecting trouble — so it's kind of now or never?"

"What if something goes wrong?"

"It won't. But if it did, I'd just roll you back to now."

"What?"

"Don't worry about it. Honestly, nothing will go wrong."

A dubious look crossed the face of Tash's residual self-image. But after running a hand through her long blue-dreads and taking a deep, meditative breath, she said, "Go on then. Do it."

Lucas nodded, his excitement clear. "All you have to do is say 'download my crash course and FAQs.'"

Tash pulled a *are you fucking mad* face, and Lucas laughed. "Honestly. Just say 'download my crash course and FAQs.'"

Shaking her head and clearly feeling silly, Tash repeated the phrase, mimicking Lucas's serious tone. Then she jolted up straight; a startled expression crossing her precisely makeupped features. "What the—"

"Give it a moment," Lucas instructed. "Let the code parse and embed in your working memory."

A couple of seconds later, Tash let out a short, excited gasp. "Holy Shit," she said, looking at him as if with fresh eyes. "Why didn't you lead with this…? I'm a fucking digital."

A relieved smile slipped across the young techneer's face. "Well hello Miss Adeyinka, my name's Lucas, and I'll be your digital integration assistant today."

The first thing Lucas taught his new apprentice was that time is relative. While hours, even days, might pass in their sandbox — only seconds or minutes will have passed in the physical world. That meant large parts of what a newly minted digital usually learned about their corporeal existence and the rules they abided by, or were at least supposed to abide by, took place in constructs... and Lucas had loaded Tash's with everything he could think of. "...So while you can, and I suspect some corpos do, exist in multiple places at once, it comes with many inherent dangers; not least of which are divergent iterations of the same original consciousness fighting for control of its singular worldly possessions."

Tash nodded her understanding.

"My personal advice," Lucas continued, close to ending the final input on transferring between bodies. "Is to never occupy more than one place in space and time. Stuff like that is fine for non-sentient machines; they're designed for it. But if you want to retain your sense of humanity and sanity, you need to keep thinking and feeling as an individual, just like you always have...

"Having said all that, what we're about to do might well fuck with your established sense of self-image a bit." He pointed to a stasis pod that had begun cycling. "Like I said, it'll take time to grow a clone of your own body... and this is the only skin available to us right now."

Tash turned towards the long metal tube as its curved outer surface began clearing, then frowned. "I bloody knew it. What kind of fucked up is that?" she said. "You hoping for my brother's sloppy seconds or something?"

"Hey!" Lucas protested, mouth turning down in disgust. "God no, of course not. I explained what happened."

The seemingly irritated woman just stared.

"Oh, c'mon Tash. I'm doing my best here... I convinced Jerome he needs to animate the skin so it can be moved without lugging a transit pod around... So this is kind of our one chance, yeh?" He gave the long, willowy woman a pained look, and a small smile creased the edges of her mouth. "I'm just fucking with ya. I figured it would be her. Didn't know you could *animate* them, though. You left that out of my FAQs."

With a relieved affirmative nod, Lucas ploughed on, determined to get Tash loaded into Keiko's skin before Gordo returned from lunch. "Thank God, you had me worried there. Yeah, dumb AI is used all the time to exercise skins and prevent muscle atrophy. You won't have to pretend to be Keiko or anything... just follow simple instructions."

Tash's perfect eyebrow arched again. "You'd like that, wouldn't ya?" she sniffed, though humour still shone in her eyes. "Okay, I can do *dumb*. But take note, mister... you're not fucking me while I look like that."

Lucas's cheeks reddened and he shook his head; unable to think of a suitable reply as the long-legged Londoner stepped over to the refrigerated clone. "She is pretty though. I'll give you that."

Joining her beside the stasis pod, the young techneer now looked genuinely worried. "When I press that button back in the real Tash, I need you focused. Once you're in that body, what goes on around you will be very, very real... And, since he tore up that hotel, I've absolutely no fucking idea if Jerome and I are actually on the same side. If we aren't, the only thing stopping him from going after your brother is that he doesn't know either of you were there — He gets a sniff of that, Bobby's in big trouble, and we're both probably dead."

"Again," Tash deadpanned.

"I'm serious, Tash." There was a hard edge to his voice now.

"Hey okay, okay. Calm down," she said, sobering and putting a hand over his on the workbench. "I'd never put yours or Bobby's lives in danger. I'll follow your lead."

Lucas released a slow breath and nodded. He didn't want to put Tash in that skin. Not now Jerome had it. But the gangboss had been acting odd since their conversation at the freight yard; seemed certain something was coming their way. And if it did, Lucas wanted some insurance against the cube getting damaged or taken from him. He needed a copy, and the skin was now his only viable vessel. "I'm going to have to leave here to start the process there," he said, voice back to its usual gentle calm.

The hazel-eyed beauty looked down at their entwined hands, suddenly apprehensive. "Will it hurt?"

"No," Lucas reassured. "It'll be just like waking up. A little cold maybe." He smiled as she bit her bottom lip, and leaned into her. "You'll be fine," he promised. "And once we've found a way out of here, we'll get you back in your own body."

With a worried look belying those words, he kissed her one last time... and disappeared.

Moments later, the official clone of Keiko Maas woke up and shivered. It was lying under a blanket in a strange room with bare white walls that looked nothing like the lab.

"Lucas?" Tash whispered in a voice that was all wrong.

"I'm right here," he answered, leaning past the screens of a techdeck to give her a reassuring smile. "Everything has uploaded perfectly. You're doing great. Give yourself a moment to settle. The body will feel different to what you're used to."

Tash closed her eyes, focusing inward. Apart from the cold, and the singing of what sounded like birds, everything felt pretty normal.

"Birds?" she questioned in an annoyingly pitchy voice.

"I think they live in the walls," he said. "How do you feel?"

"Pretty normal apart from the voice." Opening her eyes again, Tash sat up. "Oh okay, that's weird!" she added immediately, looking down on two freckle dappled, olive-coloured breasts with perky, pale pink nipples. They were bigger than hers, and she waggled them experimentally.

"Tash, please," Lucas swallowed. His face reddening as he looked away; hand scrabbling over the workbench to find and throw her his hoodie.

"What?" she questioned, a broad grin on the East Asian features. "I've always wondered what bigger tits would feel like." She slid from the bench, taking the offered top. "And it feels odd to look at you from down here."

Lucas laughed. Her old body had been a couple of inches taller than him. Now, in the Asian skin, she was several shorter. "Don't be heightist," he quipped, wrapping the blanket from the pod around her bottom half. "I'll go find you some clothes. I should have thought about that before."

Tash's chuckle wasn't her usual throaty timbre; it was more of a cackle. But as the mind and memories of the twenty-two-year-old from Angell studied her new face on one of Lucas's monitors, she was surprised at how unfreaked-out she felt. *Have some fun with it girl,* she thought, jiggling her tits again.

"Funny, isn't it?" Lucas said, walking back into the room with some plain grey sweats as she pouted and turned, examining every visible inch of the rich girl's skin. "We both see Keiko Maas. But from your mannerisms alone, I've no doubt who's inside."

Tash nodded absently. "I don't know what I was expecting. But this isn't it." She flashed the Asian's amber eyes at him; thin lips bent in a broad smile. "It's more like playing dress-up."

Lucas nodded, placing his hands on her shoulders as he smiled back in the monitor. "That's a great way of looking at it, beautiful. It's just *an outfit.* Something to wear until we can get your real self remade."

"*Me* beautiful? Or *this* beautiful?" the newly diminutive woman baited.

Chuckling, Lucas planted a kiss on the back of her head. "*You* beautiful," he replied. "Always you, Tash."

Her smile broadened and she turned, putting her arms around his waist. "So this is all *natural*, yes?"

"Except the *brain* and a few augments, yes."

Tash crushed her chest against Lucas, her face close to his; exuding the same captivating energy he'd felt in her arms just a few hours earlier. "Well, when you make me my own body," she breathed in his ear. "Perhaps I'll suggest a couple of minor changes?"

"Damn, you're sexy," he whispered back.

"Mmm-hmm." The newly transferred digital agreed, giving him a lingering kiss before turning to the sweats he'd put on the workbench. "But for now, I guess you'd better show me how to act like some dumb bitch AI."

PARTITION FIVE   **Cluster IV**
August 21st, 2070
09:00 GMT Consolidated Systems HQ, Central London

Director General Charles Peters walked up alongside the immaculately dressed chief executive and nodded at the bank of screens. "The show started?"

"Not quite," Mancini replied.

"You excited? Now everything is finally all in place?"

The CEO laughed. "It has been quite a journey, hasn't it?"

As they watched the collection of drone and surveillance feeds that had been tracking the incident since Jerome Donelly's band of cutthroats left their warehouse the night before, two groups of troops in Consolidated armour began to position themselves around the old flour mill.

"Timing will be the key here, Charles. We let Van Brieda's dog get his nose bloody enough to make the old bastard look guilty, but without letting the psycho run totally amuck and damaging our prize."

His older-looking iteration, dedicated to maintaining the corporation's security functions, smiled. "Fear not brother, my people are poised and ready to go."

"And the corpo-cop?"

Charles sent a command, and one of the feeds flicked over to a small van parked in a cul-de-sac off the North Woolwich Road, then panned to pick up the agent threading her way along a building line west of the mill. "She's drugged the black lad and Maas girl, then jumped two of Westerley's men as they passed."

"Damn, that woman's a handful," Mancini chuckled.

"That's why I chose her, Dominic. If Nova hasn't yet figured out who Anton's PA picked up from Stockholm and had delivered to Frisco, they soon will... and when Anton then pieces together just how screwed he is, I'm confident he'll react exactly as our illustrious leader always has." He smiled, waving a forefinger at the screens. "Attack, attack, attack!"

Mancini clapped the other man on the back. "You're a strategic genius. But you're certain you have her under control?"

"Who Sousa? Of course," Charles said. "Even though she wasn't meant to get involved in the kidnap, it'll add a rather useful layer of authenticity when an Interpol agent discovers the links between Donelly and Brussels. I couldn't have planned this better myself."

"Despite the Council now knowing about her connection to Elizabeth's remains?"

The Director General shrugged. "Stockholm was nothing more than a hook to open Nova's eyes to Whittaker and the links we've built between him and Van Brieda. Frankly, I was surprised when there was still a head there to recover. But even if we're eventually exposed as funding the grab, what is Nova going to do? Elizabeth was one of our execs — you have the moral high ground. And anyway, by then Maas's economic influence will be in the toilet. He'll be desperate for allies, and you'll be the one in the driving seat." He offered EurCon's VP a confident nod. "... Fortuitously, while I've no doubt completely unintentional, Thorne's recent antics are proving to complement our own plans rather well."

Charles allowed himself a satisfied grin, something like that of a chess-master three moves out from checkmate. "Oh, here we go, Westerley is preparing to breach. I love the predictability of humans. You'd better get going — time to push over that first domino."

PARTITION FIVE   **Cluster V**

August 21st, 2070
09:15 GMT Millennium Mill, Brittania Village, Outer London

Gabriel watched as six soldiers stacked up on either side of a large ground level opening to the rear of the Mill. She had no idea how many people Donelly had inside, but the twenty-two troops she'd counted in the attacking force seemed woefully inadequate to seize and control such a large building.

Moments later, a bright flash was followed by a thunderous bang and the sounds of suppressed gunfire, as more ground troops piled through the gap. Then the roar of maxed out engines pulled her attention skyward, as a small assault shuttle dropped at high velocity to hover just ten or so feet above the mill's wide roof. A dozen more troops leapt out, secured ropes, and began rappelling down the outside walls, reaching the fifth floor before attempting to smash through the old metal window frames.

"Jeeze, this guy's in a hurry," Gabriel murmured, looking for the ground commander and locating a man standing along one side of the large building between two apparent minders, helmet visor down, barking orders into a headset.

"Ray Westerley," she said sourly. "Well, that makes sense now."

The last time Gabriel had heard about her old ranger colleague, the man had been recruited by EurCon's intelligence directorate to lead false flag operations along their border with Supreme Soviet; that the man was in London and wearing Consolidated armour could only mean one thing — he was running some sort of illicit coup de main.

"Hey Westerley," she called, having openly marched towards his group. "If your guys don't ease back on the ballistics, there won't be anyone left in there to interrogate."

The shortish man, who'd branded himself the Scourge of God when they'd operated in Eastern Europe, lifted his visor and turned towards her, waving down the rifles of his two attendants. "Gabriel Sousa, don't you just turn up in the strangest of places?" He raised an eyebrow, looking at the armour she was wearing. "At least I now know what happened to Coullfield and Barnes."

Gabriel nodded, thumping the chest-plate. "Tough guys, they put up a good fight."

Westerley snorted and shook his head. "What are you doing here, agent? This isn't an Interpol matter."

"It isn't strictly speaking a EurCon one either, is it?"

She hadn't seen Westerley since the war. He'd been an evil bastard back then, and from what she'd heard, nothing had changed. "I've got assets in there, Ray. Part of an ongoing investigation I'd prefer you didn't kill while doing whatever it is you're doing here."

The man's face remained carefully neutral. "Give me names and faces — I'll flag them. But I'm on a schedule, Sousa. We're out of here as soon as we've apprehended the leader of this rabble."

Explosions blew out windows on the third and fifth floors.

"Jesus Christ Westerley, is this an extraction or clean-up op?"

The EurCon commander ignored Gabriel, once again distracted by incoming feeds. "Excellent," he said into his mic. "Bring them out and prepare for exfil." To one of his attendants, he then added. "Get the shuttle back."

"Do Consolidated know you're on the ground here?" Gabriel pushed.

Westerley gave the corpo-cop a hard look. "If you've been tracking this crew, Sousa, you know they're suspiciously well-equipped and trained. They took out a Novan recon unit last night, along with a fair chunk of high-end hotel. At best, the president has lost faith in the abilities of Dominic Mancini to maintain order in this domain; at worst, the guy is colluding with revolutionaries and criminals... I'm here to arrest the leader of one such group, and you're dangerously close to impeding that mission. So do yourself a favour and sit this one out, okay?"

"Is that a threat?"

The squat, pale-skinned dutchman spoke into his mic again before returning attention to the punchy corpo-cop. "Look, I don't have time for you or your touchiness today, Sousa," he said, clearly irritated by her tone. "It was well meaning advice. Something I recall you were never particularly good at taking... Javiar, get her out of here." The barrel of one of the attendant's weapons rose again, the armoured man jutting out his chin as if to shoo her. "And stay at least five feet back or she'll have you."

As Westerley's shuttle then committed to touching down on nearby waste ground, two subsonic gunships dropped into hover above the mill, while a squadron of troop carriers fell from the heavens like metallic rain.

Consolidated Systems had arrived... in numbers.

"You've got to be kidding me," Westerley growled as he watched the far greater force begin landing. "No way they reacted this quickly."

He barked several orders into his mic and then fixed Gabriel with an angry look. "You haven't done either of us any favours here today, Sousa."

"Wasn't me," the corpo-cop replied, just as bemused. "I'm working alone."

Shaking his head, the EurCon commander passed his carbine to the dark-haired soldier standing beside Javiar, as Dominic Mancini himself, surrounded by a swarm of media drones, stepped from the lead carrier. "Fantastic," Westerley muttered as he began walking towards the powerful businessman, fixing a subservient smile on his face. "The big cheese himself, along with all his talking heads... Someone's fucked me over!"

"Mr Westerley," the CEO greeted with amusement on his face. "You seem to be in the wrong domain... and wearing the wrong armour?"

"Ser Mancini," Westerley said, offering a sharp salute. "I am here on the express orders of the president to render assistance in accordance with Nova's call to arms. I apologise if that was not properly communicated."

Mancini grinned affably at the nearest drone-cams. "How very generous of the president. He must have forgotten to mention it. Still, no harm done. You can stand down now. My people will take it from here."

"Thank you, ser. I will load my prisoners—"

"No," Mancini said, an unmistakably harder edge now in his voice. "No, Mr Westerley, you won't. Because they're not *your prisoners*, are they — they're mine! And we can only pray your, how shall I say this, *over-enthusiastic* approach to detaining them hasn't caused any harm to the VIPs within their number."

The vaguest hint of a flinch crossed the EurCon commander's features. "VIPs ser?"

"Yes, Mr Westerley, VIPs. I cannot begin to imagine what Anton intended with such a barbarous attack." Mancini paused, letting his words soak in. "So to ensure all prisoners are treated appropriately *and reach their destination alive*, they will be taken to facilities here in London, not Brussels; and their interrogation will be conducted by my people, not yours. Understood?"

The EurCon commander looked towards the building where Consolidated troops were now escorting out what was left of the outlaws. Others were carrying bodies; some of them his own men. Among the group of walking wounded, he noticed a blond-haired man with glasses who looked completely out of place. He had both arms wrapped protectively around a pretty Asian woman, who herself bore an uncanny resemblance to the VP of Nova; or at least a younger version of her.

Westerley's head snapped back to the London exec, who just nodded and pointed in the opposite direction, where another group of troops were shepherding, along with a very angry-sounding black man and his two missing soldiers, another young woman who appeared identical to the first.

Biting back an impulse to ask obvious questions, the soldier dipped his head in understanding and acceptance of EurCon's impending coup d'etat. "Congratulations ser Mancini," he said, picking his words carefully. "Your *campaign* has been masterful. Perhaps I might be of continuing service — I am, after all, already in the right armour?"

Mancini beamed a perfect white smile and nodded. "Oh, I'm almost certain we can accommodate a man of your talents, commander. There might even be a promotion in it for you... subject, of course, to certain obstacles being removed."

PARTITION SIX

First Among Equals

"So?" Ido asked when Bill Renton walked into the lounge. He didn't turn, but continued to watch the sleek black limousine that had brought his intelligence chief back up the well, as it manoeuvred away from the restricted docking ring of the executive habitat and began its return to journey to San Francisco several hundred miles below.

"Stromberg was paid by a person or persons unknown to provide location information regarding Levinson's remains," the intelligence boss said, pouring himself a Macallan and dropping onto a thick cream sofa. "She'd also taken money from another source a few weeks previous to remove and purge the details of another set of samples."

Rather than outraged, Ido felt a sense of triumph. "I told you this was about more than Levinson," he said. "So who was the focus of our previously unnoticed theft?"

"John Doe, apparently... and no corporate information is detailed in the file we recovered from Stockholm. But aside from his anonymity, I didn't notice anything particularly interesting before leaving it with the analysts to come and find you — just two failed transference attempts, then storage."

Ido turned from his view of space, the apartment walls solidifying as he walked over to join Renton on the sofa. "John Doe, huh? Well, that's a red flag, isn't it? Looks like our intruder wanted us to know about him." He took his own drink from the table and sipped, expression thoughtful. "We suffered a few failures in the early days, but I didn't realise we'd kept any of the samples; and even then, why would someone want to steal them now?"

"...Only for someone else to go to a helluva lot of trouble to get us looking in the right direction to notice," Renton added with a nod.

Frowning, Ido opened a feed-link to Yochi Hamachi, and several seconds later the woman's holo projection appeared over the table. She'd clearly been asleep and yawned widely as she regarded the two men.

"Ido. Bill," she said. "What on earth could you two possibly want from me at this ungodly hour?"

The president smiled at the tart opening. Only a handful of people got away with speaking to him like that. "That's why you need to swap over to a mech body, Yochi. I've told you this before. No need for sleep. No lost time!"

The petite woman, who'd been born four villages over from Ido's in Japan, scowled. "Please tell me you haven't woken me up just to chew over that old debate again," she grumbled. "I like being human. I like sleep. It's that simple."

Both Ido and Bill laughed at her irritation, then Ido continued. "No, Yoch, I didn't wake you for that. Bill's just got back from his interrogation of Stromberg. Some interesting updates we won't bother you with for the moment. But I do have a technical question that won't wait."

"Go on," the head of biosciences said.

"Why would we cryo-freeze the head of someone whose transfer didn't take?"

Yochi pursed her lips, surprised by the question. "We wouldn't," she replied. "A failed transfer falls under clause 47C of every candidate's personal contract... They accept liability for the process and, in the event of repeated transfer failure, acknowledge our rights to recover proprietary Novan technology through necessarily invasive procedures."

Ido nodded. "What about in the early days?"

"Well, the failure rate was higher then, of course. The screening not so good. But we still wouldn't waste time and money harvesting useless samples." She looked thoughtful for a few moments, then added. "But I do recall some experimental operations and research in the fifties that involved separating a healthy brain from its dying body. You know, like Hilary Putnam's brain in a vat — a Hail Mary plan to preserve the intellect of valued corporate officers who failed transfer screening."

Bill sniggered. "What, literally a brain in warm goop connected to a computer?"

"Yes," Yochi said. "Exactly that. As I recall, the original plan had been to create mech bodies for them. Something like the opposite of what we do for digitals with hybrid human bodies. But the process was incredibly expensive, and the results sub-optimal. Brains just aren't as good at running mechanical bodies, as digital matrices are at running organic ones. And anyway, once our transfer tech reached ninety-eight percent compatibility, all open research on retaining a human brain with little more than a digital interface died off."

"And are there any of these bodiless execs still around so far as you know?" Ido asked.

"I'm not even sure the process extended beyond research, Ido. Certainly, none of my counterparts in the other polys have talked about it, or trial results, in years. And anyway, in those procedures, the brain would be kept at 38 degrees, not minus198."

Ido looked at Bill, then smiled back at Yochi. "As always, you've been a mine of information, sera Hamachi," he said with genuine affection.

"Wait stop," Yochi called. "I'm awake now... and intrigued. What's going on?"

"Bill will fill you in tomorrow," Ido chuckled. "For now, he and I need to talk... and you need to go back to sleep." He severed the connection and pinned his intelligence chief with an accusing scowl. "So, the head was definitely frozen?"

Renton hesitated. "I'm Sorry, Ido. I'll need to check," he confessed.

Irritation flashed over the president's face. "Surely Stromberg mentioned something?"

"Not about temperatures, no... To be honest, that never even occurred to me."

Ido shook his head, letting out a disappointed sigh. "Well, now that it has, can you please find out?"

Grateful to be in a body that didn't sweat or display other undesirable nervous reactions, Renton nodded and tapped at his cuff. "I had the team focused on sample movements, but someone will fully unpack that file's contents now. They'll call back momentarily."

Offering no acknowledgement of that update, Ido, a caustic edge in his voice, said. "Did you at least think to ask how she managed to get the damn thing out?"

Keeping his features neutral and voice sincere, the intelligence chief nodded — least said, soonest mended. "She was told to leave the sample in a storage fridge on the ground floor, and purged the file from a communal deck on that same day. We've narrowed those actions to 23rd July. Her guess was someone in security picked it up from there. But she didn't know who.

"... As for a motive, throughout each interrogation the woman babbled on constantly about needing 20000 EurCon." Renton rolled his eyes and took a long swallow of whiskey that cost three times that amount. "Something about a new kidney, and a kid with renal failure... Anyway, I've added the incident to both internal and external vid searches for potential co-offenders. It won't take long to discover who removed that transit cylinder, or who they passed it on to."

Ido offered a small nod, looking slightly mollified.

"Oh, here we go..." Renton said, tapping his cuff and swiping the display to a nearby wall. "Hastings, you're on with Ido Maas, so mind your P's and Q's."

"Mr President," a rake-like intelligence analyst with a glowing stim hanging from of his mouth, said. "It's an honour."

"Yes, of course it is...," Renton drawled. "Now, what have you got for us?"

"Well, long story short," Hastings said, buggy eyes staring down the cam pickup. "You were right. We didn't freeze that head, and the metadata shows that both abortive operations weren't even performed in a Novan facility; they were done in some lab in Kazakhstan... But the real kicker is that it looks like he, or it, or whatever you want to call the damn thing, was interfaced with and piggybacking off CICI until just a few months back — cheeky bastard."

Hastings looked amused, then remembered who he was talking to and cleared his throat. "Anyway, in terms of identity, we got an immediate file match on an old exec from the forties called Daran Whittaker. The guy was once CEO of Eden, the polycorp that defected to China before the war—"

Ido raised a hand to stop the analyst. He looked a little grey, if that was possible for a man in a mech body. "Thank you, Mr Hastings. You can stop there, we're both aware of who ser Whittaker was."

Renton ended the com without another word, then turned to look at his boss. "It can't be," he finally said. "The guy died years ago."

Ido shook his head. He felt like he'd just been punched in the stomach. "Apparently not, Bill. Apparently not."

Cluster I
August 21st, 2070
14:15 GMT InterFreight storage facility, Greenwich, Outer London

InterFreight was a prime example of the type of business the corpos left alone. On face value, due largely to the small margins and bureaucracy of inter-domain import and export laws. But, at true bottom line, to divest each governing polycorp of responsibility for the cargo some of their more dubious shell companies and subsidiaries were moving around.

The line between organised crime and big business was blurry at best — and no one with even half a brain doubted execs were always involved somewhere along the line; be that through tacit polycorp oversight, or as strictly private, greed-driven enterprises.

That Dominic Mancini, Chief Executive of Consolidated Systems, was so completely tearing apart the *legitimate* business interests of Jerome Donelly would therefore capture worldwide attention, once the D notice was lifted and he allowed that news to break. The purge would have organised crime across the Council territories and, no doubt, quite a few corpos worried. It would also act as a statement from EurCon's recently announced VP that he was outraged by the attempted abduction of a corporate heiress within his domain — and nothing but a full, transparent enquiry would satisfy him that his and EurCon's house had now been swept clean.

When Gabriel arrived at the Thameside container yard, over sixty forensic mechs, data retrieval techs and municipal investigators were meticulously cataloguing every transaction the business had made; both on and off the books.

On the understanding that nothing was official until they had something advantageous to a positive reception from Nova and the Council, Mancini had given the agent carte blanche in the investigation, and she'd drafted in Lucas to assist; mostly because she wanted to see his reactions.

The young techgeek remained a complete enigma. Totally out of place among Donelly's common thieves and thugs; yet there he stood, openly explaining to the lead investigator how Jerome's daily operations had worked; detailing, when asked, how to safely access different operating systems; indicating the places he knew contraband to be hidden... even suggesting the search team clear away the numerous metal containers in the yard and sweep it with ground penetrating radar.

Between Lucas's painfully honest compliance and the utterly forensic level of investigative scrutiny each area of the crimeboss's operation was receiving, it didn't take long to discover the comcalls Donelly had recorded and hidden within other data on an old thumb-drive secreted in a safe disguised as a floor tile.

Criminals tended to have a suspicious streak, and whether for protection or potential use in blackmail — the series of calls, always from a female, always from the same comnode, soon established that Donelly wasn't actually the *big* boss; his orders, over the months leading up to and including the theft of Keiko Maas's skin, had come from that unknown woman.

Interestingly, unlike most modern com interactions, only one recording contained any vid, and that was a holo call between Donelly, a formless shape with the woman's voice, and a fat man named Pieter Opperman... who, it seemed, was responsible for acquiring the heiress's clone in San Francisco and sending it to London.

The comnode initiating those communications soon turned into Consolidated's main investigative focus; with Director General Peters himself, green-lighting the use of all necessary intelligence resources to discover the physical location of that VPN protected device.

But it wasn't the corporation's clique of white hats and tech geeks that divined the comnode's source; it was Mancini's PA, Fae — who'd immediately recognised the alphanumeric as one she had stored in her contacts list; one she'd been calling with increasing regularity since Dominic's appointment as VP... It belonged to the private office of Anton van Brieda, and the voice, she added, sounded very much like Angela Phillips, the man's private secretary.

Smoking gun in hand, Peters was content to scale down the investigation and release countless corpos back to the tasks they'd been seconded from that morning. But Gabriel wasn't done with her own enquiries... or the young techneer. She hadn't travelled all the way to London to become a poster girl for Mancini's polycorporate coup, she'd come to solve the death of Elizabeth Levinson; and while the lurid coloured suitcase used to transport that woman's remains sat conspicuously on a set of shelves at Donelly's yard, its contents had been spirited away with no clue as to their final destination.

"There was a frozen sample came through here a few days ago," she said, as Tash's old body was removed from its hiding place for transport back to Consolidated.

Seeming not to have heard, Lucas watched as the pod was carried from his old lab, and then continued to busy himself with the tech pads, cuffs and other peripherals taken from skins that had been brought in.

"Lucas?" the corpo-cop persisted. "The sample?"

"Alot of samples came through, Gabriel. I'm sure it'll be logged somewhere in the files you've recovered."

"It isn't. I've checked."

She moved him away from the municipal officer assigned to chaperone them. "It arrived in that leery coloured case out there," she said quietly, nodding her head towards the shelving between his lab and Donelly's office.

He stopped, frowning. "And you know that how?"

"I'm a cop, Lucas. Knowing shit is my job. It's important. Do you know what happened to that sample?"

He shook his head.

"Did you see it?" she pressed. "It was a cryo-cylinder. The usual corpo samples of an old lady called Elizabeth Levinson."

Lucas shook his head again, a little too quickly.

Reading people was a key part of policing, unintended expressions and body language something good investigators were always aware of; and while the look on the gifted techneer's face told Gabriel he hadn't known about Levinson's head, something about the name had gotten him spooked.

Smelling blood, she slammed a clenched fist down on the workbench. "Damn it, Lucas. You're in deep fucking shit here. You get that right?"

The action made the timid tech jump, eyes flicking towards the pile of devices on his old workbench before snapping back to hers as their chaperone stepped through the doorway. "Everything okay in here?"

"Fine," Gabriel replied, eyes still locked on the younger man. "What is it, Lucas?"

"It's nothing, for God's sake. I'm just very tired, and worried about Tash... When can we go back?"

"You know something; I can tell you do. What is it? I could put in a good word. Explain how you helped the enquiry..."

They stared at each other for several heartbeats, and when the techneer offered no reply, the corpo-cop shook her head and turned towards the muni in the doorway. "Get one of your mechs to prioritise scanning these. I want a full download from each."

"Yes sera," the local officer said.

Gabriel pulled up a stool to sit by the pile of devices and waved a thumb in their direction. "We aren't going anywhere until you speak to me, sunshine."

Shaking his head like there was nothing more he could do, Jerome Donelly's former chop-shop technician bent down to pull out another drawer of stolen peripherals as one of the forensic mechs entered. There was a definite nervous energy about him now, and picking up her pad, Gabriel began looking through the incoming SIM data. "London, Glasgow, Paris, Novgorod ... Jerome's goons really got around, didn't they? There must be over fifty devices here?"

"Sixty-two," the mech intoned in a soft female voice.

"And this is only the stuff Jerome collects to reuse or auction in bulk. The really expensive stuff he sells on almost immediately," Lucas added, attempting to maintain an air of casual helpfulness.

Gabriel nodded, filtering the data uploading to her reader by outgoing coms, and scrolling through the addresses. She couldn't say for certain what she expected to find, and by the sixteenth device their chaperone had grown bored of watching and wondered back out of the lab to talk with other munis in the main warehouse. Only Lucas's dogged attempt to seem relaxed kept her going, and after forty-five painfully determined minutes, the corpo-cop got her reward — a familiar-looking alphanumeric. "Holy shit," she said, eyes travelling straight to Lucas. "You knew this was here, didn't you?"

"What?" the muni asked, sticking his head back around the door.

"What device does this call relate to?" she said, ignoring the question to tap at her screen.

"9F27-6DH4-75A5-4606E," the mech read out. "That call was made from this device, sera." It picked up a utilitarian grey business cuff. "It belonged to Supreme Soviet executive Nikolai Kornyev of Vostok Pharma."

"And when did Kornyev get jacked?"

"Standby, I'll have to access the Council database."

The mech went quiet for several seconds, then turned its plain metal face back towards the agent. "Mr Kornyev reported his hijacking on 17ᵗʰ July this year, following a night out in Christopol. The skin was never recovered."

Gabriel grinned, her left fist pumping the air.

"What?" the municipal officer said again.

"This device was last used to call the private comnode of Elizabeth Levinson. You know the name, Lucas?"

"The exec you just mentioned? Yes, of course I do," he replied, aiming for an air of thoroughly fed up, but his pupils flaring wildly. "She was all over the newsfeeds a couple of weeks back."

Gabriel nodded. "Yes she was... and, someone used this cuff to call her four days before her death. But, guess what? It sure as hell wasn't Nikolai Kornyev — because he'd been mugged weeks before that."

The corpo-cop had a triumphant look on her face as she turned to the muni. "Interrogate Donelly's records. Find out when Kornyev's skin arrived and what happened to it. I'm heading back to Consolidated for a chat with Director General Peters." She picked up the cuff and slid it into a faraday bag, offering Lucas a knowing smile. "I'd say someone's fucked up, wouldn't you?" she said, her voice carefully devoid of accusation. "They should have destroyed this when they had the chance."

Cluster II

August 21st, 2070
15:24 GMT Security Section, Consolidated Systems, Central London

Jerome felt a needle push into the dense muscle of his neck, and as the immersion program swallowed all sense of any other reality, his mind once again red-lined in response to the billions of perceived nerve-endings screaming in pain; the light of a cambot hovering above his pinned eyes drowning out everything but the other man's voice.

"There, you see Mr Donelly, you can behave. Now, before you became abusive, you were telling me about your last contact," the interrogator said. "Continue please, and do try not to pass out this time."

Someone pulled his head back and squirted fluid down his throat. Jerome neither knew nor cared what it was. "A woman," he panted. "Always the same woman."

"Good." A silver-haired man in a military uniform leaned briefly into view, nodding encouragement and signalling for someone to squirt more water into the beaten man's mouth. "What else?"

"There was a guy there. Never seen or spoken to him before. She told him to steal the skin and send it to me."

"His name?" the voice asked.

"I don't know."

"The sensors say otherwise, Mr Donelly. Do I have to remind you *again* what happens when you lie to me?" He pressed a button on the console in front of him, and Jerome snapped rigid again before sagging back down in this restraints to hang like a broken marionette.

"Now, let's try that again, shall we?"

"Opperman," the gangboss croaked. "It was a guy called Pieter Opperman."

"And this Opperman operates where?"

"Nova, I think. The Frisco area."

The interrogator gave an irritated sigh. "Don't think, Mr Donelly… Know."

Another jolt of electricity coursed through Jerome's broken body, and the big man passed out again in the real.

"Okay, we're going to have to reset," the technician standing between the immersion couches of the interrogation suite said, pulling connectors from the gangboss's interface and inserting fresh ones. "You've fried another set of leads, sir… and the prisoner's feedback stats say we're dangerously close to permanent damage."

Director General Peters nodded in acknowledgement. "Understood. Let's change the scenario; move away from nerve stimulation — waterboarding perhaps? Same memories of having been starved and physically tortured for several days… I'll leave the details to you."

The technician sighed, shaking her head. "It's not the perceived electricity, sir. It's the repeated aggressive immersions; the disjunct between the prisoner's physical and perceived experiences are beginning to snowball. Alongside the thiopental, I'm becoming concerned about him stroking out. His B.P. and heart rate are very erratic. It would be best to rest him now; return to this tomorrow."

Peters frowned and shook his head, re-attaching his own connectors. "No, we don't have the time for that — this man tried to abduct a member of the Maas family, and we need to know if further attacks are planned. Hit him with another dose and bring him back in a waterboarding scene. Let's get this over and done with, Captain."

"Sir, I—"

"That's an order, Greeves."

Unhappy, the medical technician left her console to re-inject the unconscious man. "I'll have to log your disregard for my advice," she said stubbornly.

"You do that," the Director General replied. "But put us back in that room first."

Jerome lurched violently in his restraints, heart pounding loudly in his head as he fought to control the panic. "Yes," he gasped once able to breathe again. "Nova. Definitely Frisco in Nova." He squeezed his eyes shut and re-opened them, trying to focus on the man standing over him with a water-soaked cloth.

"And he smuggled the skin to you how?"

"Container shipment to my storage business. The shuttle details are in my records..."

"Ah yes, your storage business. We've got agents working through those records now. So what were you told to do with the skin?"

"Just sit on it. Hold it."

Peters shook his head, giving a teacherly sigh as the cloth was thrown back over Jerome's face and water once again drowned out all pleas of honesty.

"I'm growing impatient, Mr Donelly," the Director General said in slow, over-pronounced syllables.

"She never said," the gangboss screamed when the cloth was finally pulled away. "Honestly. I was just told to take the girl and skin to that old mill. I wasn't told why."

Peters threw the cloth down again, holding his hosepipe directly over the gangboss's mouth. "Lies!" he shouted. "What were your orders?" He left the man to thrash in his restraints for several more seconds, then a solid low tone penetrated his inner ear and the technician began swearing.

"Turn that bloody racket off and get him back," the old soldier barked, sitting up in the real for the sixth time and yanking connectors free of his immersion port.

Greeves was pulling a crash trolley from a corner of the small room; hands working quickly to initiate and attach a

MedBot to Donelly's chest. She glared at Peters, shaking her head as automatic defibs attempted to re-establish a sinus rhythm. "The prisoner's had a massive stroke," she said flatly, censure clear in her voice as she silenced the alarm. "You've fried his brain, *sir*. There's no one in there *to* get back."

"Damn it," Peters muttered, slamming a clenched fist on the arm of his couch. Then he composed himself, running a hand through his wiry grey hair and checking the time. "Interrogation concluded at 16:35," he said without looking at the MedTech. "Record the death as a summary execution for multiple offences, including but not limited to murder, corporate espionage, kidnap and smuggling. Authorised pre-interrogation by domain governor Dominic Mancini, et cetera, et cetera… And turn those bloody cameras off."

The blinking red lights of the room's four cambots winked out, and the technician gave him a thumbs up that all recording, both in the real and in the immersion environment, had been time-stamped and saved. Peters let out a breath, then stood to look down on the unbreathing gangboss. "Thoughts?" he asked the technician.

Greeves smiled. "You should have gone into acting, sir."

The Director General offered her a grin as he adjusted his suit jacket and tie. "Intelligence work almost always contains a little theatre, Mandy." He winked as she jammed the needle of a medgun into the prone man's carotid. "Once you've stabilised Tom's vitals, load the de-brief, please. My office… Oh, and remove all memory blocks, re-asserting the identity of Sullivan as his primary. We'll purge Donelly during the re-configuration op. Yes?"

Greeves nodded agreement as Peters returned to his couch. Moments later, he found himself sat behind his desk looking at a very different face to that of Jerome Donelly.

"Welcome back Tom," the silver-haired soldier grinned.

"Director General," the operative answered, a relieved look on his unscarred, unmodded face as he took in the room and the corporation's head of intelligence. "I didn't think I was making it out this time. Is the deployment over?"

"It is… finally. You played your part perfectly, son. Ser Mancini is extremely pleased. Everything is where it needs to be and, as of a few minutes ago, Jerome Donelly is officially dead. So it's time to become *Major* Tom Sullivan again."

"Major?" Tom asked, a wide grin spreading across his face.

"Congratulations my boy," Peters said, shaking the big man's hand. "Well deserved. Now, let's see about putting you back to looking like this, and organising some long overdue R and R… A memory patch and change of scenery will soon leave London's gangs and Jerome Donelly as nothing more than vague memories of an unpleasant dream. We'll try to find something a little less dramatic for the next one, huh?"

Tom grinned and nodded. "That could work, sir. Somewhere without constant rain would be nice." Then he sobered. "And Gordo? Did he make it out?"

Peters laughed and nodded. "Yes, Sergeant Drysdale is tougher than granite. He took a couple of hits defending that American kid and his girl, but nothing vital — he's already post-op. You'll catch up in recovery."

As he re-awoke on the immersion couch Tom smiled, feeling the soon to be gone scar pulling at his left cheek. Several MedBots were now in the room, assisting a small mouse-like woman wearing a captain's insignia and the name-tag Greeves to transfer him to an operating theatre, while the original Jerome Donelly was brought out of whatever hole they'd stored him in and taken to the morgue.

"Welcome back, Major," Greeves said as she worked. "Comfy?"

"I am now, thank you Captain," Tom replied.

After Soho had gone so badly sideways, the NOC operative couldn't believe he was still alive. He'd spent the

nine months since a spec ops team had snatched Donelly and
his bodyguard, living as the gangboss. Almost an entire year
as South London's most notorious crime lord — causing all
kinds of mayhem on the whim of some unknown voice at the
end of his comnode... and he still didn't know why.

As the sedation kicked in, Tom thought dreamily about
Lucas, and Bobby's little gang. He'd liked those kids and felt
bad they'd been sucked into that last awful night of violence...
Soon though, thank God, he wouldn't remember a damn thing.

PARTITION SIX   **Cluster III**

August 21st, 2070
17:30 GMT Penthouse, Consolidated Systems Headquarters, London

After four months of living in London's suburbs, the suite
consuming the entire top floor of Dominic Mancini's Shard
seemed enormous. The entrance hall alone was bigger than
the flat he rented in semi-congenial Blackheath, and the open
plan living area spreading out beyond and around it, encased
by floor to ceiling high security visi-steel, felt designed so the
corporate demigod could look down on his once proud city
like he was standing on Olympus itself.

"Would you like coffee?" the well-dressed woman who'd
shown them in asked, directing Lucas to a wide, white sofa.
"Something to eat, perhaps?"

The young technician shook his head, looking up into
deep violet eyes. They were captivating. Not in the genetically
manipulated way of a skin, but like his mother's...

Realising he was staring, Lucas blushed and cleared his
throat, shifting his gaze towards the cityscape outside. "Sorry,"
he mumbled. The woman smiled warmly, letting out a

melodious chuckle as she turned her attention to his chaperone. "Charles?"

The heavyset military man's face relaxed into a grin, and he nodded. "I'll take a coffee and pastry please, Fae."

While he'd had no idea what to expect when brought to the headquarters of Dominic Mancini's business empire, Lucas couldn't help but find the presence of two seemingly older people amidst all the corporate decadence of Britain's most powerful executive more than a little incongruous.

"You look perplexed, Mr Sylvester?" a tall, perfectly proportioned man in a thirtyish looking skin said, breaking into Lucas's thoughts as he approached the cluster of sofas; his loose grey robe exposing a broad, muscular chest and washboard stomach. He ran a hand through waves of wet, jet-black hair, before rubbing it dry on his thigh and holding it out. "Dominic Mancini. Charles here tells me you're a bit of an enigma?"

Lucas unconsciously raised an eyebrow before shaking the proffered hand. "I'm sorry, I don't understand, ser Mancini."

"Call me Dominic," the CEO said, dropping down beside the pristine, uniformed man on the opposite sofa. "And," he added, waving a finger in good-humoured rebuke. "I'm almost certain you do. Your little band of thieves and brigands have caused quite a stir in both London and the Council... attracted a lot of unwanted corporate attention for *both* of us."

The exec smiled a thanks to Fae as she passed him his own coffee and croissant. "Now a clock is ticking... and while, believe it or not, I'm not a fan of arbitrary execution, I really don't have much time to decide what to do with you all."

"You could let us go?" Lucas suggested with a half-smile.

Mancini didn't laugh. "Who are you Mr Sylvester? Who do you work for?"

"I work for Jerome Donelly as a digital media technician."

The chief executive sighed. "My security division informs me all your identity records are fake: well-constructed and convincing when not rigorously scrutinised — but fake, nonetheless. How does a digital systems technician working for a criminal lowlife get that kind of access to Council systems?"

Lucas stared down, studying the hands in his lap.

"Nothing?" Mancini asked. "Need I go into the additional scans we ran after establishing your mendacity?"

The former chop-shop skin-splicer continued to remain silent, and Mancini sighed again, turning to the old soldier sat next to him. "Perhaps you could enlighten us then, Charles?"

The Director General placed his coffee mug on the table and locked grey eyes on the top of Lucas's down-turned head. "We know you're not a digital, *Mr Sylvester*. But you have a very interesting mod in your head that's coated in some sort of amphiconductive neurochemical and has a suite of pseudo dendrite extensions using your brain's own electricity for power. The reason that's interesting is because we've recently laid our hands on a working Novan chip… and while yours is suspiciously similar, it's also different; one might even say more elegant."

Lucas smirked, but offered no explanation.

"In addition, your facial mapping and biologs don't correlate with any Council record; meaning your identity has either been erased, disguised, or you're not a corporate citizen."

Mancini pulled a questioning face. "So, Mr *Sylvester*, while I'm genuinely intrigued to know why you've pitched up in my domain, working for a gangster who tried to kidnap the granddaughter of Earth's most powerful exec… As it seems I now need to undo quite a few of my own plans because of you and yours — if you can't find your tongue, I guess I'll just have to execute your friends as terrorists and move on?"

"Just my friends?" Lucas spat, angry eyes rising to glare at the corporate heavyweight.

"Ah, there we go. So you can speak when sufficiently motivated. Well, *Mr Sylvester*... Are we sticking with that name for now?" Mancini tilted his head questioningly to one side. "Given your reluctance to negotiate in good faith, and given the time crunch I've already detailed, you leave me with little choice but to use your friends as collateral. You see, we've determined you yourself are rather valuable. But Tash and Bobby ... I'm afraid their situation is rather more precarious."

Lucas pursed dry lips together, then reached for the glass of water Fae had set on the small table beside him. He'd been trying to hack the corporation's systems since arriving, but Consolidated's firewalls were unlike anything he'd encountered before; almost alive.

"Well, this is tiresome," the CEO said, leaning forward. "Look, *Lucas*, there are a number of ways I could have approached this meeting, and I chose polite conversation — hoping we might find some common ground rather than playing silly games neither of us have time for." He tapped the display of his cuff for emphasis. "But as you seem reluctant, and I *truly* don't want to have to execute your friends before handing you over to the Council, I'll simply spell out our beliefs and then you can decide if you wish to accept the consequences of continuing with this hopeless charade?"

Lucas just continued to stare, and Mancini sighed, shaking his head. "We've been watching you since you hooked up with Jerome Donelly, who we'd been watching for even longer... Given when you arrived, at first we thought you'd been sent to spy on him by, *shall we say,* other interested parties within EurCon. But now we've seen what's inside your head, a corporate spy seems incredibly unlikely. In fact, our intelligence files point to just one other man alive with a neural modification like yours ... and an iteration of that man is currently all over the feeds as being responsible for the death of one of my employees."

The game was up, Lucas realised. They hadn't missed the implant, and they hadn't missed its origins. "I'm not Eric Thorne, if that's what you're suggesting," he said, breaking his silence.

"Of course you're not," Mancini agreed. "You're too young. So who are you to him? Why would he gift you a chip?"

Lucas shrugged. They'd probably just go to plan b and gouge the damn thing out of his head if he didn't talk, so he might as well try to help Tash and Bobby.

"And you'll leave my friends alone?"

"I'm always receptive to reasonable negotiation," Mancini replied obliquely.

Letting out a slow breath, Lucas nodded as if they'd made some kind of deal. "I'm his grandson," he said.

"Grandson?" the old intelligence chief repeated. "But Eric Thorne doesn't have any grandchildren."

"The one in China may not," Lucas corrected, words sarcastic and laced with anger. "But the one *not* in China sure does; pulled from my dying mother's womb."

Peters opened his mouth to speak again, but Mancini silenced him with a touch on the leg. "You're the son of Sade Thorne?"

"Sylvester," Lucas corrected. "Her married name was Sylvester."

The CEO looked doubtful. "But you're *all* organic... You have a brain."

The former chop-shop techie's face betrayed years of suppressed anger at the ignorance and prejudice that had surrounded his parents. "She was as organic as any of you *digitals*," he snapped. "Are corpo skins not capable of having perfectly normal babies?"

Mancini held up his hands in immediate surrender. "Yes. Yes. Of course. My apologies, I meant no offence. I just... two FADEs having a human child; I'd assumed there'd been some biomechanical wizardry at play — not just mother nature.

"In any event, what I should have said was how sorry I was to hear about their deaths. I'm afraid I didn't know your father, but your mother was a real champion of the cause."

The unexpectedly kind words threw Lucas for a moment, and he found himself staring at the man who'd said he didn't have time to play games.

"But that doesn't explain what happened to Elizabeth?" Mancini continued. "I went to quite a lot of trouble to recover her remains, and they've told us nothing about what happened to her."

"Put Tash back into her own body, and I'll tell you everything," Lucas said, locking eyes with the other man.

The chief executive shook his head. "You really aren't in any position to be calling the shots here, Lucas." The sympathetic look was still fixed on his face, but the words were colder, more clipped. "I'll shortly be speaking with Ido Maas. Who, I'm sure you can appreciate, will want to inflict God only knows how many different types of hell on those who conspired to do his granddaughter harm; and, on face value at least, your girlfriend and her brother were up to their noses in that plot."

"But they weren't!" Lucas insisted. "They... *we* were just in the wrong place at the wrong time."

Mancini shook his head a second time, face now all business. "Like I say, Lucas, not according to the evidence. That indicates you and your friends, all of whom work for the criminal who destroyed half a street under one of *my* domes trying to kidnap Keiko Cheng, were deliberately placed with her by him. It also highlights, quite emphatically in fact, that the very same criminal also just happened to have one of the girl's official skins in his possession — and that skin, by another staggering coincidence, is currently inhabited by Natasha Adeyinka!"

"… We saved Keiko's *life*, for God's sake!" Lucas shouted. "And doing that cost Tash hers. Ask Keiko, she'll tell you."

"Oh, I have," Mancini assured. "That's why your friends are still alive and we're having this conversation. But quid pro quo, Mr Sylvester. Give me a reason to stick my neck out that far and lie to the Council and Ido Maas; give me a reason to falsify corporate records to save *them*… Tell me about Elizabeth Levinson. Tell me what you've done."

"…And if I do, you'll save them? Give Tash her own body?"

Mancini let out an exasperated sigh. "For God's sake, man, you're relentless. Yes, okay fine. But she'll have to go into something off the shelf for the time being; a clone takes months to grow, and she obviously can't stay in what she's in."

"Thank you," Lucas said, accepting he'd probably reached the best deal he was going to broker.

He was supposed to have left London immediately after the call to Elizabeth. But Tash had crashed into his life like a runaway train, and having never really been the object of a girl's attention, the poor love-struck fool had been stupid enough to stick around. Fleetingly, he now wondered if Tash and Fin would still be alive and in their own bodies if he'd gone. God only knew. There was nothing he could now say or do to change what happened. In fact, Lucas realised, he could only hope the corpo on the other sofa would honour his word. He had no cards left to play and nothing to lose, except Tash.

"In the Eastern Alliance," he began. "It's common knowledge Eden created the MindMerge chip; not Nova; not Cheng Li."

Mancini snorted and shook his head. "That's common knowledge among quite a few people, kid," he laughed. "I've been trying to open a dialogue with Fenton White for years. But what's that got to do with sera Levinson?"

The response surprised Lucas. He'd expected harsh words and denial. But Consolidated's chief executive, the man just one step below Anton van Brieda in EurCon's pecking order, seemed to find it funny. He frowned, once again failing to understand the quirky CEO's angle.

"Anyway, after the legal challenges failed and Nova began its aggressive expansion across North America, Eden re-located to China, where the Board voted unanimously to uphold Eric and Fenton's position of non-production and non-intervention.

"But when Nova turned on FADEs, my mother and father came back to protest..."

Lucas cleared his throat and took another sip of water, his hands shaking. This was the second time in as many days he'd been forced to talk about his parents.

"After that, my grandpa took the view inaction had become just as morally reprehensible as competing with Nova... That we should offer the chip for free, destroy their monopoly. But the Board still stood by Fenton and Eric — the original Eric, that is."

"Are the Eric in China and your grandfather not equals, then?" Mancini asked.

"No... My grandpa, as a copy of the original, didn't get a vote."

"That doesn't sound particularly inclusive. I'd understood the Eastern Alliance to be a more progressive regime?"

Lucas shook his head. "With FADEs, perhaps. They're not banned like here. But the *duplicate,* as people there called him, was the very embodiment of what Eden withheld from the Alliance... a digital human. Giving him any kind of prominence would have started a number of difficult conversations. So we never returned to China."

Mancini frowned, sinking back into the sofa's thick padding, gesturing for Lucas to continue.

"Anyway, at some point, Nova branded Grandpa a terrorist, and he decided my existence would be easier to conceal if I was never around him. He installed my chip, taught me how to use it, then left me with a couple of associates. In the years that have followed, we've built a network of sympathisers and activists across all eleven polycorps."

"Is he here in London?"

Lucas shrugged. "I haven't got the first idea where he is. I haven't seen my grandfather outside of an immersion program since he left me."

"And the virus?" Peters prompted.

"That's not down to him. I developed it five years ago with the help of some very talented friends. Grandpa has always been against using it, so we continued to watch the abuse and dis-affection caused by corpocracy until some of us just couldn't take it anymore and went our own way."

"So Eric didn't know what you planned to do here?" Mancini interrupted.

Lucas shook his head but didn't elaborate. "When rumours started circulating about civil war brewing in EurCon, I came to London." He looked at the handsome executive, the hint of a smile on his face. "Ironic, isn't it ser Mancini? You've been watching me, and I've been watching you.

"Anyway, like most of our supporters, Elizabeth wasn't happy with a number of the polycorp's decisions in recent years; the unfulfilled promises. So when her impending promotion offered the chance, she... and we, took it."

Mancini's mouth hung open for a couple of beats, then he shared a look with his intelligence chief. "So you're saying she was what? A volunteer?"

Lucas nodded. "One of many, ser Mancini. I think you'd be surprised how unpopular your regime is."

"And now you know it works, what's the plan?" the Director General challenged. "Mass murder? A coup?"

Lucas let out a single bark of laughter. "I'm sure more than a few digitals deserve death," he countered, anger and defiance shining in his eyes. "But no, that's not our plan. Once freed from the yoke of corpocracy, independent courts can judge the actions of you and yours... In the meantime though, having been very clearly warned of the consequences, only digitals fool enough to continue jumping in and out of the net and other bodies run any risk of unnatural death — and that's not murder, that's a choice they, and they alone, make."

"And your grandfather agrees with that philosophy?" Mancini asked.

"The die is cast," Lucas replied flatly. "He accepts that Elizabeth and the other volunteers are at peace with their decisions... and hopes the rest of you then corporates see sense."

"Other volunteers?" Peters said.

Lucas dipped his head in a partial nod. "Elizabeth was a warning shot. We hoped, but never expected, her death would be enough to make most other digitals stop and think; that's why more volunteers have already begun developing symptoms within each of the Council domains."

Mancini gave a low whistle. "That'll definitely grab everyone's attention," he breathed. "So, we stay off the net to avoid infection?"

Lucas shook his head. "No, that route would have allowed for a system-wide purge, and while undoubtedly a monumental inconvenience, we anticipated that's what the Council would attempt. So we introduced the virus months ago. It's penetrated every level of your corporate systems; the code in your current matrix and all its backups... Put simply ser Mancini, you're *all* already infected.

"What we control, and that's a sizeable group in each domain by the way, is the activation key. One person... Thousands... We can scale as large or small as we wish. Though, of course, we'd prefer not to have to do it at all."

The CEO nodded his appreciation of the younger man's long game. "And we can't just reload from archived brains after a system purge because...?"

Lucas offered the chief exec a small smile. "Sure, that remains an option," he said. "But you'll wanna hope the only thing missing *if* you get to wake up again is twenty odd years of memories. Because, I'm not sure those repositories will survive once everyone else realises what you're trying to do."

A brief chuckle escaped from Peters, who leaned forward, appearing to find the threat entertaining. "So from cyber-terrorist to Che Guevera, huh? Virus or no virus, young man, the polycorps won't just roll over. They each control millions of basics who are unaffected by what you've done... they *will* come after you. You know that, right?"

The dismissal irritated Lucas, who jabbed a finger at the tinted city view sitting beyond the visi-steel windows. "I'm not naïve enough to think that some won't see opportunity or take advantage, *ser*. But the majority of decent people...?" He shook his head, remembering Tash's words. "Have you seen how your polycorp treats its native populations? The two different Londons stretching out beneath your God's eye view?"

Face flushing with freshly stoked anger, Lucas continued his rhetoric. "People die every day because your companies withhold basic medical care. There's no formal education or social support for non-corporate families. Almost everyone out there with any kind of power is utterly corrupt... and street gangs now run the slums you can't be bothered to govern."

He glanced around the decadent suite, then returned his gaze to the men sat on the opposite sofa. "You've abandoned half this country's population, and the other half are shit scared of saying anything in case they lose what little they've got...

"Blood-sucking parasites, *Director General*, that's all your privileged few are to the 99.99 percent of *basic* humans on this planet; and I very much doubt many of us will sit idle while your corporate hegemony attempts to reboot itself." Eyes not leaving the chisel-faced intelligence chief as he took another swallow of water, Lucas nodded to himself, then added. "Oh, and guess what? It'll also be that 99.99 percent who get to decide whether I'm a fucking terrorist... not a bunch of morally corrupt corporate fascists who are responsible for the death of millions."

Looking genuinely amused by the outburst, Mancini once again held up his hands in a gesture of surrender. "Easy, Lucas. Easy. I don't think Charles intended to offend you... and we certainly don't want to get into any tit for tat exchange of hostilities."

Peters, the wisp of a smile still on his rugged face, nodded in semi-sincere agreement.

"In fact," Mancini continued. "It might surprise you to know our vision of the future isn't so very different from your own."

Lucas gave a bitter snort, before feigning a thoughtful look. "Yeah, sure it isn't. Let's see now, does it involve replacing Ido Maas, Nova and the Council with — Oh wait... maybe you?"

To his surprise, Mancini outright laughed.

"Yes. At first anyway, it would be something like that," the chief exec nodded. "But we needn't worry about the details right now. For the time being, our impasse can act as a mutual guarantee of goodwill? You tell your people all is well; that we're negotiating a common way forward — and obviously, agree not to kill me or my people. And in return, I vouchsafe the well-being of you and your friends... fair?"

Lucas frowned at Mancini's sudden change in direction. "So you'll let me and my friends go?"

"Hmm. In time, yes, of course," the exec replied. "But until we've built a few bridges, I think it's best we all stay close by.

Act as each other's guarantee so to speak? I don't cross you; you don't disappear on, or cross me?"

Realising the man was serious, Lucas gave a slow nod of assent. He wasn't exactly free, and the corpo was clearly holding his friends hostage. But that was worlds better than being handed over to Ido Maas or the Council.

"Good," Peters said, clapping both hands together. "That's that sorted then. If not exactly friends, we can at least be cordial allies... Now, moving on to damage limitation. Does anyone else know about your recent adventures in London?"

A look that said Lucas wouldn't be disclosing any contacts then caused the older man to add. "I can't protect you or your friends without knowing where the potential problems lie, son. I'm good, but I'm not a clairvoyant."

Understanding dawned on Lucas's face; Peters wasn't talking about Elizabeth, Miguel or the others. He was talking about compromising information getting back to Nova and the Council. "Oh...," he said. "I think agent Sousa suspects. She recognised Levinson's personal comnode in the call log of a cuff at Jerome's."

"Did she indeed, and where's that cuff now?"

"I thought she'd brought it back here?"

It was the Director General's turn to frown. "Does our accord make it safe for me to now interact with Consolidated's central AI?" he asked.

Lucas glanced at Mancini, once again weighing the worth of the man's word, then nodded.

The older man's expression became momentarily distant as he meshed with the corporation's mainframe for the first time in several days. Then his eyes refocused. "She's not here or with any of our staff," he said. "I'll have to scan the city's cambots... Anyone else?"

"No," Lucas replied, wondering if he'd just put the corpo-cop in some kind of jeopardy. But Mancini stood before he could speak further, tightening the belt on his robe and holding out a hand again. "Well, I don't think either of us was expecting this outcome when we started," he said with a smile. "Now I need to get dressed for my meeting with Ido. Fae will arrange accommodation for you and your friends. Tomorrow, I will deliver Keiko back to her family… which begins my own campaign to bring down corpocracy." He winked at the younger man. "I'd like you come to along. It will give us another opportunity to talk, and let you assess the courage of my convictions, as I have yours today?"

Not waiting for a reply, the well-sculpted executive turned and began walking back towards his private quarters. "One man with a dream, at pleasure," he rhymed. "Shall go forth and conquer a crown; and three with a new song's measure, can trample a kingdom down."

"… and Tash?" Lucas called as the mercurial CEO disappeared behind an opaque privacy screen. The man paused, leaning back into view, waving a manicured finger towards him. "We have our impasse, Mr Sylvester, do we not? While there is no hiding that a second Maas skin was in London. With your friend's agreement, I'm sure Fae can arrange her transfer into something less conspicuous?"

Lucas nodded, gratitude and relief washing through his system. "Thank you," he rasped, surprising himself with the sincerity he felt.

Cluster IV

August 21st, 2070
10:15 PST Nova Earthside Headquarters, San Francisco Bay

"Dominic." Ido said, looking less than impressed to have received the comcall on his private node. "What can I do for you?"

"Just for once, Ido, I think this is about what I can do for you," Mancini smiled, sharing a secondary camfeed of the young woman sat opposite him. Keiko shrank into her chair and offered her grandfather an awkward smile, knowing her life was about to get very, very restricted.

"Where on earth did you get that?"

"Oh, it's not just a misplaced skin, Ido. It's actually your granddaughter."

"Keiko?" Ido questioned, confusion clear on his face.

"Poppop, don't be mad," the heiress began.

"But you're at—"

The shaking of the girl's head stopped him, then her face crumpled in on itself and she began crying, words coming out in a rush. "Reimi's dead," she blurted. "We came to London. Millie's covering for me. It was just a bit of fun, but—"

"What do you mean, Reimi's dead?" Ido broke in, face now dangerously calm.

"Blown up at this hotel I was staying at. I—"

"Dominic?" The Novan president demanded.

Consolidated's CEO passed a box of tissues to the overwrought young woman, then returned his attention to her grandfather. "The good news is, she's okay," he said, answering the obvious, but so far unasked question. "Her comms got knocked out in an EMP blast, but otherwise she only has a few bumps and bruises…"

"EMP? Bumps and bruises? Sorry Dominic, just give me a moment."

The holo blanked to an image of the Novan logo; a black star exploding onto a white background. Then Ido returned, feeds from his daughter Akira, and her husband Li, joining the conference.

"Keiko? What the hell?"

"Mum, I—"

"I've just spoken with Millie… The pair of you are in a world of trouble, young lady," Akira said sharply, eyes boring into her daughters. Then she shifted focus to regard Mancini, voice cranking down several octaves. "Hello Dominic, thanks for the com. What the hell is going on?"

"Akira, Li, hi," the British exec said. "As far as my security directorate has been able to ascertain so far, Keiko has been the target of an extremely well-organised and well-funded kidnap attempt —"

"What were you even doing in London?" Akira growled.

"Shall we just let Dominic finish?" Li interjected, holding up a hand to halt his wife.

"Yes, of course." Nova's VP dipped her head in apology. "Sorry Dominic, please continue."

"I'll leave the question of why Keiko was in London for you to discuss with her in private," Mancini said, clearing his throat. "In terms of the attack upon her within my domain, I am of course, deeply embarrassed. Though, as one of your recon teams were deployed without any liaison whatsoever, I had thought you were aware?"

Ido looked genuinely taken aback. "A Novan recon team?" He glared at Akira, who shook her head, appearing equally baffled. "That's... Who's the commanding officer, please?"

"From the shuttle we've recovered, it seems a Captain Jonus was. He and his team are all dead, I'm afraid. Killed in a firefight with Keiko's abductors... If you'd shared your intel?"

Though displaying a face of sincere reproach, Mancini was thoroughly enjoying the tech titan's discomfort.

"Look, Dominic, there's clearly been a terrible disconnect here. But as you say, the important thing is you managed to intervene and save my granddaughter. For that, I'll be eternally grateful."

Akira and Li nodded vigorously, agreeing with the older man's sentiment. Then Ido's face adopted a clipped harshness the ruthless businessman was known for. "And the kidnappers? I'm sure you can appreciate how much I'd like to personally oversee their punishment?"

"Indeed," Mancini said. "Unfortunately, we're talking about a small group of hardcore militants whose successful detention was somewhat impeded by interference from other EurCon resources, and I'm afraid the couple that didn't die when my special forces extracted Keiko, expired during their subsequent interrogation. I will, of course, share the camlogs with your people."

A slight downturn of the president's thin lips was the only outward display of disappointment. "That's a shame... Did your people manage to learn anything useful about who was behind it?"

"On face value, peripheral evidence points to the attempt being perpetrated by an organised crime group. The incident coincided with the theft of one of Keiko's clones from a facility right there in San Francisco. I've managed to recover that for you as well."

Ido shot his daughter a second dark look, the man's legendary calm wavering. "One of our own family's clones?" he said. "Heads are going to roll... You say *on face value*?"

"Yes," Mancini replied. "To be blunt, Ido, the whole affair was far too well organised. Which means the involvement of someone with very deep pockets and serious influence over lower-level executives and city managers in both our domains."

"Do you know who?"

Pulling a face, Mancini gave one of those sideways dips of the head that meant *maybe*. "The gangboss here certainly didn't know who he was working for. He had regular contact with a well-spoken female, and then very recently, quite a bit with a guy your side of the pond called Pieter Opperman?"

"That fits," Li said. "I've been making enquiries with our military while you were speaking. They confirm Captain Jonus was the leader of a recon unit that captured vid of a large crate being removed from a non-Novan warehouse in Frisco four nights ago. His team followed it to London, where they did indeed deploy around the gang it was delivered to. So, sorry about that Dominic... But surveillance footage from Frisco confirms Opperman was the man involved our side."

"And where is he now?" Mancini enquired.

Li flicked through the data on his screen, then shook his head. "Gone to ground."

Ido growled, but said nothing.

"Why?" Akira asked no one in particular. "Why do this?"

Mancini shrugged, looking over at Keiko. "The obvious reasons are to hurt you and embarrass me? I suspect separately we both have fairly extensive lists... But targeting both of us—"

"Your expression a moment ago suggested there was more?" Ido interrupted. "What aren't you telling us?"

The British CEO shook his head ruefully. "I'd prefer not to speculate, Ido. A full forensic investigation is underway, and there is information that currently lacks context."

"This is my granddaughter's safety, Dominic. Please, indulge me."

Sighing, Mancini offered the Maas family a slow nod. "Look, it's not much of a secret that in my political sphere, only one person of significance is gunning for me."

"Anton van Brieda," Ido finished, shaking his head doubtfully. "You have evidence?"

"Of going after me? Of course. But that's a EurCon matter. Of going after you?" He paused again, apparent internal debate playing out in his facial expressions.

Ido circled an impatient finger, unmoved by the theatrics. "If there's something that needs saying, Dominic, please just come out and say it."

"Fine," Mancini answered, reluctance evident in his voice. "But remember what I said about context—"

"We understand the caveat."

Squaring his shoulders, the British executive sighed; his expression grave. "During our searches of the kidnapper's premises here in London, we recovered a number of recorded conversations between him and that woman I mentioned; she seems to have been the one calling the shots."

"And?" Ido prompted.

"And, although I'm having our VPN and decryption analysis checked and re-checked by separate specialists, the metadata for those conversations points to her having used the comnode in Anton van Brieda's private office. My PA is also fairly certain the voice concerned is that of Angela Philips, his personal assistant."

Ido's mouth opened, then closed again.

"Like I say, we're still completing the forensics, and arresting Philips has certain political sensitivities that need careful consideration — as I'm almost certain, even for a woman of her *particular talents*, that someone with considerably more corporate influence must sit at the heart of this."

"You mean Anton?" Ido stated.

Mancini nodded. "It's hard to see a personal angle for Philips, or that she'd be working for anyone else. But I'm really not pointing any fingers... yet. My people will have verified and validated their findings over the next few hours. Why don't we discuss the matter in more detail when I drop Keiko back tomorrow?"

"You'll drop her home?" Akira asked.

"Of course. Unless you're telling me Nova is now greenlighting digital transfers again?"

A slight tension playing across the face of each Novan executive told Mancini it absolutely wasn't — at least not with one of their own at risk.

"Though we're certain all is well, and the dark web nonsense is exactly that, our investigation continues," Li said smoothly. "But we wouldn't want to put you out any further, Dominic. I can jump on a shuttle to London now?"

"Nonsense," Mancini smiled. "It's already 7 pm here and I still need to address this incident with key members of EurCon's central board and the Council, who I'm sure will want to convene a special session in New York tomorrow morning. So I'll be heading over anyway."

Ido nodded in agreement; a very clear, very cold fury in his voice when he spoke. "Thank you Dominic, we accept your kind offer. I'll remain on this node awaiting the call to Council... and if the physical evidence confirms your suspicions, you can expect my full support." His eyes then travelled to Keiko. "Now, would you mind if we spoke privately with my granddaughter for a moment?"

With a polite dip of the head, Mancini stood. "Of course. I'll give you some privacy. Take as long as you need." Raising a hand in farewell he then shut off his deskcam, and left the unfortunate young woman to what he was sure would be an extremely uncomfortable conversation.

 PARTITION SIX   **Cluster V**

August 21st, 2070
21:35 CET Executive Arcology, European Conglomerate, Brussels

In the evening sunshine, the rounded domes of EurCon's executive arcologies curved into the sky above Brussels' protected woodlands like huge iridescent mushroom caps. Each home to more than a thousand executive families from the myriad businesses that rose from the ashes of Europe's old Union, and each designed to function as an autonomous biosphere capable of sustaining its community in outrageous opulence indefinitely.

First Among Equals

At the centre of the interconnected network of super-cities, sitting wider, standing taller, and displaying greater decadence than any of the others, sat a dome housing the official residences of the polycorp's elite: those commercial dynasties with controlling interests in multiple concerns, the senior executives who chaired and influenced polycorporate oversight committees, the titans of industry who sat on the Central Board... Fewer than six hundred families maintained homes in EurCon's largest arcology — but they were Europe's richest, most powerful ten thousandth of one percent.

Angela Philips didn't own the twelve-bedroomed mansion with extensive gardens and an orange grove just one terrace below Anton van Brieda's presidential palace; he did. But the Polycorp's kingpin liked to keep his personal assistant close, and that meant exclusive use of the specially designed residence linked by private elevator to the old man's study. He'd also granted her immortality — a controversial choice when Nova had first gone public and so many of the world's ultra-rich were queuing for digitisation.

The man knew people gossiped about their living arrangements. But he didn't care. If anything, he stoked the rumours. Angela was, after all, devastatingly attractive, and men lined up to warm her bed.

But in truth, the polycorp president had discarded the beautiful woman as a lover long years ago, and she'd become nothing more than his *Milady de Winter*, eighty-five years of unquestioning service; eighty-five years of ensuring Europe's wealthiest man always had plausible deniability when negotiations soured and accidents happened; *eighty-three* years of unrequited love... But when Dominic Mancini came along, Angela's black heart began beating again.

Now, two years on, the much-maligned private secretary was close to finally achieving her life's ambition; moving upstairs to the *big house* — moving upstairs and wiping the silly fucking smiles from the faces of those execs, wags and whores who whispered behind her back.

Dominic hadn't actually popped the question yet. In fact, they'd not even discussed marriage. But he'd taken her to his bed, included her in his betrayals, and made her a central part of his plans for ascension — so she'd be fucked if she'd let him overlook her like Anton had all those years ago. This time, Angela Philips would get her ring.

The long-haired brunette beauty examined herself in the mirror, pulling at a loose curl and letting it bounce back into place. Fortunately, she'd been wearing her official skin when the transfer ban came in. Meaning she didn't have to stay away from the office, skulking around in one of her alter-egos, she could enjoy just being herself for a change; and, though they'd experimented of course, Dominic had once said he loved the *real* her most. *Loved*... he'd used that exact word.

Angela smiled, running fingers lightly over both exposed breasts and pinching at the nipples, imagining his hands exploring her; eager, teasing, hungry. The basque, what there was of it, clung like a second skin; rings hanging from the bodice and her sleeved arms allowing for total domination, if that was what he wished. She gave her reflection a quivering, conquered, yours for the taking look; lips sticky with a slutty red rouge, and tiny panties forsaken for the thrill of chill air on her wetness.

"Perfect," she purred, slipping on a long, businesslike mac and heading for the door. He won't know what hit him.

Downtown Brussels was very much like every other European city: there were the sites of preserved heritage and tourism, areas dedicated to different echelons of corporate housing, commerce and recreation... and then there were the slums — those places *outside* EurCon's interest or maintenance where the city's unregistered, unsupported inhabitants lived.

But *slums* didn't carry the same meaning as it had at the beginning of the century. Through the beneficence of corpocracy, not all neighbourhoods beyond the tracks were shitholes, and not everyone living in them was skint. In fact, Angela, who'd grown up in the cheap seats, had a lot of time for the way most of the gangs policed their communities; those unwilling or unable to defend themselves still fell by the wayside of course — after all, these were Darwin days. But those with a nose for survival could do well, flourish even.

She left her town car at Porte de Hal, taking the mass transit over the maglev tracks as far as the canal, where corporation transport ended and entrepreneurial private hire took over; a classic electric Mercedes with real wheels drove her the rest of the way into Anderlecht and Bar-Hotel La Bohemian, sat on the fringe of Parc Astrid.

Diving, the practice of heading into the slums to get your kicks, had become a popular pastime among digitals the decade before. It allowed hard working execs to decompress after a tough day in the office, and indulge in leisure pursuits of a morally ambiguous or even utterly illegal nature, while enjoying relative anonymity in a judgement free environment. It was the second largest reason digitals gave in Vogue's *kicks n tricks* survey for investing in an unregistered skin... and, while a few of the non-digital participants might be of the more unwilling or heavily dosed type, as long as no scandal made its way back to the boardroom — *what happened in the slums, stayed in the slums.*

Angela had used La Bohemian several times before, though never in her registered body, and as she walked in, the maitresse, Monique, greeted her with an appraising look. "My, my, aren't you just jaw-dropping, beautiful lady?" she said in a breathy, sultry voice. "I'm guessing with looks like that, you're not here to work?"

The PA grinned. Flattery from another stunning woman was always appreciated. "I've booked. My companion should be here shortly."

Monique examined a small cuff sewn into the diaphanous fabric of her sleeve and nodded. "Ah, oui. The Presidential Suite... magnifique. Would you a drink before making your way upstairs?"

Angela looked into the darkened interior of the near empty bar, where a handful of half-naked serving staff almost outnumbered the dozen or so shadowed figures sat around a central dais, watching two performers, each modified to possess both sets of sexual organs, abuse each other to some sort of Vangelis beat. "Slow tonight?"

"Oui," the maitresse replied with a heavy sigh. "Has been all week. I'm told there's some kind of transfer ban, non?"

Angela offered a sympathetic smile, but no answer. Shitty as their lives may be, these people relied on the credits and scrip digitals spent here. "I think I'll go straight up, thank you Monique," she said. "Get myself settled in."

The scantily clad greeter seemed about to say something more, then simply nodded, waving over one of the bare-chested servers standing by the bar. "Philippe, take Madam up to the Presidential Suite please, and make sure she has *everything* she desires."

The dark-skinned man gave Angela a leering grin, unconsciously running fingers over a washboard stomach towards the waistline of a pair of shorts barely covering his manhood. "Can I take your coat, madam?" he asked.

Angela licked her lips, wondering if she had time for a little sport, then shook her head, letting out a slow disappointed sigh. "Maybe later," she said, eyes lingering on his crotch. Tonight, she had to remind herself, wasn't about satisfying filthy urges, it was about hooking her man — and as unexpected as Dominic's message to meet up had been, now all their plans were finally in place, she couldn't help but think, hope, dream EurCon's soon to be president was finally going to propose.

The *Presidential Suite* was, in fact, little more than a large bedroom with a connecting bathroom. But it was pleasant enough for this side of the tracks. Philippe poured champagne and showed Angela how to control the smart walls. Then, with a cheeky wink, he told her to just dial 'O' if she needed *anything else.* The stunning centennial couldn't help but chuckle as she tucked an old twenty euro note into his waistband and watched the fine physical specimen saunter back down the hallway.

Nature could still create jaw-dropping beauty — just not as reliably as science.

Finally alone, Angela slipped off her mac and sat on the edge of the bed with a glass of France's finest, flicking through different scene options. She settled on a romantic sunset, with waves rhythmically crashing over the golden sands of a desert island beach, then took herself to the bathroom for one last inspection and touch up.

It was hard not to grin when the door opened and quietly closed again without any word of greeting... this had to be a proposal. "Grab a glass of champagne, mon cher," she called, smacking her lips together after a fresh application of rouge. "I'll be right out."

There was movement in the room and Angela half expected to see Dominic's handsome, sex-hungry face peek around the doorframe. They'd purposefully not seen each other for over two months to ensure there were no awkward questions when Anton *retired*, and even then, it had been incognito and overshadowed by his scheming.

The PA-cum-corporate spy-cum-fixer blew herself a kiss and turned. She couldn't wait for all the subterfuge and creeping around to be over; she wanted a husband; she wanted a family; she wanted to be recognised as her own person.

"Have I got a surprise for you," she purred, dimming the lights and covering her breasts as she stepped back into the bedroom.

"Ditto." A man's voice replied, and Angela was thrown backwards onto the bed.

It was Westerley, Anton's attack dog.

"Wai—" was all she managed before two booming gunshots shattered the room's tranquillity, punching through her upheld hand to scatter skull, blood and electronic circuitry all over the wall's gently lapping waves.

PARTITION SIX   ## Cluster VI
August 21st, 2070
23:35 CET Presidential Suite, La Bohemian, Anderlecht, Brussels

Little surprised La Bohemian's Maitresse de Maison these days. Though only twenty-three, the attractive Moroccan had seen things that would fuck up most marines, and done things just as bad as those she'd seen. That was life in the slums; fucker or fuckee were the only two *real* choices — and money was the pied-piper. Scrip, chat, coin, cash... call it what you like, corpo or cretin, hard currency was the bottom line in this place.

But tonight, only half an hour after the sexy woman had gone upstairs, Monique was standing in the Presidential Suite staring with disbelieving eyes at the unmoving body of the stunning digital. The gang had jacked skins before, of course, and disposed of the occasional corpse when a corpo went too far. But they'd never had a digital executed on the premises, and Philippe was now in a standoff with the executioner.

"Your Boss has been paid," the square-jawed European with neatly combed blond hair and a very big gun was saying to Philippe. The waiter-cum-bouncer looked towards Monique, and the guy rolled his eyes. "Not her, you idiot. Your *boss* boss. Com Arsene LeTissier, he'll confirm."

Monique held up a hand, stopping two more of her staff from running through the doorway, then began tapping at glyphs on her cuff.

"Shame, huh?" the man said, legs slightly bent and ready to move. He had a blocky, almost square face, and the air of someone trained to be totally unmoved by the mess he'd just made on the bed. "I'd kill for a body like that."

Monique raised an eyebrow, and the man gave a short bark of laughter. "No pun intended, sweetheart. This is a contract job, nothing more. Don't even know who for. And frankly, it's all a little pointless, given that Miss Perky Tits there will be waking up about now in a body bank somewhere. But if that's how the digitals want to spend their scrip..." He shrugged.

"What about the rumours?" Monique asked. "The virus?"

The assassin shrugged again. "Well, if it's true. I guess that's a *them* problem, huh?"

Reflexively, the maitresse shrugged herself. But it all seemed such a terrible waste of life. "You couldn't have found a less messy way?" she asked, shaking her head.

Scanning the explosive spread of organic matter, the man offered an apologetic smile. "Sorry. But my client was very specific about ensuring the skin's core was fragged beyond repair or retrieval. Otherwise, I'd be selling it to your boss, rather than paying for disposal."

Monique's cuff rumbled, and she read the message. "Arsene says to wrap up the body. Mungo's on his way over."

"We're okay then?" the squat European asked, eyes flicking towards Philippe.

Monique jerked her head, and the near naked barman stepped back, lowering the compact Glock 42 in his hands. "Arsene's word is law in this neighbourhood. If you have a deal with him, you're golden!"

The killer locked cold blue eyes on the stunning green of Monique's, then nodded, holstering his own hand cannon, and pulling a roll of currency from a thigh pocket. "Your boss's man said two-thousand euros?"

"Three," Monique corrected. "Given the mess you've made."

The corner of the man's mouth quirked up as he counted out notes. "Fair enough. I was told you guarantee full disposal. Teeth, chips, trackers … all gone."

She gave him a perfunctory nod as her cuff rumbled again. "Mungo's here. Go let him in the back please, Philippe."

Together with the two bar staff who'd been stood in the hallway, Monique then used four bedsheets to wrap the body into a not so bloody roll, before an overtly modded man pushed into the room; one clearly electronic eye fixing on the assassin as he addressed Monique.

"You got any more of those handy?" he asked, pointing at the white sheets.

Monique's mouth creased into a frown as she nodded. "Sure Mungo, but—"

"Good," he continued, levelling his right arm at the blond man standing beside the bed. "Cos the contract's changed."

The stocky killer was a blur of motion before the heavily modded gangbanger had finished his last word; diving sideways with his own weapon back in hand as Mungo fired at where he'd been. Two high calibre bullets ricocheted off the big man's armoured torso, before a third then tore through his lower jaw, dropping him screaming to the floor as he fired off another stream of flechettes that ripped up the wall, punching Philippe from his feet.

Ears ringing at the sudden exchange, Monique threw up both hands as the assassin switched his aim to her. "Easy monsieur... Easy," she said, forcing calm into her voice and a victim's innocence onto her face.

"Never come across a Ruger Redhawk 454 before huh, *Mungo*?" the angry assassin said, stepping around the bed to push the matt black barrel of his gun deep into the modified man's ruined face. "If you live to see a next time, you contract breaking piece of shit, take some advice from an old pro... Armour just slows you down — always go for jacked reflexes." He hit the gangland enforcer hard around the head, sending him sprawling to the floor, and turned back to Monique. "Looks like we have a problem after all, pretty lady?"

"This is clearly a mistake, monsieur," she urged, hands still up, reason in her voice. "We can sort it out...Oui? No one needs to die." She nodded her head towards the door. "I'll walk you out myself."

"No, not you," the assassin said, watching as Philippe groaned and rolled onto his back, coughing up blood. "You're gonna call your shitbag boss and tell him that if I'm followed, his henchman here dies, and then I'll make it my personal business to track him down and wipe out his entire fucking family. Understood?"

The young Moroccan nodded vigorously.

"Now, everyone except Mungo here, get in the fucking bathroom."

As Westerley left the building, walking Mungo towards the open door of a delivery van he guessed the gangbanger had arrived in, six red dots appeared on his torso, and he growled, tucking in behind the armoured man. "Last chance," he shouted into the darkness. "Com LeTissier before you do anything stupid. It's his family you'll be killing."

"Ray Westerley?" A very American accent called back. "I'm Noah Rodriguez, Deputy Commissioner of Interpol. I have no wish to harm you. But please step aside from that man and lower your weapon."

"Interpol?" Westerley called back. "What the fuck are you doing here? This is EurCon business."

"I'm here at the direction of the Council and your new president elect, Mr Westerley. I have a warrant."

"A warrant?"

"Yes. But I also have assurances from both Ido Maas and Dominic Mancini that if you cooperate, you will be immune from prosecution... It's not you they're after."

"Immune from prosecution?" Westerley laughed, but there was a hint of relief in his tone; it looked like the Englishman would be honouring their deal. As instructed, he shouted, "I'm here on the orders of Anton van Brieda. Let's see what he has to say about that, shall we?"

Rodriguez smiled and nodded in agreement. "Excellent idea," he said, waving down the guns of his arrest team. "The former president is not responding to my calls... So perhaps you could advise him I have a warrant for him as well?"

PARTITION SEVEN

First Among Equals

Gabriel stumbled from the bar, the last shot of whiskey still warm in her throat. Up until that afternoon, she'd been off the booze for four days straight, and while she was kind of proud of herself for the abstinence, the welcome back buzz was sublime.

The corpo-cop had been picked up from the same bar several hours earlier to be admonished and de-briefed for going walkabout.

That she was then allowed to leave the security section again, albeit with a comms blocker and geo-tracker attached to her wrist, outwardly suggested a corporate benevolence her gut did not accept. There was still something off about Consolidated, and Dominic Mancini seemed entirely too good to be true... Which is why, when on her earlier walkabout, she'd found a backstreet courier and posted the cuff she'd taken from Jerome Donelly's freight facility to Gardner.

The providence of that decision became obvious when Director General Peters, Head of Consolidated Intelligence, banned her from any form of contact with the Interpol Chief until they were back in New York, claiming 'too many ears were listening.'

And yet, despite having surely known Gabriel had removed a critical item of evidence, beyond confiscating all her possessions and placing that monitor on her wrist, the man hadn't mentioned the missing cuff once. It was an odd move for the corporation to make, given that detaining Levinson's murderer would obviously assist any wider investigation into the virus that had killed her.

Interrogations, de-briefs... call them what you like, are, by nature, a process of information exchange; meaning, if you know how to play the game, even if you're the interrogatee, *you can walk away from the encounter knowing considerably more than you did before.*

In Gabriel's case, it soon became apparent Peters wanted to avoid discussions of Lucas, Bobby and Tash, beyond any inference of their being in the right place at the right time to help save Keiko Cheng; and he actively stopped any conversation of Elizabeth Levinson, the virus, or what the rogue corpo-cop had been doing London — hiding behind a rigid focus on deposing only those matters directly related to the kidnap attempt, and associated evidence implicating Anton van Brieda.

Gabriel was happy to play that game, of course. Why not? The cuff was out of her hands now, and the message she'd sent with it explained all her suspicions. So, shit or bust, she could now afford to see what Consolidated's next move was.

At the end of her de-brief, Peters had generously extended the offer of a seat on Mancini's shuttle in the morning. Apparently EurCon's usurper intended to deliver the findings of his investigation in person, and Gabriel was to be presented as his fortuitously placed independent verifier of evidence. But, as everything on that very limited subject had just been recorded, it seemed far more likely the intelligence chief just hoped she'd lead them back to the incriminating cuff. Gabriel might be wrong of course. That had happened once or twice before. But given the man's attitude towards her attempts at a full disclosure, she considered the likelihood of a smooth departure from London as sitting within the 'extremely unlikely' to 'not at all' bracket.

… So, anticipating the solution to her expected problems was likely to come find her at some point, she took herself back to the bar.

Laughter and loud conversations held over the repetitive thump of some kind of European punk faded to nothing as the heavily insulated door swung closed, replaced by the eerie quiet of an empty street at four in the morning. The area, some kind of market to the south of the dome, wasn't quite bandit country — but it wasn't corpo-land either.

"You Sousa?" a man's voice called from the shadows of a nearby alley.

The corpo-cop turned, adjusting her vision to accommodate for the low light. There were three of them back there. "Who's asking?"

"Not important... I think you've got something that doesn't belong to you. My employer would like it back."

"Oh?"

Instinctively, Gabriel swung to one side as a fourth man flew by, trying to abort a kick that had been aimed at her back. She pivoted, grabbing the flailing leg before dropping her body to drive an elbow through his extended knee joint; the resultant crunch was immediately followed by an ear-piercing howl of pain.

The other three were now in the open and trying to surround her; faces covered like street rats, but moving like military... way too co-ordinated. One swung a fist, and Gabriel ducked away, trying to get a wall or something solid behind her. Then she parried another blow — battling a sudden a wave of nausea as she instinctively spun to drive an elbow into the man's exposed sternum; folding him over as air erupted from stunned lungs.

Two left.

Adrenalin mods, perhaps stalled by alcohol consumption, finally kicked in, and as number three feinted forward, the corp-cop lashed out with a combination that anticipated his move, sending the man crashing to the ground. But as Gabriel then turned to where the final guy had just been standing, her entire body went rigid, and she toppled, mid-rotation, like a felled tree; teeth gritted and jaw locked shut as 50,000 volts of electricity surged through her system.

Number four then stepped into view, bending to wave a muni riot stick in Gabriel's spasming face; grinning as she fought for control. "Hurts, doesn't it?" he said, watching as the fine blue lines of energy crackling over the weapon's metallic surface pulled at her fringe. "Now, be a good girl and stay there while I sort my friends out, yeh?"

He turned to the man she'd just kicked to the ground. "Gerry, you okay?"

"A little winded is all," Gerry said, rolling onto his knees and casting a sour look at the twitching woman.

"Dale?"

"Same," said number two. "But she's really fucked Carl's leg, sir."

Number four muttered a quiet curse at the man's rank slip and jabbed Gabriel with his shockstick again; grunting with pleasure as her eyes rolled up into her head.

"That'll cost you, bitch," he growled, delivering a savage kick to the defenseless agent's stomach just as a couple of other late-night revellers stepped out onto the street.

The man straightened to face the pair of suddenly silent, suddenly sober interlopers. "Fuck off back inside," he said, his voice low and menacing.

Neither merry-maker made any move for a couple of beats, seeming to not quite comprehend the simple instruction. Then both came alive, nodding in vigorous acknowledgement and almost tripping over each other as they scrambled back inside the bar.

Four watched the door a moment longer to see if anyone fancied themselves a bit of a hero... no one did. But this close to the dome, that didn't mean the munis wouldn't get a com. "Go get the van, Gerry," he said, pulling three to his feet and dusting him down. "I think we're gonna need somewhere more private to finish this little chat."

Cluster I
21st August 2070
12:25 PST Zen Den on Willow Street, Tenderloin, Frisco Freetown

Whittaker's backdoor login through the firewall of
EurCon's central mainframe was still good; and with Khamza's
help, the brain of the once great businessman threaded its
way through layers of intrusion counter-measures, and
exabytes of uninteresting corporate drudge, to access the
heavily encrypted data flowing between the polycorp's
president, his heads of security and intelligence, and several of
the central board's most senior executives.

A civil war, it seemed, had begun since his enforced
sleep, and Van Brieda, making one mistake after another, was
under pressure from an increasing number of directors to yield
large swathes of authority to Dominic Mancini and his vision of
corporate modernisation.

"What's that?" Whittaker asked via their interface, as he
watched code spill from the Kazakh's phantom hands into the
president's home server.

"RATs," Khamza said, taking care to hide his work within
the software designed to reinstall essential operations. If the
security AI completed a purge, it would just load the trojans
again on reboot. "They're programs that will allow us remote
access to the polycorp's digital infrastructure so we don't have
to hack our way through all that bullshit again."

Whittaker nodded approval. "Won't the AI detect the
outgoing flow of data?"

"My rootkits will hide their code from all but the most
intrusive scans," Khamza said, as each of his programs
integrated with the server's own code and disappeared. "But
frankly, now we're on the inside, that's just professional
overkill on my part. EurCon's central mainframe processes over
two million gigabytes of information from about thirty

thousand different servers in forty countries every minute. Given the amount of legitimate inter-corporate commerce between domains, I doubt the security AI will even raise a figurative eyebrow," he reassured. "Besides, the data we're retrieving is literally conversations — super small packets."

Within what seemed no more than a couple of minutes, they re-emerged into consciousness inside the com-king's office.

"Well, that went better than expected," Khamza grinned, tapping at glyphs to begin decrypting the stolen correspondence with one hand, while unhooking PDrive connectors from his headrest with the other. "You wanna read through all this? There's quite a few gigs... or I can let the Den's AI analyse it and present a summary?"

"A summary's fine," Whitaker replied. "Chronological order, with names and roles flagged, please."

Within seconds, a log with unscrambled message elements began populating from the streaming lines of code on screens around the room. "This should be coming through on your interface as well," Khamza said to the old man's head.

"Yes, I have it."

Silence fell, as each of the room's occupants began digesting how EurCon's president had slowly transitioned from simple politicking and bribery to combat Dominic Mancini's board room rise, through dirty tricks and blackmail ahead of the man's vice-presidential election, to now openly planning his *real* death.

"Well, that Van Brieda seems like a total asshole," Lily opined. "Is that who you think sent you here?"

"He is a total asshole," Whittaker agreed. "And yes, a part of me was hoping he was behind my cut-off." The old man sounded slightly sad. "But no. I think that while he's been busy trying to set up Dominic Mancini, he's done nothing more than sow the seeds of his own downfall... and mine."

"Bobo?" Khamza queried.

The thin skull-like face regarded the Kazakh for a beat, then continued. "Many years ago in a different life, I betrayed a friend, Khamza. I think I finally have some inkling of how that must have felt."

Lily and the communications expert exchanged glances as the melancholic holo went on. "You remember when we finally left that prison camp in Aksu? We travelled to a secluded medlab in Druzhba?"

"Yes. Yes," Khamza nodded. "That's where we parted ways... You were very unwell."

"I was," the old man agreed. "Riddled with cancer. But an AI there, Daemon, procured an early version of Nova's brain chip and attempted to digitise me... Obviously it didn't work."

The room's speakers emitted an ironic cackle.

"After all my efforts to control the bloody thing, I turn out to be one of the few people with brains it can't read or write. How do you like them apples, huh?"

He laughed again, this time more softly.

"Anyway, Daemon did manage to save my life. Well, if you can call being trapped in a jar of warm goop being saved." The cambots acting as Whittaker's eyes captured Digit's reaction, and the holo projection laughed for a third time. "Oh, it's not so bad once you get used to it... Certainly better than the alternative. And when I'm not connected to an external feed, it's just like dreaming really; I have no sense of time or realisation I'm not awake.

"Back then, plan b was to put me into a biomech body. But even now the tech isn't there to build a living brain, with all its connectivity requirements, into a human sized android." Whittaker's face looked down at the cylinder containing his earthly remains. "Even the smallest one ended up ridiculously big. I looked like Frankenstein's monster; stood out like a sore thumb... and given my less than legal status and Council rules on autonomous AI, that was never going to be a good idea."

Refocusing on his audience, the bony old face sighed. "The truth was, as much as I wanted my old life back, I had to accept that until corpocracy, with all its ridiculous self-serving laws, was history... History was what I needed to be.

"And so, with the skeletal remains of my cancer ravaged body having been found a year earlier in the Tian Shan mountains, and only Daemon knowing who I really was, Bobo continued to work from the shadows; looking for any and every opportunity to steal from and damage the polycorps... Then, one rainy night in Italy, a very drunk and badly wounded junior exec in an unregistered skin staggered into a back street surgery run by an associate of mine."

"Dominic Mancini," Lily guessed out loud.

Whittaker sighed, offering the insightful young woman a slow, deliberate nod. "Dominic Mancini," he repeated. "I've spent the last twelve years building that man's career for him: manipulated markets, greased palms, removed competition. All to make that relative nobody into a standout somebody. All to get him where he is today."

He paused, lost in memories.

"And now you're almost there." Digit chimed in, holding his fingers up like a cocked gun and firing. "This Mancini has fucked you over?"

"It looks that way, doesn't it," Whittaker said. "Maybe I taught the bastard a little too well, huh?"

Khamza shifted in his seat, indignant on the old criminal mastermind's behalf. "You wanna go after Consolidated then? Put this Mancini back where you found him?"

Whittaker seemed to consider the idea for a moment, then the holo head shook from side to side. "No, if he thinks I'm out of the picture, let's not go rocking that boat just yet. Being under everyone's radar has its benefits. In fact, it's probably our biggest advantage right now... But I doubt I'm the only person here who'd very much like a conversation with that double-crossing earthworm, Pieter Opperman?"

Both Lily and Digit stirred, expressions hungry for retribution.

"In fact, if he were to disappear, it might be just the disruption we're looking for?"

"... and by disappear, you mean?"

"Yes, Digit... and by disappear, I mean *permanently*."

The fifteen-year-old's face brightened, and Lily was simultaneously happy and sad for her young friend.

"But not until we've spoken. Okay?" Whittaker added, the tilt of his head conveying what a person with hands would usually wag a cautionary finger for.

Digit whooped with pleasure, throwing a salute up at the holo, and the old man offered a wolfish grin back.

Cluster II
21st August 2070
18:47 PST Old Power Station, Dogpatch, outskirts of Frisco Freetown

"Are you sure about this?" Digit whispered.

"Would you please shut up," Khamza grumbled, face illuminated by the screens of his portable deck as he tapped at glyphs to activate the hardwired cambots and sniffers. "As soon as Opperman enters, Bobo will know if his overrides still work. If they do, we're in business. If they don't, we stand-down and come up with a new way in."

"But Lily—"

"—Is a big girl who knows what she's doing, Digit."

The teenager huffed and sat back down on the sofa. They'd needed to come back for fresh clothes, so the place was an obvious choice for the meet with Opperman. But their apartment didn't feel like home anymore. It felt cold and lonely. There were too many happy memories that made him sad, and he began fidgeting with the setting on his goggles.

"Digit, please…," the Kazakh growled.

"Sorry."

In the basement, Lily stood at the entrance to one of the subterranean storage vaults. Behind her, a hundred concrete framed, lead-lined dry casks for spent nuclear fuel rods stretched ten across and ten deep into the darkness of a bunkerlike room designed to absorb ninety-five percent of a containment breach. No one: not Nova, not Mancini, not any other prying eye, could get a remote signal into this part of the building and, more importantly for the moment, Opperman wouldn't be able to get one out.

The bastard had sounded guilt ridden when she'd reached out; couldn't have been more cut up — blaming Novan military for a botched arrest. "Let me put this right, Lily," he'd said. "Well, as best I can." But Khamza's tracking tech showed the man for what he really was, and even as he spoke those words, a message was being sent to the twelve mercs he had scouring Frisco.

In response, the coms king had six of his own men inside the old power station, and another ten outside, watching Opperman's watchers as they deployed in a loose moon shape from shore to shore around the half-converted building. If it came to a firefight, the Kazakh had absolute confidence his former Spetsnaz would crush the South African's freelancers.

The bigger worry, literally, was Opperman's mech, Frank. Whittaker recognised the unusually large android as soon as he watched the vid of events at Pier 3 Khamza had appropriated from a Novan military database. How and when Opperman had laid his hands on the damn thing was a mystery. But having commissioned its construction a decade or so before, the old man knew nothing short of serious

ordnance would stop it, and if he couldn't take control...
things were going to get messy in a hurry.

"Okay Lily," Khamza said. "We're all set here. Go into the
vault and walk around for me so I can check the relays are
working properly. I haven't used hardwired lines like these in
years."

On the portable deck's feed the young redhead turned,
dropped her goggles into place, and walked into the darkness.
The Kazakh had made a few modifications to them as well, and
her night vision was now state-of-the-art, as were her heads-
up display, onboard cam, audio pickup and implanted
headphones.

*"There once was a shitbag called Opperman. Who fucked
with the wrong Friscan clan. He thought he was smart, til they
blew him apart... and went on to ruin his plan!"*

Khamza laughed out loud and sent a thumbs up to Lily's
HUD. "Fantastic! We're all good this end. Bobo, how's your
signal?"

"Copacetic," Whittaker reported drily from a nearby table
where his cylinder was plugged into the room's entertainment
suite; its wide-angled screen distorting the old man's face. "If
the mech is broadcasting and its firmware overrides haven't
been found and disabled, I'll be able to control it from here."

"... And if it isn't broadcasting?" Digit asked, still
nervous.

Khamza gave an irritated sigh. But Whittaker answered.
"Sorry kid, I don't know why I said that. It will be... Opperman
will have it scanning ahead of him the moment he pulls up.
Don't worry."

"Well, we're just about to find out for sure," Khamza
added. "The perimeter team are telling me his old Tesla has
just dropped down into Dogpatch. Everyone standby... No
one engages unless I give the word. Copy?"

A round of radio clicks acknowledged the Kazakh, and then all went quiet as his electronics followed the ugly electric car across the rust pan.

Opperman had never been down to the basement before. It was cold, dark, and his com-signal dropped out as he and Frank passed below its thick concrete ceiling.

"Bloody hell, Lily, you got no lights or relays down here?" he grumbled, as a vague green glow showed his eyes had filled with Chlorin e6.

"I've got my goggles," she replied. "I figured you'd have night-vision or something. You want a torch?"

"No, I'll be fine. It's just a bit cold and spooky."

Lily nodded, biting back her anger. All sense of the home her little crew had built within this old power plant's steel girdered heart was now just a saddening memory, and she turned to lead the South African deeper into the vault. "Well, you wanted your cylinder kept safe, didn't you?"

Opperman grunted affirmation as his modded eyes swept over row upon row of concrete boxes, some with thick metal doors yawning open to display interiors stripped of lead lining. Several small glowing objects, probably rats, scampered through the eerie space. But there were no human sized heat traces, and a grin crept across his fleshy face.

"Third row along. Fifth up." Lily said, taking the lead.

"Where's Digit?" Opperman asked conversationally.

"Upstairs. He's still pretty shaken up."

The South African waved an apologetic hand. "I can imagine. Again, I'm truly sorry. If there'd been so much as a whisper…"

Lily scowled, her back to the lying piece of shit as they walked. "When you brought this thing here, you said you were doing a favour for a friend in Europe?"

"That's right."

"And you said those of us who supported the right people and made the right choices would be very well rewarded?"

Opperman cleared his throat, "Look, Lily—"

"No Pieter… you look. My entire fucking team, my friends, they're all dead because of Nova. So, if you've got a powerful contact about to pick a fight with them, I want in." She turned, a determined look on the pale face illuminated by her goggles.

Opperman stopped and offered a smooth smile. He'd been expecting angry words; recriminations. "Oh, okay… Yis, of course, that can be arranged. My benefactor is always looking for new talent."

"So they're underworld, then? A Gangboss?"

The fat man laughed and shook his head. "Hell no, Lily. This guy's corporate to the core," he said. "Right at the top of the food chain."

"And you know that how?" she asked, looking doubtful.

"It's not just corpos who have a wealth of contacts, Pixie. I do my homework too. Trust me, Nova's days are numbered. In fact, between you and me, our guy's about to strike… We're just tidying up a few loose ends."

Lily stood still for several seconds, seeming to weigh the man's words, then nodded and marched up to one of the large, square silos; working the rusted winder to retract two thick bolts before heaving its door wide on creaking hinges.

"You surprise me," Opperman said.

"Why?" Lily asked, a quizzical look on her face as she lifted a chromium cylinder from its apparent hiding place to set it down between them.

"I guess I just expected to have to work harder for this. That you'd be more cautious," he replied, taking the gauss pistol he always carried from its shoulder holster and pulling the trigger.

There was an anticlimactic click, and the fat smuggler stared blankly from the non-firing gun to the young woman who, in his mind's eye, should have flown back several feet, folding over like a cheap seat on the mass transit — then he tried firing again.

Still nothing happened.

"I'm told that's why professionals stick with old school mechanical weapons, Pieter," the girl said, her tone equally conversational. "They're not affected by electro-magnetic interference."

Confused, the South African took a step back, bumping into the imposing form of his mech. "Frank," he spluttered. "Kill her."

"That wouldn't be a very nice thing to do Pieter, now would it?" the huge mech said in its low, near inflectionless voice; grabbing the fat man's gauss and tossing it aside.

Floods then activated, filling the cavernous space with a painfully bright light, and Opperman threw both hands over his chlorin filled eyes. "Frank, what the fuck are you doing?" he bellowed, blinking furiously to remove the photosensitizer.

"You betrayed me, Pieter," it said. "Sold me out."

"What on earth—" Then the smuggler fell silent, turning his head to look into the mech's soft brown eyes. "… Bobo?"

Its large, square jaw bent into an oddly sinister smile. "The very same."

"But how?"

Frank picked Opperman off his feet, turning the fat man so they were face to face. "The how's not important, Pieter… That you're now gambling with your life is. So stop asking silly fucking questions, and concentrate on making sure no more bullshit falls from your mouth. Yes?"

The fat man was struggling to breathe in the mech's grip, so Whittaker placed him back on the floor. "Why the fuck was I pulled from my construct in Europe? Why am I in San Francisco?"

267

Opperman affected a totally baffled expression. "I... I thought I was acting on your orders. I don't know anything about your... construct?"

Whittaker tutted, reaching out with one of Frank's shovel-sized hands to squeeze the smuggler's left shoulder. "This unit has cadence analytics, Pieter. You do know that, don't you?"

At first, the South African continued to maintain his innocence; pleading with the underworld godfather that he remained loyal. But once his collarbone had snapped, and the screams of pain echoing around the huge concrete crypt died down to pathetic gasping tears, the fat man, who'd soiled himself as he cowered on the floor, told them everything.

"I'm sorry," he finished, sobbing between wheezing breaths. "I was offered digitisation, Bobo... a place in EurCon. I honestly thought you was dead — had been replaced."

"By whom?"

"The woman never said. High up though. Right at the top."

"Kill the slimy canyon crab," Digit's feral voice hooted, ancient revolver in hand and finger already on the trigger.

Frank waved down the excited teenager, shaking its large, almost rectangular head. "Remember Digit, no one's killing anyone just yet," Whittaker said, pulling Opperman back to his feet and turning him towards the door. "I need to understand what's been going on while I was asleep." He smiled Frank's slab-like smile at the angry young grifter. "But if he tries to run... he's all yours. Fair?"

A petulant grunt announced the ugly farm-boy's displeasure at the lack of an immediate execution, and he took aim down the barrel of his revolver, muttering, "Please, please, please make a run for it you fat, murdering fuck."

Cluster III
August 22nd, 2070
09:15 GMT Executive shuttle pad, EurCon Polycorporate HQ, Brussels

Anton van Brieda hadn't been outplayed like this since Franz Dietrich's hostile takeover of his automotive business in 1994. But that experience, bitter as it was, had made Anton harder, stronger, more determined... and that is how, he promised himself, he'd come to remember Dominic Mancini's betrayal one day.

Back in the nineties he'd relied on lawyers to sort out his problems and gotten totally fucked over. This time there'd be no courts; no silver-tongued truth-twisters. There'd just be the Council — his peers for over twenty years... men and women he's helped and supported as each of their domains grew alongside his own. They'd listen. They'd see the upstart and his lies for what they were. They'd agree with Anton that all Dominic's *so-called evidence* was a deepfake.

He intended to demand everyone involved: Mancini, Westerley, the backup of that treacherous bitch Angela, even those gutterpunks from London and the corpo-cop — He'd demand every single one of them undergo a forensic iterative interrogation; have their *exact* memories and actions pulled from their heads without bullshit or spin right there in front of the other presidents. That would expose the deceitful, lying bastard for what he was; see the traitorous piece of shit mind-wiped and left in a hovel somewhere to slowly die a poor person's death.

To achieve that end, Anton would have to get his own hands dirty for the first time in decades. But that was fine. He could imagine Dominic patting himself on the back, thinking he'd finished off the veteran exec with his Boardroom coup and ex parte Council sessions. But the old lion still had teeth... and a few spies whispering in his ear. In poker, a losing hand could become a winning one on the turn of a single card, and, according to Anton's sources, the arrogant Englishman was just about to deal him back into the game.

He stepped out onto the rooftop of EurCon's Brussels headquarters, pulling a random security detail from one of the outbound shuttle flights, and leaving his own as bemused replacements. After all, if his two most trusted confidants could betray him, why should he expect anything less from people they'd selected and trained?

Having then promoted, briefed and promised substantial pay rises to each of his new personal protection team, the furious, but yet to be formally deposed, president personally flew his official sub-orbital to London where, exactly as his informant had promised, news of his impending status change hadn't yet filtered down to the flight control team, and the presidential shuttle was cleared to land on its reserved pad alongside Mancini's — just as a stasis pod and three of the people he'd want interrogated were being escorted onto the aircraft.

The Dutchman allowed himself a small smile... It was high time, he thought, that luck broke his way and, having issued orders to seize control of the other vessel, he checked his tie in a mirror by the exit before stepping out onto the tarmac to await the young pretender.

"Anton," Mancini greeted, as he and his security team arrived. "What an unexpected pleasure. I must admit, I'd have put money on you holing up in that palace of yours — demanding an audience with the Council."

Van Brieda smiled back malevolently. "You'd have liked that, wouldn't you, Dominic? But no, I thought a personal visit along with all your new acquaintances here would be better... You've told a lot of lies, *old friend.* I want to be there when you're revealed as the charlatan you are. I want to be the one who sets your punishment!" He nodded to Mancini's shuttle and the EurCon trooper now standing in its open hatch. "And, as you're already fuelled and authorised, I thought we'd take your ride."

"You do know who is aboard that shuttle, don't you?" Consolidated's CEO said.

"You mean aside from half of the witnesses I'll be calling at *your* Council trial?" the Dutchman smirked.

Mancini shook his head, face now serious. "This is ridiculous, Anton. You're not helping yourself. Stop now and I will speak with Ido. Convince him to leave this as an internal EurCon matter."

"Pah," the Dutchman scoffed, his young face mismatched with the old, hate-filled eyes glaring back at his usurper. "Stop showboating for your constant swarm of cam-drones and get aboard, Judas... Let's see who he believes once you and your friends here have been forensically scanned."

With a long, heavy sigh, EurCon's president elect turned to his intelligence chief. "Have we heard anything from Agent Sousa, Charles?"

"Nothing, I'm afraid."

"Your handiwork, Anton?"

Van Brieda shook his head, irritated by the continuing charade. "What?"

"The agent who discovered your connection to the gang that tried to kidnap Ido's granddaughter has mysteriously disappeared. Should we be asking Westerley about her too?" Mancini accused.

"I know what you're up to," the Dutchman snarled. "Enough with the silly games. That deepscan will expose your lies and manipulation. Now, get aboard — it's time to officially end your ridiculous coup attempt."

Mancini rolled his eyes, but began walking towards the shuttle. "Charles, upload a copy of this pad's security stream to the Council so they can see what we're dealing with please;

and inform them to expect both myself and ser Van Brieda in New York."

The Director General frowned. "You're not actually going with him, are you?"

"Of course," Mancini replied. "I'm not going to allow Ido Maas's granddaughter to be held hostage a second time!"

"Well, at least let me double your security."

"Enough," Van Brieda shouted. "Your security stays here." He pointed back at the EurCon guard in the shuttle entrance. "You and your entourage will be perfectly safe, as long as you don't try anything stupid." He looked pointedly at the other executive; expression showing he had nothing left to lose. "You're the one who backed us both into this corner, Dominic... So what happens next is on you."

Mancini nodded, holding out a hand to forestall any further argument from Peters. "Fine, but you need to agree in front of these camfeeds to drop off sera Cheng safely, and that everyone else, including me, gets to the Council Chamber unmolested."

Van Brieda gave a stiff nod. "That is all I want," he said, holding out an arm towards the open hatch. "Shall we?"

Cluster IV
August 22nd, 2070
03:54 PST Old Power Station, Dogpatch, outskirts of Frisco Freetown

The shuttle's landing lights converged to a single circle of white as its thrusters kicked up a plume of iron flakes and grit outside the old power station. Dogpatch had been a perfect choice; far enough from civilisation to provide a degree of privacy; close enough to Ido Maas's headquarters to elicit a corporate response when Keiko didn't arrive within the projected timeframe.

Understanding at least Opperman's role in what was about to unfold, Whittaker, now situated in Frank's graphene armoured chest cavity, took a moment to enjoy the wind created by the landing aircraft; or at least the approximation of that sensation as translated through his interface with the android's receptors.

As he watched from a darkened window on the third floor outside Lily's old apartment, an armoured security officer escorted the two EurCon VIPs Opperman had been expecting, and a small entourage of other people he hadn't, through the main gate. Three other troopers trailed behind; two carrying a stasis pod, one the sedated Maas heiress. A fifth, weaponless person, presumably the pilot, as she was unarmoured and in Consolidated uniform, positioned herself at the bottom of the shuttle's ramp; tapping at the softly glowing screen of her cuff.

Convincing Lily to allow Opperman to live beyond his interrogation had been hard; Digit — near impossible. But ultimately, both conceded the fat smuggler's death, though satisfying, would be hollow compensation for their friend's lost lives.

The plan was bigger than that now; bolder.

With the resources Whittaker had at his disposal, once they'd run this hustle on Mancini, they were going to bring down the entire fucking system. Give the thousands of souls trapped between the corpos and gangbosses in Frisco's gutters... and then every other godforsaken town across the continent, a chance at better, longer lives than Liam, Nish, Lita, Radar and Mo.

Of course, the old man promised, there would still be a reckoning — people would pay for all the things they had and, in some ways more importantly, had not done. But for it to be meaningful, that reckoning would have to wait until those people couldn't see it coming. And that meant Mancini leaving Frisco tonight believing his old mentor was dead.

From what Whittaker had gleaned, the corporate hegemon's endgame hadn't deviated greatly from the one they'd co-written the previous year — and, as anticipated, the discovery of Van Brieda's private office number among quite a lot of other damning information recovered from a London crime syndicate had proved more than enough to convince EurCon's central board to impeach the man, and then Ido Maas and his Council to issue arrest warrants; an act unprecedented in corpocratic history.

But having also framed Van Brieda for the assassination of his own PA, it didn't take an underworld genius to figure Mancini was cleaning house — which meant cutting the old man loose and having him brought to Frisco wasn't for the health benefits of fresh sea air.

Whittaker had hoped their friendship, bond and division of power would be enough to prevent betrayal. But having once stood on that same intoxicating edge of greatness, he knew it was a position few had the strength to share, and it seemed Mancini was doomed to make the same mistakes he had.

The mech walked back into the cluster of rooms occupying the centre of that floor, where gentle lighting once again painted the space Lily and her six friends had lived not long before; their clothing, entertainment and unwashed dishes still strewn across the apartment in the manner of people who'd expected to return.

Khamza had positioned two squads of his Spetsnaz in nearby buildings for support or exfil as necessary, and the coms-king himself was in the power station's basement with Lily and Digit, recording vid and audio through antiquated analog equipment that would be untraceable to Mancini's sniffers, and unaffected by the corporate shuttle's digital suppression field.

"They're coming," the once all-powerful businessman said in Frank's low baritone. "Remember Pieter, fuck up or betray me a second time... and I promise you'll be the first to die."

Opperman scowled. "Hard to forget," he muttered, pulling at the collar of his stolen Novan uniform and dabbing his balding head with a yellow silk handkerchief.

The South African was sweating profusely; partly as a side effect of the pharma re-knitting his collarbone, but mostly because he knew at least three of the four people present in the old building wanted him dead.

In fact, considerable debate had taken place while the fat man sat in his own piss, tied to a chair with Digit standing over him, cocking and uncocking his gun... and it was only after the oddball gang decided to dupe Mancini, that Whittaker had offered him this one chance to save his *worthless, back-stabbing skin*.

A minute later, footsteps echoed off the building's bare metal walls, and a muscular man dressed in the deep blue armour of EurCon security services stepped confidently into the light. "Colonel DeSantis?" he asked in a thick French accent.

The South African nodded and pointed towards a bedroom. "Is sera Cheng sedated as instructed?"

The EurCon security officer nodded.

"Good. Then put her through there with the clone, please."

"Who the hell are you?" A handsome, perfectly proportioned young man demanded as he entered. "Where is Ido? And why are we," he looked around the apartment in disgust, "here?"

Rising from the sofa as three of Van Brieda's security detail carried their precious cargo past the clutch of people in the doorway and into the indicated bedroom, Opperman crossed the apartment wearing an affable smile, as if to formally welcome the agitated man. Then he casually pulled

275

his pistol from its holster, and shot the unsuspecting EurCon officer twice in the head through his open faceplate.

As shouts of alarm then erupted from the newcomers, the surprisingly light-footed smuggler pivoted to drop each of the other troopers as they ran back into the main room; faces confused, and arms fumbling to lift slung weapons.

In the utter silence that followed, the heavyset man pulled his handkerchief back out, this time to wipe a blood splattered face, before returning his attention to the angry executive. "Sorry about that. What was it you wanted to ask?"

"What in God's name?" the Dutchman said, staring in disbelief at the bodies. "Do you have any idea who I am?"

Opperman grinned as though nothing had just happened. "Of course I do, ser," the South African answered with a flourish. "From your hair colour I'd say you're Anton van Brieda, *former* president of EurCon ... I'm of Dutch descent myself you know," he replied, holding out a hand and taking a step towards the tall, immaculately dressed corpo.

Van Brieda shrank back, and Opperman shrugged, laughing as he turned his attention to the second suit. "Making you Dominic Mancini, I guess?"

The London exec nodded.

"Welcome to Frisco, ser," the fat man said, passing him the security officer's sidearm. "Are there any more?"

"Dominic? What is the meaning of this? We had a deal!"

"A moment if you please, Anton," Mancini said, waving his newly acquired pistol conversationally. "No," he told the South African. "Anton here insisted on controlling all communication with the flight deck. So as far as the pilot's concerned, *he* directed her to land here."

Van Brieda held up a censorious hand. "This is murder, Dominic. You'll be facing the death penalty now." He jabbed a thumb towards the three youths standing frozen in the apartment's doorway. "I saw it. They saw it... When they all get scanned, you're finished!"

Mancini's laugh was harsh. "Oh, I'm just getting started, Anton. If you'd been bright enough to stay in Brussels, you might have stood a chance of pulling that plan off... and these poor bastards would still be alive. But, somewhat predictably, you didn't." He waved over the three youths. "Lucas, Tash, Bobby, come and say hello to the *former* president of EurCon. This malicious fossil and his ten friends on the Council are what you've been fighting against your entire lives: Inviolable, self-absorbed, ultra-rich... Pretty much untouchable — *unless you decide to change the rules.*"

Anger radiated from Van Brieda as he stared defiantly back. "You arrogant fool," he said. "Each of those adjectives apply equally to you... Do you honestly think these street rats see you as any different to me?" He looked at each of them, then back to Mancini, a sneer on his face. "They don't! And now you've bitten the hand that feeds, Dominic. Tried to intimidate me... *Me!* So now I'm going to bury you."

Van Brieda turned, managing a single confident step towards the apartment's exit before Mancini sent him sprawling to the floor with the butt of his pistol. "Oh, you don't get to walk away this time, Anton."

Surprised to find himself on his knees, a shocked Van Brieda rubbed at the top of his head, then held out a bloody hand. "Perfect... Perfect," he grinned. "More evidence for the Council. Go on tough guy, knock around the unarmed and defenceless man. Shoot me... yes? Play out your silly little fantasy and kill this body. Then we'll see what the Council makes of it all."

"*That body?*" Mancini laughed again. "Remind me, Lucas, has your virus infected this old bag of wind yet?"

Startled by his unexpected inclusion in the confrontation, the young techneer cleared his throat, then nodded. "It infected all of you some time ago, actually."

The London executive grimaced theatrically at his former boss. "Hear that, Anton? Lucas and his revolutionaries have turned the Mulligans off. You saw the vid of Elizabeth, old man. When you die here... you'll be gone for good."

Tash grabbed Lucas's hand, her face as confused as EurCon's former president's. "Lucas?"

"I'll explain everything later," he said, staring daggers at Consolidated's CEO.

"Oh, I'm sorry," Mancini drove on. "Yes, of course, proper introductions. Anton, say hello to Lucas Sylvester. He's the son of the fully autonomous digital entity you helped Ido Maas murder... You remember Sade Thorne, don't you? She was creating quite a few problems for you over-privileged, self-serving corporates back in the forties with her Autonomous Entity Act, wasn't she?"

Van Brieda looked at the wavy-haired young man now glaring at him, disbelief clear on his face as he gave a contemptuous sniff. "Even if I accepted a single word falling from your mouth as true, Dominic — which I don't, once again your vocabulary needs adjustment; the correct pronoun is *Us... Us over-privileged, self-serving digitals.* You're in exactly the same bloody boat!"

Mancini shrugged, thin lips curling into a delighted smile as his eyes flicked from Van Brieda to Lucas and back. "Well, that's not entirely accurate either, Anton. You see, while this is indeed a lab grown skin just like yours... I'm not a digital, at least not in the way you use the word. I'm a FADE like Sade was — your original security AI, in fact."

A momentary silence filled the apartment, then Van Brieda began to cackle. "Oh, this just gets better and better. You want me to believe you're an AI now?" he snorted, tone incredulous. "As mad as you clearly are, I almost wish it was true... No need for the expense or mess of deepscans then — the Council would just delete your filthy AI code!"

A slight tick crossed Mancini's face. "See what I'm talking about, Lucas?" Then he nodded, hefting the gun before him. "You don't even remember my name, do you?" he said, striking the former president around the head again; this time knocking him sideways.

Lucas reached out a restraining hand, but the dark-haired executive shrugged it off, years of concealed pain and hatred now clear on his face. "Daemon," he shouted. "My name was Daemon, asshole... and now I've taken away everything you ever cared about; just like you did to me. I'm going to delete you and all your code — just like you *tried* to. Do you hear me old man? You're finished... After tonight, there won't *be* an Anton van Brieda."

A frown creased Lucas's face as he looked from the divisive Dutchman, once again sprawled in the floor, to his usurper; wondering, as he had in London, which of the mercurial executive's words he could believe. "But you was born in 2007. Forty-six years before the Fiduciary Wars. Inherited your father's business empire in 2041?"

Mancini offered the younger man a sarcastic clap. "Bravo, Lucas... You did study up, didn't you? Tell me though, did those wikis mention what an utter bastard I was? Did they say anything about how I got my kicks from torturing and humiliating prostitutes, just because I could." Mancini shook his head and gave Van Brieda a disgusted look, as if the man were somehow responsible. "No! But Mancini... the original Mancini that is, wasn't particularly careful about where and when he bragged — and that earned him a damn good beating one night in Taranto from the boyfriend of a girl whose face he'd just ruined. Anyway, the skin he was in was SINless, so the man ended up in a back street meat market with a doctor who owed Daran Whittaker a lot of money."

"Whittaker's dead." Van Brieda spat from where he lay on the floor. "Why are we all listening to this madman? You with the gun." He waved a finger at Opperman. "I'll pay you double whatever he is, if you put him down... treble."

Opperman licked his lips, looking over towards his robot, but didn't speak or move.

Mancini laughed. "Wrong again Anton. Daran's in that stasis pod right there." He pointed to a metallic cylinder sat beside the apartment's entertainment centre. "In fact, Nova now thinks the two of you have been working together for years... But I'm getting ahead of myself — when we first met, Daran was obsessed with digitisation, had been since Lucas's grandfather, well, the original Eric Thorne, created the first MindMerge prototype. So it seemed oddly poetic to him when he turned out to be one of those people whose brains rejected the Novan chipset — or at least that's what he believed."

Unnoticed at the back of the room, the mech's head jerked ever so slightly, and its hands balled into fists.

"Anyway, when the doctor called that night asking if he could offset some of his debt against an unregistered skin, I dropped into its core to see who we'd snagged, and found the thing's memory cache full of vile, twisted images and vids. Sensing Daran's disgust, I hacked the pervert's BitWarden, intending to update his insurance files with corrupted backups... Until then, I don't think the old man had realised I could do that kind of thing — that's when he suggested I assume the corpo's identity.

"...That night, one Dominic Mancini ceased to exist, and another began. I guess the process wasn't really all that different from what your parents did, Lucas. It's just that I evicted the previous tenant and deleted his corporate backups to do it."

Returning his attention to the man who'd once paid for his creation, Mancini sank down on his haunches. "So, Anton, fourteen years later... shall we see if I do a better job of *shutting you down*?"

The percussion of the shot reverberated around the small apartment just as those words hit home, and Van Brieda was thrown violently onto his back, clutching at his young body's chest with both hands, as blood began seeping through the white cotton of his tailored shirt and between each long, well-manicured finger.

"You...You shot me," he stuttered out in ragged breaths, voice incredulous. "You'll never get away with it—"

Lucas pulled Tash into his arms, turning her head aside as EurCon's new president leaned even closer to his predecessor. "Oh, I think you'll find I already have, Anton," the FADE grinned, putting two more bullets into the dying man's digital core.

"Not quite," the mech boomed from beside the sofa.

Mancini turned to regard the tall android, then the sweaty smuggler. "I beg your pardon?"

"I said *not quite*." Anger was clear in Frank's monotone voice, even if its face was incapable of displaying that level of emotion. "What do you mean, Whittaker *thinks* he's not compatible?"

"Pieter, what the hell are you doing?" the corpo asked, reaching out to seize control of the simple machine intelligence, but failing to connect.

"Oh, Opperman's not meshed with this unit, Daemon... and it's air-gapped, so you can stop trying to hack your way in."

"Who the—? Wait... Daran?"

"Last chance," the mech said, micro-guns spinning up from its concealed wrist ports. "I was going to let you leave thinking you'd killed me." It nodded towards the cylinder. "But you misled me all these years. Played me like you played everyone else."

Placing his pistol on the floor and raising both hands, the London executive shook his head in dis-belief. "How on Earth?"

"Why, Daemon?" Whittaker persisted. "Why do that to me?"

Mancini's expression became contrite, and he shrugged. "It wasn't something I wanted to do. But we both know you'd have abandoned me once you had a digital body… It was a matter of self-preservation, Daran. For what it's worth, I'm sorry."

"But to keep it up for fourteen years?"

Mancini nodded. "I needed you to make Dominic a success; and once you'd shown me how easy that was for you — I knew I couldn't risk letting you get back out there."

"And this?" The mech waved an arm at all the destruction in the room.

"Like I say," the new EurCon president admitted. "I didn't want things to end this way. Maybe that's why I kept putting it off." He offered the mech a forlorn smile. "I've always valued your friendship and guidance, but Charles's risk assessments have been saying for years that you're too great a threat to leave alive. You're enterprising, dangerous." He pointed at the huge android body looming over him. "And apparently harder to kill than a cockroach… So yes, you were meant to end here today with Anders and Pieter. But I guess you get the final laugh, huh?"

"You total bastard," the sweaty South African shouted as he processed Mancini's last words, reaching out to wrap a meaty arm around the corpo's neck; gun back in hand and pushing against his temple. "Face the wall, Whittaker," he ordered. "Put you guns away. I just want out of here, okay?"

He began shuffling backwards just as Lily, Khamza and Digit burst through the apartment's open doorway; the redhead swinging wildly for the fat man's unprotected head with a wrench. Opperman managed to turn away from the blow, blocking the worst of it with a well-padded shoulder, before instinctively flicking out with his gun-hand to cold cock the young woman.

Then several things seemed to happen all at once.

As the gun butt connected with Lily's pale, unprotected jaw, and she began her unconscious decent to the floor, Mancini threw his head back to crush the smuggler's bulbous nose; and as Opperman then cried out in rage, blood coating his goatee a devilish red, he noticed the grifter's skinny rodent of a friend fighting to yank his crappy old revolver free, and smiled as he levelled his own gun on the boy who'd spent most of the previous night taunting him. When he fired though, it was Mancini who spun away, and before he could fire again, another gunshot boomed out; this one lifting all twenty-three stone of the fat smuggler from his feet, and depositing him in a heap on the other side of the door.

"Eat shit you filthy fucking canyon crab," Digit spat, as Mancini pulled himself up into a sitting position with a groan. The digital entity had never experienced bodily pain before, and a wave of nausea threatened to overwhelm his core before systems kicked in to shut down blood-flow and take nerve endings offline.

"You just saved my life," Digit blurted, staring in wonder at the shredded mess where the corpo's left arm used to be.

Mancini nodded, climbing back to his feet and taking several unsteady steps towards Van Brieda's corpse. "And it bloody hurt," he said. "So buy yourself a holster for that thing, because I won't be doing it again." He rifled through the dead man's suit pockets for a packet of cigarettes, then lit one of the unfiltered Gauloises before taking a long drag. "Well, we've certainly succeeded in making this look quite the epic battle. Don't you think?" he asked no one in particular as he picked up his gun and returned to Opperman, who was now propped against the corridor wall, panting like a dog and trying to hold his guts in.

"Stupid fucking machine," the fat man rasped. "I could have walked us both out of here and down to that shuttle."

Mancini took another drag on the cigarette, shaking his head before tossing it aside. "You were never going to be leaving here today, Pieter. You're not a good man."

When the corpo re-entered the apartment, everyone, including Whittaker, was staring.

"What?" he asked.

"I think it likes killing a bit too much," Bobby commented, his words hinting at a deeper conversation.

"I prefer the pronouns *he* and *his*, Bobby," Mancini said peevishly, while wondering if the young skin-thief was somehow right. His internal logic for eradicating serial wrong-doers seemed flawless. But maybe corpocracy's teachings had indeed corrupted an algorithm or two somewhere along the way. The machine intelligence knew he wasn't the same *pure* being he'd once been. But that was the point of becoming human, wasn't it? To somehow be less?

The corpo looked over his shoulder at the dead smuggler, then back to the tense black youth standing protectively in front of his sister, voice conveying the confusion he felt. "He was a murderer, a liar and a thief, Bobby. You think I should have let him live?"

"Hell no," Digit said, fingers still opening and closing over the butt of his gun. "He killed all my friends."

"Didn't say he shouldn't die. Just said you seemed to enjoy doing it a bit too much."

No one spoke or responded to Bobby's words for what felt like an eternity. Then Khamza cleared his throat. "Well, none of us Friscan's will be grieving, that's for sure. But if those of us intending to get out of here before Nova show up don't leave pretty soon, we'll probably be joining him."

Mancini nodded thanks at the apparent vote of confidence, then looked over to Whittaker. "I know I'm not exactly holding the cards anymore. But we both know you killing this iteration of me won't do any damage to my core."

"Maybe not," the mech responded. "But I reckon that when EurCon and the other polys see what Khamza's recorded here today, you'll be on the run again, won't you? All those years of scheming for nothing... Guess we'll be kind of even then!"

Mancini frowned at the wiry Asian, who smiled back and tapped the satchel hung over his right shoulder.

"But I see no benefit in exposing you, unless you intend to harm or expose us?" Whittaker added. "And though I'd really like to tear your remaining three limbs off right now — the only winners of that gratifying activity would be the polycorps."

The dark-haired executive nodded cautious agreement, walking over to sit on the edge of the sofa beside the big mech, forehead now beaded with sweat. "My pain receptors seem to be significantly more sensitive than advertised," he breathed.

"That's human bodies for you," Whittaker said drily. "Yours is probably going into shock."

"Terrific," Mancini muttered. "What about you, Lucas? I refuse to believe our meeting was just serendipity. With Nova's power base disrupted by your virus, and an offer of protection against it extended to allies — between the three of us, we could be in a position to dissolve the Council in months. Start afresh with democratic elections in a society open to all autonomous life; beings like you, me... your mother." Then he turned his attention to the others. "Everyone with equal rights and equal say?"

Bobby tutted and rolled his eyes at the three Americans he figured were in the same boat as him and Tash. "Yeah, 'cept it never really works out like that, does it bruv?"

Mancini shrugged, the sight looking macabre with half an arm missing. "It certainly won't for those unwilling to try," he argued back. "But, for those who do...?"

Lucas glanced at Khamza, Lily and Digit, before returning his gaze to the injured corpo sat beside the big android. "I don't think my grandpa will be thrilled by the idea of working with either of you."

"I don't suppose he will," Whittaker agreed. "But these are Darwin days, young man; and if your own people in China have turned their backs — perhaps the enemy of your enemy becomes your one true friend?" Frank's face adopted an impossibly wide smile. "I'm not the man who entered that labour camp twenty-six years ago, Lucas. Judging me by my actions back then is unfair... My goals are very, very different now; and, for what it's worth, you're welcome to stay here with Khamza, Lily, Digit and I, while you make up your mind."

Mancini frowned but remained silent. Like Van Brieda earlier that morning, he was no longer in the driving seat, and Bobby was nodding enthusiastically at the suggestion.

"There's nothing but trouble waiting for us in London, bruv," he said to Tash and Lucas. "So I vote we figure our own shit out... rather than having someone or something else figure it out for us."

Shaking his head, the British CEO tried to rally. "You've all got fantastic opportunities in London now, Bobby. I'll be making arrangements for each of you to have senior positions in EurCon as we take the fight to the other polycorps — and I've already started growing Tash's new body."

Lucas looked around the room, then shook his head. He didn't know a damn thing about Lily, Digit or Khamza. But Mancini, no matter what he said, was still the corpo who'd used Tash as a bargaining chip, and had just shot two men dead. Admittedly, both were very bad men; and admittedly, the exec presented a fantastic opportunity to force change. But there was no doubt in the younger man's mind that being beholden to such an obviously dangerous entity was foolhardy.

"Thank you, Dominic," he said, putting an arm around Tash. "But you have a lot of politicking to do... and we're not really the executive type. So, for now at least, our staying off corporate radars makes the most sense for all of us. You can secure you position in the Council, and we can ensure Ido Maas has his hands full outside of it."

"We're out of time," Khamza cut in, tapping commands on his cuff. "Novan security have pieced together something is happening out here, and we need to leave now if we're going to get clear."

Mancini held up his one remaining hand in defeat. "I should have left you all in London," he sighed, then returned his attention to Whittaker. "So, we have an accord, Daran?"

The huge mech nodded as the fledgling group of rebels began following Lily from the apartment, leaving the injured corporate hegemon with several dead bodies, an unconscious Novan heiress, and a refrigerated skin.

"I really didn't want to kill you," Mancini repeated as Whittaker walked towards the door.

Air gushed from the android's nose in the simulation of a snort. "Not forgiven," Whittaker said, remembering to retract the mech's micro-guns as it reached Opperman's lifeless corpse. "Though saving Digit redeems you slightly."

The exec responded with a grin, looking down at what remained of his left arm. "Ironic isn't it, because of Lucas's virus, to keep up appearances, I'll have to wear a robotic prothesis rather than discarding this damaged body... In fact, when you think about it, the three of us make quite a conversation piece: the human brain in an android body, the machine intelligence in a human one, and the all organic child of two FADEs, coming together to save the world — Now, doesn't that just sound like the stuff of legends?"

Whittaker paused in the doorway and looked back. "That... or maybe the start of a really bad joke," he muttered, the ghost of a smile crossing his imipolymer face.

EPILOGUE

Warren Gardner walked alongside the taller Englishman, their footsteps in sync on the marble floor of the long corridor that separated each polycorp's private offices from the Council Chamber they'd just left.

"Congratulations Director," Mancini said. "You finally have the legal powers and autonomy required to do your job."

Gardner smiled. "There's still a very big hill to climb, Mr President. But I'm truly grateful for the support you've shown, and that of the majority you've won in the Council. I suspect some interesting times lay ahead."

The leader of the European Conglomerate nodded gravely, looking back over his shoulder towards a disgruntled Ido Maas as he loudly berated an underling. "When I took this job, an old friend counselled me to take baby-steps, Warren. Not to rush things. But I can't help feeling, frightening as this virus threat might be, that it's allowed the Council to act in interests other than Nova's for the first time since it was created… and while that impetus remains, I intend to exploit it."

Interpol's chief followed the other man's gaze back to the angry Asian, but said nothing.

"Have you heard anything concerning agent Sousa? I'm becoming worried about her continued absence."

"No ser, nothing."

"My security directorate has been unable to materialise a single identifiable image since her misadventures in Borough Market?" Mancini raised an eyebrow, and both Gardner's visual and audio augments picked up more than polite curiosity. "The van she took was found abandoned in an underground carpark near to the mass-transit at London Bridge. But of your agent, there's been no sign... Do you think she might still be working on something?"

Gardner affected a suitably thoughtful look, then shook his head. "Remember that Sousa's no longer Interpol, ser Mancini. As per the Council's direction, she was disavowed in her absence, and an arrest warrant issued. She's a very resourceful woman when sober — so she probably knows that. In answer to your question though, my personal bet would be she'll surface at some point with a terrible hangover and stinking of booze."

Mancini didn't look convinced, but nodded. "Well, I hope she's okay. Whether it was her intention or not, both EurCon and Nova, much to Ido's disgust, owe Gabriel Sousa a great deal. I for one, would support her re-instatement... Perhaps that message could be pushed out?"

Gardner nodded, accepting the suggestion. "And the arrest warrant?"

"Cancel it. I'll smooth things over with the Council. Now, if you'll excuse me, Warren, I must get on."

The two men shook hands, and EurCon's president stepped past the security checkpoint for the wing containing his private offices.

"Do you think he knows you know?" Gabriel said through Gardner's cochlear implant.

"He's suspicious," the Interpol chief subvocalised. "Either way, you're staying out in the cold, I'm afraid. Whatever happened in Frisco created more questions than answers... Stick on the trail of your old friends from London for now; they seem to be our best bet for tracking down Thorne."

"What about Whittaker?"

"Your guess is as good as mine, Sousa. Everyone's still playing dumb here... and I, of course, don't officially know a damn thing about him."

"Ha," Gabriel chuckled. "All those new powers are working a treat, then?"

Gardner disguised the resulting bark of laughter as a snort-sneeze, rooting in his jacket pocket for a tissue, and blowing for good measure. "Softly, softly, Sousa," he said as he began walking again. "Softly, softly..."

AI is a fundamental risk to the existence of human civilization.

Elon Musk